Praise for

"One of the most unique and quirky interactive novels of the early 21st century."
—Dene Grigar, PhD, Director, Electronic Literature Lab

"Funny, crazy, ultra-postmodern satire."
—Mariusz Pisarski, hypertext scholar, translator, publisher

"Belongs in the tradition of screwball comedy, but it raises that tradition to the level of metaphysics—a cross between Borges and the Marx Brothers."
—Michael Tratner, author of *Modernism and Mass Politics; Deficits and Desires;* and *Crowd Scenes*

"Blurs the boundaries between fiction and reality."
—Dr. Chelsea Miya, University of Guelph, Ontario

"A comic, frantic narrative that recalls Monty Python in its absurdity and erudition."
—Mark Bernstein, Eastgate Systems

"Trippy epic built with mathematical precision and profound insight into the psyches and odysseys of a murdering grad-student-ex-con, a matryoshkan cross-dressing international spy, and a paralympian-level Vietnamese cup-juggler."
—Bill Bly, author of *We Descend*

"Magic in the lasting, a rubbery kind of elastic stretched to the limit of the funny bone."
—Rob Swigart, author of *Little America* and *Mixed Harvest*

"Whoa . . . Wow . . . Hmmph."
— Frank "Many Pens" Figurski, at Findhorn, on Acid

Also by Richard Holeton

HYPERTEXT NOVEL:

Figurski at Findhorn on Acid (figurskiatfindhornonacid.com)

TEXTBOOKS:

Encountering Cultures: Reading and Writing in a Changing World

Composing Cyberspace: Identity, Community, and Knowledge in the Electronic Age

AVAILABLE IN THE BRAUTIGAN LIBRARY DIGITAL COLLECTION:

Lumber World: A Novel

Lumber World: The Rejection File

STEP AWAY FROM THE PIZZA

Fictions, etc.

Richard Holeton

The Fictitious Press

Montara, CA

Step Away from the Pizza: Fictions, etc.

Copyright © 2025 by Richard Holeton

All rights reserved. No part of this book may be reproduced in any form or by any electronic or mechanical means, including information storage and retrieval systems, without permission in writing from the publisher, except by a reviewer who may quote brief passages in a review.

Book layout and cover design by Kate Winter / From Manuscript to Book Cover image by Richard Holeton, created with the assistance of DALL-E 3

The Fictitious Press
Montara, CA

ISBN 979-8-9990042-0-8 (hardcover)
ISBN 979-8-9990042-1-5 (paperback)
ISBN 979-8-9990042-2-2 (ebook)

Library of Congress Control Number: 2025915837

First Edition

Disclaimer: This is a work of the imagination. The names, characters, places, and events portrayed in this book are either wholly fictitious or, in the case of actual or historical persons or events referred to, used in a purely fictitious, satirical, and/or parodic manner. Otherwise any resemblance to actual living or dead people, places, or events is unintentional and coincidental. Literary collage and erasure techniques have been used in some pieces to create transformative works of the imagination using published texts which are in the public domain and/or fully cited.

The author gratefully acknowledges the following publications where these works originally appeared, and whose editors sometimes honored them with awards or prize nominations. Most are available to read online via links from richardholeton.com. Fellowships and residencies generously awarded by The Henfield Foundation, the California Arts Council, the National Endowment for the Arts, MacDowell (Michael Chabon and Ayelet Waldman Fellowship), and the Museum of Fine Arts Houston/ Maison Dora Maar (Ménerbes, France) provided invaluable time and space for much of the work published here.

"Afterword(s): Take a Book/Leave a Book" first appeared as a print poem in *Forklift, Ohio*, and then as a multimedia slideshow in a hybrid edition of *Notre Dame Review*.

"Calling Fruits and Vegetables" first appeared in *The Fish Anthology 2007: The Winning Stories from the Fish Short Story Prize* (Runner-Up, Fish One Page Prize).

"Chance Meeting Between Cambodian National Amputee Volleyball Team, Stephen Hawking, and Black Mothers Displaced by Hurricane Katrina" first appeared in *Cult Magazine*.

"Counting" first appeared in *Gargoyle Magazine*.

"Frequently Asked Questions about 'Hypertext'" first appeared, as an actual hypertext, in *The Electronic Literature Collection, Volume 1*. A quite different, print version of the story appeared in *ZYZZYVA* as "Understanding Hypertext."

A different version of "Ham Again and Again" first appeared in *Neon Garden*.

"Henry Revisited" first appeared in *Cult Magazine*.

"June Swoon, 1994" first appeared in *Tupelo Quarterly*.

"The King's Summer Palace" first appeared in *Transfer*.

"March Madness, 1974" first appeared in *OPEN: Journal of Arts & Letters* (Pushcart Prize nomination) and was republished in *COG* (Finalist, COG Page to Screen Awards).

"Postmodern" first appeared, in multimedia form, as "'Postmodern'—An Anagrammatic Slideshow Fiction" in a hybrid issue of *Vassar Review*.

"Product Placement" first appeared in *Mississippi Review* (Honorable Mention, Mississippi Review Prize).

"Sonnetizing the Singularity" first appeared in *Unlost: Journal of Found Poetry and Art*.

"Spam Pantun" first appeared, as "September Spam Pantun," in *YU News/Poetry Hotel*.

"Step Away from the Pizza" first appeared in *Poor Yorick Journal*.

"Streleski at Findhorn on Acid" first appeared in *Grain Magazine* (First Prize, Short Grain Postcard Story).

"Thanks for Covering Your Lane" first appeared in *Indiana Review* (Finalist, Indiana Review Fiction Prize).

"Transient Encounter of Chilean Miners, Benjamin Netanyahu, and Girl Scouts from Boulder" first appeared in *Delphinium Literary Magazine*.

"Tunneling" first appeared in *Litro Magazine*.

"Velcro World" first appeared in *Cimarron Review*.

"Waif OD" first appeared, in different form, in *F(r)iction* (Best American Short Stories nomination) and was republished by *YU News/Poetry Hotel*.

"The Winograd Matrix" first appeared, as an interactive fiction/Twine game, in *Kairos: A Journal of Rhetoric, Technology, and Pedagogy*, and was republished in slightly different form in *voidspace*.

"Unlikely Convergence of Danish Animal Rights Activists, Rigoberta Menchú, and Multi-Level Marketers" first appeared in *Delphinium Literary Magazine*.

"Year of the Pig" first appeared in *Tattoo Highway*, was republished in *The 8th Annual Writer's Digest Short Story Competition Winners* (6th Place), and was anthologized in *The Rosetta Screen* installation at the Martin Luther King, Jr. Public and University Library, San Jose, CA.

For Roni, Rachel, and Miranda

To the reader

One story, one poem, and a flash fiction make their debut in this collection; another piece was self-published as an online slideshow. All the rest were published in print and/or online literary journals, sometimes in different form from what appears here, between 1986 and 2025.

This nearly 40-year span makes it tempting to order the work chronologically, an arrangement that might show some artistic or temperamental evolution (for better or worse) over time. I also considered organizing the pieces by style, because they range from fairly conventional-appearing, character- or plot-driven stories to more experimental forms such as a Choose Your Own Adventure-type narrative, or a text made by erasure or redaction of a famous work, things that may "look funny on the page" (as Flannery O'Connor described unconventional writing).

Indeed, several of these works also appear online not in static form but as interactive, hypertextual, and/or multimedia texts—digital or electronic literature, "translated" here onto the printed (or e-book) page. URLs are provided for readers wishing to experience those born-digital, e-lit versions.[*] In addition, I've republished several of the pieces online on the Medium platform (medium.com/@holeton). Why then this collection? Because I still love print, and I still love books as physical artifacts (and the e-book format, mimicking the book, still allows me to pull together these decades of writing).

---

[*] My e-lit works are collected and archived by the Electronic Literature Organization at The NEXT (the-next.eliterature.org/collections/19).

Alas, you will see that I've chosen to arrange the pieces neither chronologically nor stylistically, but rather thematically. The themes (*father, found, future,* etc.) are all "f-words"—the "f" (though not the theme) being more or less arbitrary, other than also beginning the word *fiction*. Thus if you read straight through—which probably few people do, but just in case?—you may experience some formal vertigo as you bounce from a "normal" narrative to one composed of anagrams or found text or Frequently Asked Questions, then back again. In any case, these pieces are happy to be all gathered here, and no matter how you read, I hope you enjoy some or all of them.

P.S. Many many thanks to Kate Winter, Book Wizard, for her inspired design of this publication.

—RH

Contents

To the reader ix

FUTURE

Plastic Life 1

Tunneling 11

Velcro World 25

Counting 49

Sonnetizing the Singularity 61

FATHER

Step Away from the Pizza 67

Product Placement 85

Henry Revisited 97

Do You Have Balls? 109

FOUND

Waif OD 119

Ham Again and Again 121

March Madness, 1974 125

June Swoon, 1994 143

Spam Pantun 157

Afterword(s): Take a Book/Leave a Book 159

FROLIC

    The Winograd Matrix   171

    Postmodern (Play in One Act)   189

    Frequently Asked Questions about "Hypertext"   193

FLASH

    Calling Fruits and Vegetables   223

    Streleski at Findhorn on Acid   225

    Hero's Journey with Enlarged Prostate   229

    Chance Meeting Between Cambodian National Amputee Volleyball Team, Stephen Hawking, and Black Mothers Displaced by Hurricane Katrina   233

    Unlikely Convergence of Danish Animal Rights Activists, Rigoberta Menchú, and Multi-Level Marketers   237

    Transient Encounter of Chilean Miners, Benjamin Netanyahu, and Girl Scouts from Boulder   241

FAUNA

    Year of the Pig   247

    The King's Summer Palace   253

    Thanks for Covering Your Lane   273

    Pelican Stamina Triple Double Dactyl   297

About the author   299

FUTURE

(something that may occur in time to come,
or in a state that does not yet exist)

Plastic Life

Soon you, and the whole world, will know what I know. Or at least some of what some of us know. Which is that life as we know it will never be the same. At the same time I wonder, who am I to say—ten years after barely finishing high school, a Lab Tech III working the Night Crew, while I supposedly get my associate's degree in nanobioplasticology? Before all this, no one even know such a field existed.

"Good morning, Donny," Melvin says through his shit-eating grin, the second I walk through the door at 9 pm, "morning" for us. I nod instead to Gary and Larry, our crisply uniformed, buzz-cut Marine guards. I thought I'd like Graves, i.e. graveyard shift, with its more limited social interaction. But it doesn't matter if you avoid eye contact with Melvin, or even if you're facing away, he insists on verbally acknowledging every entry and exit, like the aggressively polite maître d' of our windowless bunker. You almost want to tip him.

"Tomorrow, eh Donny?" Melvin says to the back of my head.

During the day, when the rest of us third-shifters are sleeping, he's working on his Air Lot Real Estate license. Literally selling the vertical space above the ground. So what the fuck is he doing down here in a subterranean Level 9 Gov Biolab?

"Yeah, yeah, tomorrow Melvin." I give him a token jerk of the chin. "Token jerk," that seems appropriate. I don't know why I'm so annoyed by Melvin. Maybe he reminds me of myself back when I was a goody-goody kid running for middle school student body president. Which I lost BTW, before I started huffing grak and skipping class, claiming the election was rigged.

"Hello, Dora!" Melvin says before she's even lifted her ID badge off the scanner. Dora is our Night Shift Supervisor, a postdoc studying Nanoscale Depolymerization and, as she's the first to admit, much better trained in science than in personnel management.

"Dr. Yang will be here at 0500 to pick up a Conehead sample," Dora says matter-of-factly, before lining up her carefully calibrated Tupperware snacks to input the calorie counts into her activity tracker. Gary and Larry sit up straighter at the mention of Dr. Yang, then resume monitoring their security feeds. It's the mention of the Coneheads that sends a quiver up my spine and out the top of my head, a warm, almost electric buzz I can't remember ever getting from my own species—very hard to describe, and even harder to explain, but give me a little time and I will try.

Tomorrow Dr. Zixuan Yang, our PI and Lab Director, will be receiving the Baekeland Medal, following closely-guarded deliberations by the reclusive and anonymous Baekeland Jurors, and the secret will be out. Given the epochal significance of the revelation, according to Dora, it was no contest and the verdict was unanimous. Yes the Coneheads are involved. Big Media will be there to Shape the Narrative. The ceremony and press conference will take place in a nondescript Gov building nearby, so as not to risk exposure (public and microbial) of the Lab, whose location is unfindable on any map and whose physical details and staffing I am required, according to my NDA, to "cloak, disguise, obscure, obfuscate, and even fictionalize when called upon to portray." Which seems ironic given that everything we do is recorded.

"So, are there any questions?" Dora dons her white lab coat, nitrile gloves, and hairnet. She seems uncertain what additional prep might be required for the big event. The Gov venue, chosen for its high ceiling, has been outfitted with a 24-foot cryogenic transmission electron microscope for a Live Demo. We've been diligently nurturing the Coneheads for weeks. Actually the day shift does most of the heavy lifting, the real research, while we clean up their messes, monitor the Rapid Robocloners, maintain the Milliflex Metamembrane Debunker, and sanitize the Spectral Sequencing Nanobator. That doesn't mean we aren't invested in the little buggers.

"Will Dr. Yang be wanting tea?" Of course Melvin raises his hand with an ass-kissy question. Gary and Larry exchange a barely perceptible eyeroll. They make an odd couple—Gary descended from diminutive Irishmen, Larry a long lanky Jamaican—together spanning the extremes of the allowable height range for Marines, 56 to 86 inches, a distinction they seem proud of.

"Nice thought, Melvin, why don't you ask her," Dora snaps. Dora's intermittent fasting makes her a little cranky, and she barely tolerates Melvin's passive-aggressive geniality. Everyone knows Dr. Yang will have tea when she arrives. IMHO Melvin wants desperately to make himself memorable so that, some day when he becomes a fully licensed Air Realtor, people will think of him when they want to buy or sell an Air Lot ("Air Rights are the future," because of the increasingly toxic condition of terra firma, Melvin's told us repeatedly). Well I will think of him all right. What I will think is, Melvin is the last person on the fucking planet I will ask to get involved in my Air Estate transaction, if I ever have one.

I admit my prospects are doubtful, given my track record. Before the Lab, I drifted for a decade—you know, a puppet, a pauper, a pirate, a poet . . . up and down and over and out, etc. Drifted like the first Great Pacific Garbage Patch, merging occasionally with other collections of microplastic refuse, exchanging contaminated Forever Chemical-laden bodily fluids while slowly killing the oceans. The Predacious Online College Placement Office said if I declared the science major, in this barely-imagined discipline, they could refer me for lab jobs (which they did) that would lead to a "guaranteed lucrative starting salary" in a "fast growing, cutting-edge domain" etc. (which is bullshit because a Level 9 Lab is Q-Level Confidential, meaning I can never add it to my weak-ass Competency Profile). Although it does turn out that having zero close human relationships helps you get a Top Secret Security Clearance. The 100-page application form, for me, was mostly blank. "I am like Old Teflon, before it was banned following the Third Petrochemical War—nothing sticks to me, while I contribute to the destruction of the environment," I wrote on the questionnaire.

So anyway, we proceed to clean up after the day shift, monitor the Rapid Robocloners, maintain the Milliflex Metamembrane Debunker, and sanitize the Spectral Sequencing Nanobator—all in service of the Coneheads—until today becomes tomorrow and

Dr. Yang buzzes in at exactly 0500.

"Good morning, Dr. Yang!" Melvin greets her. This time of course, it really is morning.

"Call me Zi," Dr. Yang says reflexively, probably something she learned in Conversational English, since no one ever calls her Zi.

Dr. Yang perches on the high stool at her preferred lab table and commences rapid foot tapping against the bottom rung, making a hollow metallic sound from her wooden clogs, which keeps a sort of metronome time with her shoulder twinge, gut clench, and facial tic that scrunches up half her face at regular intervals.

"Would you like some tea, Dr. Yang?" Melvin says (there he goes). When asked a question, even a routine one, Dr. Yang looks up quizzically and tilts her head so that her short black hair hangs straight down above her ear, as if returning to Earth from far, far away and needing a moment to reoccupy her body in order to interact with other humans.

"Dr. Yang is a brilliant scientist, but, I mean *and,* as you will observe, she is multi-neurodivergent," Dora had heads-upped the Night Crew early in the grant.

"She's still learning English," I offered, but Dora scowled at me for trying to deny or downplay neurodiversity.

"Mul-ti-neu-ro-di-ver-gent, adorable word," Melvin had said, as if we were all dying to hear his opinion of Dora's terminology. Then he tossed a turd into the punchbowl by repeating with emphasis, "a-DORA-ble!" Making us, especially Dora, cringe. Though I wouldn't describe her as *adorable*, I saw Dora once on the outside, a little place I sometimes go for a morning beer after work, and I barely recognized her in street clothes with her long brown hair over her shoulders, maybe a little makeup, looking very . . . normal.

FWIW my thought is that neurodiversity is related to biodiversity, therefore the fact that Dr. Yang, way out on the spectrum, has discovered the most extreme life form ever found, makes total sense. Where do I fall on these spectrums, I wonder? Or are they *spectra?* Dr. Yang struggles to interact and communicate with people, and I struggle with wanting to. Maybe I am just not a People Person, and that is why I feel such a visceral connection with the Coneheads.

As Melvin brings the tea, I consider asking Dr. Yang: Which is more difficult, converting octylaniline and catalytic aldehyde into membrane precursors for living systems, or bonding with other humans?

Right, too personal.

Dr. Yang looks at me and blinks rapidly, and for a second I think she's read my mind, but instead she says, "Bring bunnysuit please!"

I snag a suit from the cubbies, scan and unseal it. Bunnysuits are the fully encapsulating sterile X51-class hazmat gowns we have to wear in the Cleanroom that adjoins the Lab. They say our Cleanroom is 20,000 times cleaner than a hospital operating room. Really, 20,000? Who calculates these things? I find it funny that our 20x Cleanroom is filled with toxic sludge from the Stupendous Pacific Emulsive Waste Archipelago, the SPEW, which subsumed the Great Pacific Garbage Patch following the First Petrochemical War.

Even with Dora helping, it takes a half hour to get Dr. Yang scrubbed and sealed up, booted and hooded. Our bunnysuits are bright bioluminescent green, and I note they are made of the very same polymers and fluoropolymers that have (a) poisoned the planet and all its inhabitants (according to Dora, people ingest about a credit card per week worth of microplastics), and (b) formed the Plastispheric substrate in which novel structured microbial assemblages have begun biotransforming and depolymerizing those plastics—then miraculously reproducing.

"Stay tuned!" Dr. Yang says, a favorite English idiom. Her voice sounds distant through the full-facepiece self-contained breathing apparatus. She disappears into the airlock to enter the Cleanroom. She's back in a flash, carrying the package we have meticulously containerized, like nesting Russian dolls: a hermetically sealed polypropylene receptable, inside a polycarbonate canister, inside a polyethylene box, inside a polystyrene package. I am momentarily dumbstruck, flummoxed, gobsmacked—I don't have the words—at the sight of Dr. Yang finally bringing the Coneheads out of the Cleanroom. As the world is about to learn, an entirely new life form has emerged from the SPEW. A tiny slice of Plastic Life.

In simplest terms, *Polydubiousillium zixiosa*, a kind of polymer-based viral-bacterial hybrid, both consume and are partly made of nanoplastics. *P. zixiosa* were incubated and visualized from SPEW samples in a process too technical for me to share, even if I were allowed to, except to say that nanometer-scale ion spectrometry, metafusion chromatography, and irradiated kinetic hyperbolic biomass epiflourescence (or something like that) were all involved. I can tell you that we had an Emergency All Hands meeting that the Night Crew joined by video link, in which Dora had muted Melvin (how I wish I could mute Melvin!), although he managed to "comment" continually with pesky or pointless emojis. Anyway, after much animated discussion led awkwardly by Dr. Yang, the nanoscale critters were informally dubbed Coneheads for their uncanny resemblance, under 500,000x magnification, to aliens from the planet Remulak. Their unique structure of elongated, cone-shaped "heads" and "faces" also evoke the Moai of Rapa Nui, the mysterious megalithic stone torsos of Easter Island, but the name Coneheads just stuck. Look, there's microscopic Beldar, Prymaat, and Connie! I can almost hear them:

"Beldar has returned to the humo-fossil fuel planet."
"Join us for mass consumption of plasticized flesh strips."
"They have knarftled the garthok!"
Etc.

Now as a hastily de-bunnysuited Dr. Yang and the Coneheads are whisked away to the ceremony, we Blunt Skulls of the Night Crew are silent. Even Melvin. We all know that something has changed. What have we unleashed? Among other unspoken questions, will the first known plastic-based life form eat through their own plastic containers? Given that the little devils are wrapped in their own food. Sometimes, and this is one of those times, I want to shrink down, down, down—like the microscopic submarine crew in *Fantastic Voyage,* but even smaller, as small as the subatomic, quantum-realm Ant Man—and join the Coneheads in their inexhaustible polymer soup.

Gary loses the roshambo, so we gather around Larry's security feed to watch the event. We have to huddle uncomfortably close, touching shoulders (actually, Gary's shoulders reach only to Larry's hips, his head at Larry's belly). The Baekeland Medal is named for Leo Baekeland, the Father of Plastics. Bakelite, which Baekeland named after himself and patented in 1909, was the first successful moldable plastic resin, the ancient forebear of Tupperware and Teflon and the entire Age of Plastics.

"Baekeland sold General Bakelite Company to Union Carbide in 1939," Dora tells us.

"And the rest is history," intones Melvin melodramatically.

As we watch them strap the Baekeland Medal around Dr. Yang's neck, Dora adds that for many years the medal itself—like vintage radios and telephones, AK47 magazines and German Luger grips, pipes and cigarette holders, domino sets, poker chip caddies, prayer beads and Buddhas, toys and games and musical instruments and countless other consumer items—was made of genuine Bakelite, polyoxybenzylmethylenglycolanhydride, until recipients of the award became uncomfortable with its asbestos content, and it was replaced with "Fakelite."

Dr. Yang is alternately beaming and facial-ticcing. All the Global Newsfeeds light up as the giant microscope streams a 3D image from the sample. Could the Coneheads clean up the oceans? Save the planet? I know they could make mincemeat of that Fakelite medal. I miss them already. I don't know what I will do without them.

Tunneling

Weasel is following me, panting, on hands and knees, through a passage we call Route 66, even though it's only a hundred feet long, the diameter of a barrel hoop, and made of clay.

"Do you think I want to die in here?" I say. I dim my headlamp to save batteries.

Weasel only grunts under her facemask.

"I'd rather die up in the World," I say, "even though the World is fucked up. In case you hadn't noticed."

"I noticed," says Weasel, as the tunnel finally deposits us into the cramped cubicle we call the Meeting Room. "That's why I'm here, in case *you* hadn't noticed."

Feisty White sister, or privileged snow bunny? Too soon to say. Why Weasel is here is another matter. My immediate concern—*our* concern—is that the Extractors are getting closer. With my pickhandle braced against a rock, touching it to my skull, I can identify the specific harmonic signatures of their machines and robots, their TurboSuction Excavator, Gigatron Saw,

Corkscrew Hammerhead, and Wormbots.

Feeling the earth's vibrations and interpreting their meaning—that's what I'm supposed to be good at.

"Well, I suggest you finish your story and get the hell out," I say.

"How much time do you think we have?" She pulls down her mask and immediately coughs from the gritty dust. So young, I think.

"Isn't that always the question." As I've already warned Weasel, long stays underground, in the dark, can alter your perception of time, not to mention your vision, your stamina, your cognition and memory.

"I read about the hallucinations," she says.

"You *read* about them." Like *reading* about the experiences of another culture or another race, doesn't mean you can write about them. Anyway—even if we make it through our full shift, dust ourselves off, and return to civilian life on the surface—it will be only 12 hours underground, not long enough to start hallucinating.

I didn't invite Weasel; the request came from higher up, so to speak. Her real name is Ricky-something, but I insisted she take a Protest Name like the rest of us, even though she's a journalist and not officially part of our Action. She's going to tell our story to the World. "Bring it into the light," as Weasel says.

Good luck with that, I say. Though we can use the publicity.

She rubs the grime off her goggles, rapidly blinking her pale blue eyes. "According to my research, lack of sunlight . . . can make you prone to anxiety, fear, and depression."

"Ha, the *prone* part is right for sure!"

"Oh I get it—ha, no place to stand up."

Is she making fun of me? So far, I wanted to say to Weasel, you've only scratched the surface, no pun intended. I notice she's careful not to use the c-word, i.e. claustrophobia. I can spot the neurotics, the hysterics, the phobics, a mile away; like racism, or homophobia, everything's amplified underground. I'm not sure she'll last the day.

"You don't know anything about me," Weasel says out of nowhere. She's probably right, although it's not my job to know about *her,* I can only speculate about how she acquired her fear of confined spaces from, say, hiding under the bed from an abusive sibling, or about her barely-integrated upper middle class high school with her sports and her proms and her AP courses, about her private college and liberal-guilt-thesis on the techworld neo-liberal order, about how she learned she was adopted or that her mother was bipolar or that her father was having affairs, about her scraping by living with roommates in the city working as a bartender, or about her getting a few freelance pieces published concerning climate change and sea-level rise and then persuading a swashbuckling editor of a progressive journal to assign her to write about *us.*

"Maybe so," I say, "maybe not." We hear the scrabbling and the muffled voices of Muskrat and Rabbit before they clamber down from the recently-completed Pacific Coast Highway and join us in the Meeting Room. The New Jersey Turnpike is still under construction. Working at night, starting from the dwindling, oxygen-starved forest outside the fences, Vole Team 6 had worked our way in from south, west, and east, spadeful by spadeful, like a reverse prison break: breaking *in* instead of breaking out. Breaking in to the construction zone, to disrupt the construction of more destruction of the environment. Breaking in—or technically, digging under—to help set the planet free. And like The Great Escape with its Tom, Dick, and Harry tunnels, our plan includes three redundant passageways.

"How was the traffic on Route 66?" asks Rabbit, under her shamrock-green full face bandana.

"A little slow," I say, pointing at Weasel.

Muskrat nods a greeting to Weasel, as if to apologize to her for my impoliteness, then tilts his head toward me for an update.

"Their Extractorbots are closing in from the south," I say.

Above us, where the temperature is already sweltering, above us in the World where I imagine Weasel will soon return to her day job in an air-conditioned bar, inside the fences they are building—they *were* building, until our Action stopped them in their tracks—another Megatronic Fabulizer Farm that will decimate more trees, poison more habitat, generate more toxins, and kill more people.

The four of us barely fit in the Meeting Room, twenty feet underground. They all have to hunch over. Everyone except me. I'm short and slight as a jockey, another dangerous and underpaid occupation, if that's what you can call this. My stature I got from my daddy, along with my Black skin, the same combination that made him the perfect Tunnel Rat back in the Asiatic Wars. When available, they used Mexicans for that distasteful job—sounds familiar doesn't it?—Mexicans who later leveraged their underground skills to burrow under walls into the country they used to own. But a small Black man was even better. Daddy was celebrated by "our" side (*exploited* would be the better term, Weasel, I'm sure you agree) and feared by the otherwise fearless Enemy Negrito Tunnelers, who called him The Black Rat of the Rainforest (*Nesh-kur nu'ri-masu-laptra*), back when the Rainforests still provided cover. He could maneuver underground as proficiently as the ENT themselves, detect and dismantle their booby traps, and flush them from their own tunnels. He freaked them out with his shaved head, his skin several shades darker even than theirs, blending in with the shadows, appearing silently, and deadly, out of the blackness. The Legend of The Black Rat grew along with his dozens of kills, until one day he disabled a punji stick trap, two Molly bombs, and a venomous viper pit while mapping a fresh tunnel network, used up all his ammo chasing down a Negrito colonel, then had to kill the colonel's whole extended family in a burrow in hand-to-hand combat. Evidently you could hear the screams all the way up on the surface. One of the colonel's family poked out my father's eye with a stick. Finally the ENT set off an alarm blowing up the whole complex section by section, burying Daddy alive. Somehow he dug his way out, strapped on an eye patch, shipped home, and for years barely spoke to anyone, including my mother, until I was a teen and came out as gay and he said to me, "That's fucked up, little man."

So here I am following in my daddy's footsteps, I guess you could say, except for the gay part. I am Mole, aka The Black Mole. Because: moles are small and black, they have powerful arms and extra thumbs for digging, and they have a special kind of hemoglobin in their blood for survival in low-oxygen environments. Some ignorant people think my father's blood—my blood—doesn't bleed red. But it's true enough (another throwaway line I offer freely to Weasel for her story) that as The Black Mole I too am renowned among a certain audience, as a Protest Tunneler par excellence, much as The Black Rat was renowned in a different war.

Of course I'm hoping not to lose an eye, or get buried alive.

And here we are too, three seasoned members of Vole Team 6 plus one young bartender/freelance journalist—naive or brave, or both—crammed in the Meeting Room below the building site where we've managed temporarily to derail the erection of their Megatronic Fabulizer Farm, because the MFF Cartel has calculated, for the time being at least, they cannot risk killing us outright by violently collapsing our tunnels. Tunnels which in any case they have not yet found, and which directly underlie their foundation. The Cartel has also calculated that every hour, every minute that goes by with construction halted, they are losing gazillions. So they have deployed their small army of Extractors, including robo-machines poring over the terrain above us boring exploratory holes and planting sensors. Mercenary Human Operators, armed to the teeth and trained in counter-resistance, are poised to follow any lead.

To minimize potential collateral damage (to borrow their Orwellian euphemism), we keep only half the Team underground during the 12-hour daytime shift when the Extractors are active. Our motto for this Protest Action: Fuck the Fabulizers. Please ask your readers, Weasel: does the World really need another Megatronic Fabulizer Farm? Can the World afford it?

Rabbit breaks out some cheese and crackers. Outside, in the light, sans tunnel gear, her name is Ursula and she's a raven-haired Irish lass with luminescent green eyes.

"Yum!" says Muskrat (aka Cormac, freckled, also from Dublin), affecting an American accent as he delicately passes a cracker sandwich to Weasel with his filthy fingerless gloves.

Up in the World, Ursula and Cormac are lovers. I can't help wondering if, after all this time beneath the surface as burrowing mammals—I've lost track of how many weeks it's taken us to reach this point—above ground they might be furtive Furries, going in costume to Furry conventions, later mounting and humping away making beastly noises while wearing animal head masks and calling each other by their Protest Names. Furry seems like a White people fetish to me. And pretty gay, I admit, though I was never tempted. Anyway, down here we are all business. Or try to be.

"Pacific Coast Highway is foiled!" announces Rabbit, slapping hands, or paws, with Muskrat. Foiled, as in aluminum foil. With Weasel recording them ("not for attribution"), Muskrat and Rabbit explain how we attach strips of household foil along our tunnels, randomly so as not to reveal a pattern, as microwave shielding from the Extractors' ground-penetrating radar.

"Extractor GPR signal strength is already limited by the high electrical conductivity of the clay content here," says Muskrat. "So this is supplementary shielding."

"And to generally fuck with their sensor data," adds Rabbit.

I think, they're showing off for the writer now, with all this electrical conductivity of the clay. Let me jump in here.

"The same clay," I say, "that gives structural stability to our tunnel complex."

"*Complex?*" says Muskrat. Gotta challenge me. He's right of course that we don't exactly have a vast underground network.

"A *simple* complex," I say, and everyone laughs. Besides the Meeting Room at the intersection of our three superhighway crawlspaces, there's only a tiny adjacent Kitchen with our stockpile of battery packs and fans, dried and canned food, and the jocularly named Restroom, off the New Jersey Turnpike, where you hold your nose above a hole to poop in plastic bags.

"Anyway, I've worked in all kinds of soils, above and below

the water table," I continue, "and what we have here is some *bad-ass* clay." I want to make it crystal clear this isn't my first subterranean rodeo. Nothing against Rabbit and Muskrat, per se, but as a Black man, not to mention as a small and gay Black man, I've found that if you don't speak up, it will be assumed that all the available knowledge and expertise resides in the White people present, whether they're talking or not. The same knowledge and expertise, I might add, that directed my daddy down under the jungle humus to do the dirty work.

I tell Weasel that this reddish, iron oxide-laden clay is ideal for tunneling. It requires minimal bracing. It's also on the dry side, which keeps down the humidity and thus the microbial contamination from bacteria, viruses, and fungi. *Fungi*, so fun to say.

"Those are just the *natural* hazards," I say. "Be sure to tell your readers about the human-made, xenobiotic contaminants in the ground, the pesticides and petrochemicals, the microplastics and nanoparticles, the asbestos, benzene, creosote, lead, mercury, and radon. Tell them how the soil is *the Earth's kidneys,* collecting and filtering all the planetary toxins from agriculture, dumping, industry, and waste disposal."

A chunk of gooey dirt plops onto Weasel's shoulder, giving her a start. We feel the earth tremble, and we hear a high-pitched whirring in the distance.

"TurboSuction Excavator," I say. We tighten our masks and goggles thinking about those nanoparticles, but we all know that the bigger, badder threats to our underground Action are structural failure, flood, fire, and asphyxiation. Especially from human intervention: sabotage, arson, the interjection of toxic materials. Such as, by the Extractors. We do not know what they will stoop to, if and when they find us. As a Protest Tunneler, I have analyzed the Daegu subway arson fire, the Moscow subway suicide bombing, the Chicago freight tunnel flood, the Tokyo subway sarin gas attack; I've researched the secret Knights Templar tunnels under Acre, Israel, and the medieval underground network of Provins, France; and I've studied modern tunnel warfare, from the Red October Factory (Battle of Stalingrad) to Cu Chi (Vietnam), Mosul (Iraq), and the Azovstal Steelworks in Mariupol, Ukraine. We have implemented numerous defensive and counter-counter-resistance measures, clever little tanktraps for their Wormbots and camouflaged trapdoors for their mercenary Operators, but we have no devices to detect chemical or biological agents; we are the canaries in this coal mine.

"What should we do?" asks Weasel, brushing off her shirt. Her courage appears to be flagging. I knew it. She's getting cold feet in the cool clay.

"It's okay honey," says Rabbit.

The ground shakes again. A small crack appears in the ceiling of the Meeting Room.

"Do you smell something?" asks Weasel, her voice quavering. We lower our masks to sniff the chalky air.

"No," I say.

Rabbit, Muskrat, and I must decide, as we do daily and sometimes hourly, whether to remain or to vacate. I brace my pick against the wall and touch it to my head. The handle's made of dense old-growth hickory, now rare, inherited from my father; modern carbon fiber tools will not transmit the acoustic frequencies.

"Here comes the Vulcan Mind Meld," says Muskrat.

"I knew it was coming sooner or later," Rabbit says to Weasel. "He has to bring *Star Trek* into everything,"

It's more than that, I think. Muskrat wants to be in control of the narrative, to wear the mantle of authority from centuries of oppression of his Irish forebears. We've had this discussion before. I respect what they went through, I told him, but it was still White people oppressing White people, and what the English did to your ancestors is not the same as what they did to mine. Only a culture of White colonizers could dream up a *Star Trek* universe, with a militarized Federation spaceship seeking out "strange new life forms and new civilizations." Such as the Klingons, with their dark, dark skin and large bony ridges in their skulls like "lower" primates. To an African American, I had told Cormac, it's obvious that Klingons are *Star Trek*'s Black people, and as such, they're portrayed as an exotic, primitive, highly sexualized, and violent warrior culture who can barely control their passions. To which Cormac responded by sharing with me his theory that Mr. Spock and indeed all Vulcans were gay. "Gay as fuckin' Tinkerbell!" he said. Well, I said, the actor who played Spock in the later movies *was* gay. But what you're actually revealing, or excavating, is your Catholic culture's construction of homosexuality—along with Blackness—as *alien*.

"Add those up, and you get me," I'd told him.

"Keep digging, Mole," Ursula/Rabbit had added, "and you'll uncover as well the historically unmentionable Irish *women*." And to their history of invisibility and struggle—the policing and censorship of female sexuality and reproductive rights, the legal relegation of women to domesticity—what could I say? That my Black sisters have had it worse?

"The vibrations have stopped," I announce presently, having

completed the "mind meld." "They must be recalibrating."

"Their Extractorbots are like the Horta creatures on Janus VI," says Muskrat. "If Spock didn't mind-meld with the Mother Horta and learn about the threatened extinction of her species, the Federation miners who'd colonized the planet would've kept destroying her eggs."

"Here we go again," sighs Rabbit, who must've sat through all the episodes of all the *Star Trek* series with Muskrat. She turns to Weasel, who looks perplexed. "The Horta were a highly intelligent silicon-based life form who lived underground and looked something like giant tortoises without appendages. Natural tunnelers, they chewed through solid rock like an army of Ms. Pac-Men, forming perfectly tube-shaped passageways in their wake."

"So," I say, "the Gay Vulcan Spock saves the ugly alien species of rock creatures from the ignorant human colonists, a double strike against imperialist and anthropocentric narratives?" I don't know *Star Trek* as well as you, but I went to college too, I want to say to Muskrat and Rabbit. Unlike my father, who was dispatched for war and damaged by PTSD right out of high school. Maybe he's looking down posthumously on the proceedings with his one eye, like a perpetual wink.

Are we competing for Weasel's deference? Vying for the attention of the claustrophobic writer caught in the cultural crossfire? I wonder if Weasel will figure out what the real story is here, how characters with diverse backgrounds and identities like Rabbit and Muskrat and me, The Black Mole, would be thrown together underground in a fight for the future of *our* species. Not to mention the other members of the team (Beaver, Shrew, and Squirrel—I hope Weasel *does* mention them) who are out of the spotlight, outside the fences, patrolling the exterior, engaging in diversions to keep the Extractors guessing, to keep our tunnel portals hidden, and to keep our air supply fresh. I'm guessing that she can faithfully depict the actions of our Action, that she can describe the details of our fragile underground landscape—but can Weasel really capture the lived experience, the subjectivity, the phenomenology, of being The Black Mole? I think what I most want to ask is: should Weasel, should this Ricky-something the snow bunny writer, even be *trying* to do that—veering so outside her lane, trying to conjure The Black Mole in words across the void, across the chasm, of our differences?

Weasel sits on the hard, damp clay to change the batteries on her voice recorder. If she starts crying or has a panic attack, we'll have to evict her, I think. Instead she rubs her fingers together, holds them up with something slimy from the cave floor. She has an idea.

"The fungi—the fungi are not only a *hazard*," she says. "The soil is not only the Earth's *kidneys*. It's also the planet's nutrient recycling center . . . and global communication network. Right?"

"The mycelial hive mind!" says Rabbit. Yes, the tiny fungal filaments that co-evolved with plant life in a billion-year collaboration to break down and redistribute organic matter and contaminants . . . the cognitive network of fungal threads that make intelligent decisions about how to branch, respond to threats, navigate in space, interact and communicate with plants, and reallocate resources throughout the ecosystem. We had a unit on Mycelium for our Pre-Action Orientation, taught by Rabbit herself, right after the program on the Ancient Persian Qanat Tunnels, led by Muskrat, and a brief component on Unconscious Bias, delivered by me.

"I read that fungal colonies also have *memory*," says Weasel.

"They can actually remember stressful experiences for up to 12 hours."

"Uh-oh, colonies again!" says Muskrat.

"Same word, different meaning," says Rabbit. She dropped out of med school, but she knows her science. "In biology, a colony is formed when individuals live closely together, but if separated, they can survive on their own."

"Sounds like us," I say. "And 12 hours—the short-term memory of fungal threads—that's our stressful day shift, almost over."

"But hopefully not soon forgotten," says Muskrat.

"Maybe . . . the mycelial network can even help *humans* reconnect," says Weasel. The writer trying to pull the threads together. Seems doubtful to me. Maybe in a science fiction world?

"Yes, that's exactly what the fuck we need," says Muskrat. Wait for it. "The Spore Drive!" Of course. In *Star Trek: Discovery*, as Rabbit reluctantly explains, the mycelial network has become in the future a vast intergalactic ecosystem comprising its own subspace domain that spans multiple universes and also powers the starship's displacement-activated spore hub engine, aka Spore Drive, an organic propulsion system capable of quantum jumps around the multiverse.

"Plus . . . " says Rabbit.

"Wait," I say.

"Stop," says Weasel.

The red clay over our heads drips with condensation from our collective expiration, not to say hot air. The ceiling crack yawns wider. The rumbling starts in the west.

Then it hits us, a massive shock wave of wet dust and hot air, almost knocking us over.

"There goes Route 66," I whisper when we catch our breath.

"Fuckin' Extractors!" says Muskrat, and just like that, for the moment anyway, we're all on the same team, helping each other scurry down the Pacific Coast Highway and hoping to fight to live another day.

Velcro World

"Friday's the day," I say, as I turn on the compressor and load up the nebulizer.

Vanessa's back is turned so I can't see her expression. She's fiddling with the salad. It's not like she doesn't know. I squeeze the ampule to get the last drops into the reservoir.

"What does Ganesh think?" she says.

"Fucking Ganesh," I say. I suck in the mist and pass her the mouthpiece.

"Only a few vials of Quaker's Quark™ left," she says. That will not be our only concern when Dungfield-Obiwan takes over Velcro World. Vanessa puts the Tube on Classics. We like to watch Classics when we huff.

Early in the week I'm paired with Kellogg on two-hour Greeter shifts. Rotating the jobs at Velcro World is part of Team Building, which creates Trust. Trust is one of our recently-installed Core Values, as Ganesh frequently reminds us, along with

Competence and Service. Behind Ganesh's back, Kellogg calls them Continence and Cervix. Kellogg is sagging middle-aged, but his sense of humor hasn't advanced much past adolescence.

"Cervix with a smile!" Kellogg says to me, grinning goofily, as a family of four approaches. They happen to be four females, two moms with two daughters. I assume Kellogg knows what Continence means, or at least *In*continence, since he lives with his 95 year old aunt, and as a Death Metal fanatic he's very conversant with excretory functions, but I doubt he could locate the Cervix on an anatomical chart.

"Welcome to Velcro World, *The Stickiest Place on Earth!*" I extend the customers, whom we call Guests, the standard greeting. The moms look a little dubious, but their preteen daughters are bursting with excitement. We remind them we're currently in Plague Phase 6, at Level 5, with the air today at 11,000 ppm, and we hand them preadjusted K5000 BioMasks. The staff, i.e. Facilitators, wear full X51 gear since obviously we are nose to nose with the Public. The family are first-timers so Kellogg registers and retina-scans them, gets their DNA samples, all the waivers signed. He explains the ticket tiers, pointing to the sign above the welcome booth.

"Plus for New Guests, we have a special on the Platinum Passport," Kellogg says in his best fake-enthusiasm, "which includes *every one* of our Sticky Experiences, *plus* Extended Time on *Jump & Stick!*" *Jump & Stick!* is by far our most popular Sticky Experience—even newbies have heard of it, or maybe the old David Letterman stunt that inspired it. Yielding to overpowering pressure from their daughters, the gals opt for the Platinum. I issue them their velcro suits, hats, gloves, shoes, etc., and Kellogg directs them to the Ready Room.

"Friday's the day," I say to Kellogg.

"Judgment Day," he says. "*By your words you will be saved, and by your words you will be damned to fucking hell.* Something like that."

"From the Bible?" I guess. I'm surprised that Kellogg would paraphrase Bible verses, until I realize that they're just as filled with fire and fury as his favorite Death Metal lyrics.

"Well, what have you heard?" he says.

"Ganesh says there won't be any immediate changes."

"That's bullshit. They always say that," Kellogg says. I'm not sure where Kellogg gets his extensive experience with leveraged buyouts, but he seems quite certain about this.

"Yeah," I say. At least Kellogg does not seem to think I am also "they," one of Them. As Assistant Manager, I'm the one who actually interacts with the Guests and Facilitators and keeps everything running, while Ganesh sits in the Back Office looking at spreadsheets and whining to Raylene the bookkeeper about South Asia this and South Asia that. South Asia is how Ganesh refers to his brothers or uncles or cousins in India and/or Pakistan—he never specifies, and no one asks—who are his not-so-silent Silent Partners and the co-owners of Velcro World.

That is, until Friday—when Dungfield-Obiwan Private Equity (no, it does not use the acronym DOPE) from New York City officially takes ownership.

Vanessa and I turn the Tube to *Rocky and Bullwinkle.* Besides the lovable flying squirrel and moose, Vanessa adores the show's "Fractured Fairy Tales" and "Dudley Do-Right of the Mounties," while I'm partial to Mr. Peabody and Sherman's "Improbable History" segments. An ad shows a middle-aged woman in obvious but vague discomfort, hunched over the edge of her bed in a darkened room. Outside her suburban window, men are barbecuing, women chat, and children play. Quick cut to image of a white-coated doctor handing someone a brightly packaged medication. Fast forward to the woman, now outside in the bright sun looking cheery and healthful, nuzzling one of the men, laughing with the women, and throwing a ball with the children. "If you suffer from Manifold Maxiphasic Schitzach's Disorder, talk to *your* doctor about Solvatol® from Dharma Pharma . . . ." Vanessa and I look at each other, sharing our surprise at the commercial involving a disease that strikes only 1 in 100,000—which we know because Vanessa actually *has* Schitzach's Disorder.

Last year when Phase 2, Level 8 of the Plague threatened to shut Velcro World down, we had calculated the full retail price of Solvatol® from Dharma Pharma. "Looks like eighty thousand," I said.

"Per year-gghh?" Vanessa said, with exaggerated throat-clearing guttural sounds.

"Per *month*," I said. "Er, is that a German accent?"

Vanessa is not German. She's from Chicago, daughter of Greek Americans, but when she gets migraines, she lapses into various European accents, usually not very good ones. It's called Foreign Accent Syndrome, some kind of temporary rewiring of the brain's Language Center triggered by the migraines. The migraines are a side effect of the Solvatol®, the only known treatment for Schitzach's Disorder. So her Foreign Accent Syndrome is a side effect of a side effect.

"Dot eez like *vun meellion* per year-gh," Vanessa had said, like a mezzo-soprano Sergeant Schultz from *Hogan's Heroes*.

"Did you take your paracetamol?"

"Yah, yah, yaaeh!" she'd said, and I remember the accent veering toward Swedish Chef. I pictured her short-circuited Language Center like some neuronic Tower of Babel. Usually the Solvatol® migraines produce a British or French accent, not too unpleasant, but in a way I think the German is more appropriate, because Schitzach's Disorder is named after Adolf Schitzach of Zurich, the first to identify the nasty, debilitating symptoms that Dharma Pharma's Tube ad doesn't show and that I won't describe except to say they are usually fatal if left untreated. In 1941, Schitzach could not foresee the rare genetic variation causing the disease, but when he and his suffering wife Milka returned from a painful walk in the Alps covered in sticky burrs and he put a drop of her blood under the microscope, he discovered the tell-tale adhesive "hook-and-loop" structures of advanced Schitzach's Disorder. Wait, I think I am mixing up Adolf and Milka Schitzach with Swiss engineer George de Mestral, inventor of velcro.

"Solvatol® is not for everyone," the ad concludes. "If you experience life-threatening seizures, or if wart-covered horns suddenly sprout from your buttocks, you should call your doctor." Or something like that. We squint at the fine print of warnings and side effects at the bottom of the screen; Bad European Accents is not listed. I recall we'd figured the actual cost of Solvatol® (which clearly does not solve it all) at something like 1,000,000 per year, or 25 times my annual salary. Which Velcro World's health insurer, Amalgamated Wellness, has been paying since Vanessa got the diagnosis and was forced to stop working.

We reload the nebulizer and watch the serialized cartoon adventures in which Bullwinkle J. Moose replaces the disguised Boris Badenov as a circus lion tamer after Boris is fired for trying to burn down the entire Bumbling Brothers Circus, Rocky the Squirrel gets tied to a flaming stake, and evil couple Boris and Natasha try to bankrupt the circus before Rocky makes peace with some Indians and saves the day. We crack up at a Dudley Do-Right segment sandwiched between episodes.

"Lonely defender of justice and fair play!" and "Handsome, brave, daring, and hopelessly lost!" we say along with the narrator, as Dudley Do-Right bungles his rescue of Nell, tied to the railroad tracks by Snidely Whiplash.

I think Vanessa loves Tube Classics even more than I do. Those old shows are like going back in time to some magical worlds that maybe never existed but are still preferable to our current reality.

"Can I have a second?"

Ganesh holds up a hand. "Talking with South Asia," he stage-whispers.

I look at Raylene, who shrugs. She holds a pencil between her teeth but has no paper, rather two giant computer displays filled with columns of numbers. She swivels her head and bouncy gray curls between the monitors, ample bosom lagging behind.

"Pivot tables," Raylene says through the pencil. She rotates her eyes toward Ganesh, as if to say that this is all I'm going to get from *her*.

The Back Office is a converted double-wide trailer, a step up from the modified shipping containers that house most of the Sticky Experiences. The rest of us work outside in the increasingly hostile and parched elements, except for brief respites in our dilapidated Breakroom Trailer, which like the Back Office has sputtery air conditioning. Ganesh pockets his phone and gestures for me to sit on the lawn chair by his desk that serves as his visitor accommodation. Raylene hunkers down under giant headphones that look like coconut halves.

"Obviously, I am knowing there are concerns," Ganesh says. "You're concerned, the other Facilitators are concerned, I'm concerned, and South Asia is concerned." He avoids looking at me as he sucks in his breath. "But we're getting at Yes. It's going to be a win win win win. We're having a vision and we're having our Core Values to guide us, as together . . ."

". . . As together we remove obstacles and achieve optimal results by turning challenges into opportunities," I finish the refrain, almost singing it, to Ganesh's annoyance. According to his wall hanging, the Hindu god Ganesha also overcomes obstacles and brings good luck.

Up until recently, Velcro World has been an obscure, ramshackle roadside attraction, more curiosity than corporate enterprise. So last year when Ganesh—as Managing Partner, with the encouragement of South Asia—began taking management courses and leadership workshops, it seemed like overkill.

"We only have thirteen employees, most of them part-time," I had reminded Ganesh when he introduced daily All Hands Meetings and began talking about Relationship Building, Emotional Intelligence, Stakeholder Engagement, Supply-Chain Bottlenecks, and Strategic Roadmaps. I guess we should have suspected something was up.

"Basically, South Asia and Dungfield-Obiwan are making a collaborative, data-driven decision," Ganesh says, emphasizing *data-driven* as if he's invoking the Vedas. Raylene taps her coconuts and attempts a teeth-clenched, pencil-filled grin that comes out more like a grimace. Is she listening to pivot-table music? If

Kellogg were here, he would whisper to me an immature joke about the coconuts being better placed on Raylene's chest, ha ha.

"Simply, we'll be joining the Dungfield Family of EPAs in a major upgradation," Ganesh continues undaunted. "We'll be having the cash to be finally making Capital Improvements while increasing operational efficiencies and at the same time helping consolidate and commoditize an industry that is . . . *highly fragmented*."

"Are you practicing for the Transition Meeting on Friday?" I ask. "I think you've drunk so much of it, you're choking on the Kool-Aid, Ganesh." The *highly fragmented* industry that Dungfield-Obiwan is consolidating and commoditizing is Essential Physical Activities (EPAs), a category of non-health club small businesses created during Phase 4 of the Plague to counter rampant lockdown-induced Cabin Fever and keep the populace, Public Facing and Info Elites alike, from erupting. Ganesh managed to secure the Government's Emergency EPA designation, patching together grants and loans to keep Velcro World afloat—and, perhaps unintentionally but to the ultimate delight of South Asia, make it a prime target for acquisition by Dungfield-Obiwan.

"To be sure, I am hearing you, and truth be told"—Ganesh glances over at Raylene's columns of numbers and lowers his voice—"the EPA thing has been a lifeline, but we are drowning without the New Yorkers! They are actually basically saving our asses."

My regular rotation takes me to *Jump & Stick!*, our showcase Sticky Experience, where I'm paired up with Becky Ann. Sure enough, the family of four females arrives for their Extended Time, waving their Platinum Passports.

"I'm your Spotter," Becky Ann says. She sounds far away through her X51 helmet as she instructs the gals and reviews the safety protocols. She does little tap-dance steps for emphasis, which through the baggy suit look like spastic leg seizures. Becky Ann can be quirky, but she takes her responsibilities seriously. A grainy video of the David Letterman stunt from 1984 plays on continuous loop above the wall of velcro.

"Who wants to go first?"

"I do! I do!" they all say at once.

"Okay, you two," Becky Ann points to the tweenage daughters, "Rock Paper Scissors—two out of three!" She narrates the contest like a sports announcer. "You are sharp, Scissors Sister! . . . And you rock, Rock. Smash those shears!" etc.

The winning sister steps on the platform, and I cue up the drum roll sound effect.

"Remember to spread wide so you hit the wall with max body surface. And turn your face to the side!" Becky Ann says. The girl leaps onto the trampoline and gets a huge bounce, almost the height of the video monitor, before slamming and sticking solidly to the wall.

"Whoopee!" the girl screams. "Ooof!"

Becky Ann and I go into action. What people don't recall from the original Letterman stunt (and which we have edited out of the video) is that it takes practically the entire TV crew to dislodge him from the velcro wall. That is why, at Velcro World's *Jump & Stick!*, we have devised our Fast Release Wall, requiring only two Facilitators. With a lever, I activate a pulley system that yanks the whole wall away at an angle, at exactly the same time that Becky Ann slides a long-handled spatula tool, like a human-size pizza paddle, under the girl's velcro suit, peeling her off and depositing her, Ker-plunk!, onto the padded floor. It's a thing of beauty, like a well-choreographed dance, in the hands of skillful Facilitators such as ourselves. Becky Ann and I slap gloves.

The terrific tearing sound of all that velcro coming apart, when you separate the Guest from the Wall, is my favorite part. You have to be careful, though, not to generate electric sparks from ripping so much velcro at once. As we remind newbie Facilitators, NASA's first moon missions may have helped make velcro famous, but it was an electric spark that caused the fire that torched three astronauts in the capsule of Apollo 1, which was filled with staticky, highly flammable velcro. So Best Practice for the Fast Release Wall is to treat the spatula tool, for every Guest, with copious amounts of anti-static spray.

"Spray before they splay," is how Becky Ann instructs trainees. "Spray before splay! Now say that ten times fast!"

Once upon a time in the PPD, the Pre Plague Days (also BSD for me and Vanessa, Before Schitzach's Disorder), Vanessa and I were working *Jump and Stick!* together and we mis-timed the Fast Release Wall. I yanked the wall lever before she shoveled in the giant spatula tool, leaving our Guest, a former All-Pro Tight End, splayed precariously. The Tight End's many titanium joint replacements held up okay, but when I raised the wall back to vertical, it conked him on the head, resulting in his forty-somethingth concussion, apparently one too many for his chronically brain-injured noggin. After we got him on the mat he went a little crazy. Vanessa and I retreated to the Breakroom Trailer, and the medics had to strap him down. His family sued Velcro World for gazillions, agreeing to a settlement at the upper limit of the liability coverage from Amalgamated Casualty.

"That is fortunate," I said to Ganesh at the time.

"Tell that to South Asia," he said.

The Fast Release Fuckup was not the reason that Vanessa no longer works at Velcro World. Before *Jump and Stick!*, Vanessa and I had worked nearly all the Sticky Experiences together. We'd met on *Gravity Buster!* We really hit it off during our shifts on *Fly on the Wall!*, arranged our first date on *Spider Man!* (since renamed the gender-neutral *Arachnid Adventure!*), and then hit our stride in *Sticky Balls!* Soon after we moved in together, the Plague began spreading like wildfire and she got the Schitzach's diagnosis. The problem was, while Solvatol® controlled her symptoms (Language Center side effects notwithstanding), Schitzach's supposedly made her super-susceptible to all the Plague Variants, so it became too risky for her to Face the Public, even in full X51 garb. Thank goodness for the Plague Insurance provided by Amalgamated Casualty, or Vanessa and I would be, in Ganesh's words, Out of the Pocket.

After Ganesh got the emergency EPA designation and business picked back up, he hired Kellogg to cover for Vanessa—like trading your Queen for a Pawn in our *Life Size Velcro Chess Experience!*

Friday afternoon we close early for the Transition Meeting. The Detox Tunnel involves stripping off your X51 apparatus, which like astronaut gear contains a boatload of velcro, tossing it in the sanitizer tub, getting scrubbed down by the twelve-barrel decontamination shower, goggling up for UV irradiation, and throwing on your fresh clothes, all in quick succession like the conveyer-belt shower system that Vanessa and I love on *The Jetsons*. I pop out of the Detox Tunnel into the Breakroom Trailer, where Becky Ann and Kellogg are already waiting.

"Well?" Kellogg says. I squint to decipher the gothic lettering on his teeshirt, featuring the Death Metal band The Burning Butthairs and their album *Frantic Disembowelment*.

"Well what?" I say.

"Well you're Management, sort of," Kellogg says. "You know, Continence and Cervix and all that."

"Leave him alone," Becky Ann says to Kellogg. She waves a hand like she's conducting an invisible orchestra.

"Ganesh will enlighten us all shortly," I say. The meeting was called for 4:00, in fifteen minutes, and the other Facilitators trickle in shiny-cheeked from the Detox Tunnel. We know that Ganesh will keep everyone waiting so he can make a dramatic entrance. I'm relieved when Raylene arrives, in a rare appearance outside the Back Office, hoping she'll distract Kellogg from pestering me.

"How they hanging Raylene?" Kellogg says right on cue, putting on a puppy-dog face but not, fortunately, hanging out his tongue.

"Shove it, Kellogg," Raylene says, frowning at his *Frantic Disembowelment* teeshirt. She and Becky Ann shoot Kellogg a look like he's the lowest cretin from Raging Cretin Hell, not realizing that Raging Cretin Hell is probably his favorite band after The Burning Butthairs.

"Okay okay, people people people," Ganesh says, springing through the door. Everyone quiets down, then low grumbling can be heard as he rotates the whiteboard to the side that is slightly less marker-stained. Kellogg whispers "Whiteboard!" sarcastically in my ear as Ganesh draws a two-by-two grid which we all recognize by now as a SWOT Analysis diagram, with quadrants for Strengths, Weaknesses, Opportunities, and Threats. He writes a couple things in each quadrant.

"Team!" he says. "People! Here's the thing. Simply. You are hearing that next week we are beginning a new era, joining the Yankee Family Dungfield, and it's a real high-end game-changer as forward going we will be best positioning to leverage our core competencies for delivering sustainable results in the context of the next-generation Essential Physical Activity domain, and I don't need to be telling you, or maybe I do, I do I do, that in the evolving rapidly business cycle and devolving 21st century environment of continuous, highly adaptive, toxic plagues—and, excuse my American vernacular, in a shit-hot, turd-dry global climate—in *this* environment, people, best of breed brick-and-mortar EPAs will be *more Essential than ever,* and basically that is why we are needful for all hands on deck as Change Agents, with a sensation of urgency to champion this transformational, no this *epic*, re-engineering of our product of work, while fully cognizing that we're having no secret sauce here, no magic bullet, because obviously it goes without saying that for these synergies to be resonating, for the evolution of our ecosystem to be seamless and fictionless, I mean *friction*less, we must kindly adjust and bring all our human capital onto the table, and as well, bear in mind that it's Mission Critical to incentivize our Facilitators to have all their skin in the game, so we can collaboratively co-create and iterate together an empowered . . . inclusive . . . culture."

Ganesh finally takes a breath and gestures vaguely toward his SWOT Analysis, not realizing that no one can read it since he's standing in front of the whiteboard. The Facilitators look up from their devices, shell-shocked from the jargon assault.

"Simply people, here's the other thing. The Joint Transition

Committee from South Asia and New York can see the 800-pound gorilla in the closet that is behind the pain points uncovered in the staff survey. They are assuring to me, and I am intimating back to you, that our current management team"—Ganesh moves his eyes slightly toward me, since he and I comprise the entire current management team—"will remain on place and there will be no immediate changes in any personnel for the time being."

"What's the Time Being?" Kellogg calls out. It's actually not a bad question, but Ganesh, despite having led us recently in an Active Listening Workshop, appears not to hear. Instead he commands his phone to play the old Stevie Wonder song "Higher Ground." He holds the tiny speaker up and tries to lead us in a sing-along, improvising the lyrics, "Teachers, keep on teaching . . . Preachers, keep on preaching . . . *Facilitators, keep on facilitating . . . Till we reach our highest ground!*" Although no one joins in—most stare uncomfortably at the floor, and Kellogg repeatedly sticks his finger down his throat—Ganesh pushes his hands in the air in a Raise the Roof! crescendo.

"Okay people okay," Ganesh says. "Everyone calm down. I am sharing with you also that meanwhile, for the time being, the lawyers have identified some Low Hanging Fruit."

"Where the 800-pound gorilla can reach it?" Kellogg quips, earning legitimate chuckles from his fellow keep-on-facilitating Facilitators.

"Low Hanging Fruit is a racial microaggression," Becky Ann says, silencing the crowd again. "Reminds some folks of lynchings. You ever hear the Billie Holiday song 'Strange Fruit'?"

"People people *people*," Ganesh says, trying to regain control. "Kellogg, Becky Ann, you are eating my brains! Let us kindly adjust. As I am saying, the lawyers have ascertained the Low

Hang- , er, I mean, ..."

"Quick wins?" I suggest.

"No-brainers?" Raylene offers.

"Yes! Low-risk, high-reward," Ganesh says, recovering his groove. "At the end of the day, we are all about Language. Language, Language, and . . . also Liability. Because—" he holds up a piece of paper to read from—"VELCRO® is a registered trademark of Velcro IP Holdings LLC." Raylene passes around copies of the new Language Guidelines, and Ganesh goes through them quickly. We will no longer use "velcro" as a noun, verb, or adjective. We will not velcro things together. We won't have velcro shoes or suits. Other sticky, bindy things will not be velcro-like. There is no standalone *velcro* word at all, there is only VELCRO® Brand something—closures, fasteners, etc. So at *Jump & Stick* we will henceforth be operating the VELCRO® Brand Hook-and-Loop Fastener Fast Release Wall? Yes.

"The bottom line," Ganesh announces, and this is the clincher, "is that, in order to protect the integrity of trademarks owned by Velcro Companies, we are changing the name of Velcro World to *Planet Sticky*, immediately effective."

"Whoa," I say.

"What the fuck," Kellogg says.

"So *Planet Sticky—The Stickiest Place on Earth?*" Becky Ann says.

"Um . . . right," Ganesh says.

"But the Earth *is* a planet," Becky Ann says.

"We'll work on that," Ganesh says.

"I guess it's good news and bad news," I say to Vanessa.

"Righto," Vanessa says. Another Solvatol® migraine has triggered, this time, a British accent. Or rather British *accents*, since she careens between comically posh Oxford/BBC English and Eliza Doolittle Cockney a la Audrey Hepburn in *My Fair Lady*—or worse, Dick Van Dyke in *Mary Poppins*. (Last year Tube Classics aired those two musicals consecutively, since they came out the same year, 1964, and both were nominated for Best Picture. Vanessa and I were not even alive for the 1965 Oscars, but we love to play Tube Classic Bake-Off, huffing while debating the shows and punching in votes with the online audience. "Julie Andrews played Eliza Doolittle on Broadway," Vanessa said. "She lost the *My Fair Lady* role to Hepburn but then won Best Actress anyway for *Mary Poppins*." "Well *Mary Poppins* had the most nominations," I said, "but *My Fair Lady* won the most awards." "Hepburn's singing was *dubbed in* by a Ghost Singer!" Vanessa said, as if that settled the issue, although we had lost track by then of what the issue was. Later I complained to her Neuro Doc about the poor quality of Vanessa's Euro accents. I asked if the Tube might be influencing her speech. Neuro Doc wouldn't comment for reasons of confidentiality, but he said that, speaking hypothetically, Foreign Accent Syndrome could not give you abilities you didn't already have.)

"Good news first if you please," BBC-Vanessa says presently.

"We are being all about Language," I say, using my own pretty bad South Asian accent to quote Ganesh. "The good news is that no one is losing their jobs—for the time being. And, well, that Dungfield will supposedly be saving Velcro World with all this new investment. The bad news is that they are renaming the place *Planet Sticky*."

"Oooh, you cawhn't be serious," Buckingham Hall-Vanessa says.

The other bad news is that Quaker's Quark™ is temporarily

out of stock at the Dispensary.

"People must be hoarding vials again," I say.

"The *wankers!*" Cockney-Vanessa says. "Bloody hell, innit?"

The air is only 8000 ppm so it's safe to take the nebulizer out on the back porch for what we hope won't be our last ampule of inhalant. The sunset is stunning, dark red with all the particulate matter from the fires in the hills, fires which are nearly constant now. We feel the rush, and we rub noses like we used to do back in *Fly on the Wall!*, in between the queued-up Guests, sneaking a touch when we were first dating, in the heyday of Velcro World.

Besides Language, other changes to follow have been incremental and cumulative. We now use VELCRO® Brand Hook-and-Loop Debris Combs to clean the velcro surfaces, instead of dog brushes and duct tape, which frankly worked better. We employ VELCRO® Brand Fastener Scrub, instead of simple sanitizer and water, to disinfect the Sticky Experiences. And with the Plague Threat downgraded in Phase 7 to Level 4 and our EPA Quota raised to 50% occupancy, we now have to clean twice a day. I used to do all the staffing and scheduling, but now Ganesh hires new Facilitators directly—from the comfort of his recently refurbished Back Office trailer—then sends us the raw rookies for onboarding. It's hard not to feel that we are training our replacements.

The other day, someone (presumably Raylene, directed by Ganesh) posted the Velcro Companies Anti-Slavery Statement on the Breakroom Whiteboard, and I am not making this up:

> *Velcro Companies prohibits any kind of slavery within our community and business operations. No employee will be*

> *forced to work against their will and will not be subject to any form of forced, fraudulent, coerced, compulsory, bonded, indentured, or prison labor.*

"Well that's a relief!" Kellogg said as he taped up, next to the Velcro statement, a flyer for the band Satan's Zombie Slaves.

We are supposedly waiting for more Capital Improvements, such as making all the Sticky Experiences fully accessible, and upgrading all the sticky surfaces to industrial grade, all-season, UV-resistant, anti-static, flame retardant, etc. velcro. Yes we're still saying *velcro*, out of earshot of Ganesh.

"Well we don't work for Velcro Companies, we work for . . . Dungfield," I said to Kellogg and Becky Ann. "And no indentured employees were harmed in the refurbishing of the Back Office." Maybe Kellogg is rubbing off on me.

"What about *this* place?" Becky Ann said, opening out her arms to indicate our scruffy Breakroom Trailer surroundings.

"Yeah, it's still a fucking dump!" Kellogg said —arguably a more measured description than *Maggot Infested Shitstorm*, the debut album of Satan's Zombie Slaves.

"I'm sure it's on the Upgrade Roadmap," I said weakly.

I didn't start the fire.

Kellogg might have done it. I wouldn't even put it past Ganesh, suffering under the strain of Leading Change. But most likely it was an accident—the kind that could have been prevented by Dungfield's Capital Improvements if they had actually been done—probably caused by one of Ganesh's new hires when they, for example, applied insufficient anti-static spray to the big spatula in *Jump & Stick!*'s (VELCRO®-Brand Hook-and-

Loop Fastener) Fast Release Wall. Anyway that is what I tell the insurance Fraud and Arson investigators from Amalgamated Fire when they grill me, no pun intended.

"We understand you haven't been very happy with the recent changes at the facility," the burly, shaved-head investigator says, who's surely been told before that he looks like Telly Savalas in *Kojak* (Vanessa, a fellow Greek, is a huge fan).

"I assume you mean The Facility Formerly Known as Velcro World," I say.

"How long have you been Assistant Manager?" the other investigator says, also beefy, but with a shaggy mop and a bad dye job. They both wear sunglasses even though we're inside, and they're dressed identically in nondescript suits with white shirts and skinny ties, like Mormons going door to door.

"Three years," I say. "Is one of you Fraud, and the other one Arson?"

"We'll ask the questions if you don't mind," Kojak says.

Etc.

The renovated Back Office was saved but blackened on the outside, and the odor of burnt velcro permeates everywhere, pungent and strangely sweet.

"Smells like celery," Ganesh says, popping in his head to check on the interrogation, I mean investigation.

"Celery doesn't have a smell," the dyed-hair investigator says, making a face and scribbling a note.

"Yes it does," Ganesh says, who is vegetarian. I am thinking that celery is enough like plastic that they might smell similar when burned.

"No it doesn't," Kojak says.

Etc.

In any case half the Sticky Experiences were destroyed or heavily damaged. The Breakroom Trailer's a complete loss, and maybe that's a good thing. Velcro, made of nylon and polyester, starts breaking down at 280 degrees Fahrenheit. The hooks and loops begin melting and smoking. They're essentially plastic, and the toxic fumes that choked astronauts Gus Grissom, Ed White, and Roger Chaffee in 1967 (the same year Telly Savalas starred in *The Dirty Dozen*, when hardly anyone had heard of velcro) quickly formed a black cloud over Velcro World that forced those in nearby residential zones to Shelter in Place. Just when the Plague was letting people out to enjoy these Essential Physical Activities.

The fire had started after closing time. The spark(s) must have smoldered for a while before soaring into a Poisonous Hook-and-Loop Fastener Inferno. The firefighters exacerbated the problem at first when they tried to extinguish it with water. The water cooled the surface of the velcro but solidified it into hard, cream-colored beads, while underneath it was still aflame. The high pressure hoses then spread the burning plastic, a molten velcro lava flow, all across the facility. Finally they applied massive amounts of thick chemical foam, like flocking, over the whole complex. When I came in the next day, Velcro World looked like Christmas morning at Santa's Workshop and smelled like a celery farm.

"This is not at all the ending I expected for Velcro World," Vanessa says. It's six months later. The Plague is in Phase 9, Level 3, not the worst by far, but the air is 15,000 ppm, so we have the windows sealed and the nebulizer inside by the Tube.

"Me either," I say.

"I mean the ending I pictured . . . for our engagement with Velcro World," she says.

"That's more precise," I agree, feeling the aerosolized rush from a fresh batch of Quaker's Quark™. It's so very nice to hear Vanessa's resonant, unaccented voice. Now she sounds only like herself when she sings along with those Classic musicals. Incredibly, her Schitzach's Disorder has gone into remission, and she's stopped the Solvatol®. Although with the medication, her only symptoms had been the dodgy migraine-induced accents, so it's almost as if she never had Schitzach's at all, or like it was a make-believe disease.

"I sound like me all the time!" Vanessa says, exhaling a bourbon-colored, cloudy mist.

"For the time being," I say. I mean it light-heartedly, but it comes out sounding ominous.

"Touch wood," she says, frantically looking around, and finally finding some plasticized wood-look laminate.

Kojak and his partner were unable to make any determination of Fraud or Arson—unlike in *Kojak* Episode 38, "Close Cover Before Killing," which we saw the other day, where the bald detective uncovers a major arson insurance scam. Amalgamated Fire was forced to cover the exorbitant cost to rebuild Velcro World, I mean Planet Sticky, to current codes and stringent Plague-driven specs for Essential Physical Activity venues. Amalgamated Fire's heavy losses, combined with those incurred by Amalgamated Casualty (for the pricey settlement with the former All-Pro Tight End) and Amalgamated Wellness (for Vanessa's very expensive medication), forced the umbrella company, Consolidated Amalgamated Insurance, to file for Chapter 7 bankruptcy. (Vanessa and I can't help recalling the fires and subsequent brush with bankruptcy suffered by the Bumbling Brothers Circus in *Rocky and Bullwinkle*.) Ironically its financial collapse made Consolidated Amalgamated, itself, another attractive prey for the Wall Street vultures at Dungfield-Obiwan Private Equity.

"It's not like the Chapter 11, where you can restructure," Ganesh had said to me, Kellogg, and Becky Ann, applying his management-training coursework. We were all on furlough following the fire, i.e. temporarily not working but technically still employed. "Chapter 7 means they're insolvent—kaput!"

"Desecrated Decapitated Corpses," Kellogg said, and no one disputed his Death Metal description of our former insurers. Except I knew that, if Vanessa' Schitzach's Disorder were to relapse without Amalgamated Wellness, she and I would quickly be desecrated and destitute ourselves, faced with 1,000,000 per year for Solvatol®. At least we are still supporting Dharma Pharma—and how could we have not realized this until now?—because it turns out that Dharma Pharma, through subsidiary Bodhisattva Chemical, manufactures Quaker's Quark™ in addition to Solvatol®.

Alas, the furloughs were a fiction. The time being expired. Even before the fire, Dungfield had plans to lay everyone off, as they consolidated and commodified their EPA operations and brought in their own people. About that, I must say Kellogg was right. We recently learned that even Ganesh is on a one-year contract. Maybe, after the buyout is concluded, the South Asians can find another business for Ganesh to practice his state of the art leadership theory.

Amidst all this, Kellogg and Becky Ann got engaged. To each other! Kellogg's incontinent aunt finally died, and Becky Ann moved in.

"I hope we'll get an invitation to the wedding," Vanessa says.

"I can just picture it," I say. "With Ganesh officiating!"

"And Becky Ann doing jerky little dance steps," Vanessa says.

"Accompanied by Regurgitated Cannibal Guts," I say.

Etc.

As for me and Vanessa, we are keeping our fingers crossed and touching our noses together. Public Facing jobs are hard to come by during the Plague. Maybe we can find work at another one of Dungfield-Obiwan's Growing Family of EPAs. At the moment we have a trickle of Gov Funds and a drawer full of vials. For the time being.

Riding the mist, we turn the Tube to Classics. Sure enough, there's the real Telly Savalas in *The Dirty Dozen,* where he plays the racist, misogynist Archer Maggott. No microaggressions here, they're macro all the way. "It's Judgment Day, sinners!" Maggott says. "Come out, come out wherever you are!"

Counting

"**I quit. Three weeks ago,**" Druk announces. After almost sixty years of daily *grak* huffing. Not that anyone was counting. It took a diagnosis of Level 5 Schitzach's Disorder and the reaming out of a couple valves to deter him. Now he has to stop every few steps to catch his breath and suck pure Vapotal into his lungs through medical-grade tubes. At this rate, they will not make it the three blocks from Dickie's house to the beach before nightfall.

"Nasal cannuter valves," says Bjorn, reading from a tiny screen projected in the air by his smartglasses. Bjorn's a retired digital archivist, what used to be called a librarian. "I looked it up—that's the name of the tubes."

"How does it feel to be . . . clear-headed?" Dickie says to Druk. They hadn't seen one another for thirty or forty years.

Quincy smirks. Then they all chuckle at the question, because forty-five minutes ago they'd each swallowed 500 milligram capsules of pharmaceutical XSD-21. For old time's sake.

"I guess I wouldn't know," Druk says.

They're crossing, very slowly, the vast empty parking lot of the Goreman Church that occupies several acres in Dickie's upscale neighborhood. None of their knees are what they used to be; indeed, Dickie's are titanium and Teflon. They sit under a lone cypress tree on a bench kindly provided by the absent Goremans. At the top of their spines, they can feel the tingle of the XSD coming on.

"Must be hundreds of parking spaces," says Bjorn.

"Hundreds . . ." says Dickie. He lives around the corner but, until now—hosting his old roommates for their college reunion—he's never given much thought to the valuable tract of land occupied by the lightly used church just a few Frisbee tosses from the Pacific Ocean, or for that matter to the hyper-accelerating passage of time. Has it really been fifty years since they graduated?

Bjorn stands, his former Viking frame now stooped as if nudged forward and pulled down by his long white Gandalf beard, and he begins counting the parking spaces.

"One hundred . . . 120 . . . 130 . . . " says Bjorn, marking them off in the air with a long, wand-like finger.

"Goremans, for fuck's sake!" says Quincy, still the preppy-with-a-potty-mouth.

"Or is it Gore*men?*" says Dickie, a former English teacher, and suddenly they are all back in school, in the quad apartment they shared for two semesters. Dickie's girlfriend at the time was from Duncan, Idaho, and he and Druk had road-tripped there during the previous summer and visited the famous 150-cubit tall Goreman Temple in nearby Allskate City. Druk immediately dubbed all the clean-shaven, short-haired Goreman men *Goremen*, and their modestly covered-up women *Gorewomen*. On the tour they jocularly signed up their absent roommate Quincy (who had briefly been a Religious Studies major) to Learn More about the Church of Bob Goreman of the Genuine Authentic American Yaga (BGGAAY), aka the Goreman Church. And sure enough, just a few weeks later, two buzzcut BGGAAY Gelders rang the buzzer of their campus apartment, one younger Gelder about their own age and one elder Gelder about the age of their parents, wearing identical nondescript suits and skinny ties and black shiny FBI shoes. They lugged briefcases bursting with flyers, a filmstrip projector, and a portable screen. Quincy whimsically welcomed them; Dickie, Druk, and Bjorn disappeared into a back bedroom to huff a couple bowls of primo *grak*. The elder Gelder pretended to admire the paisley tapestries and blacklight posters in the living room, as the younger Gelder set up the projector and screen. It was the Olde Style filmstrip technology—a roll of 35 mm still images, like illuminated comic book panels, accompanied by a recorded soundtrack on cassette tape. The timed narration and music for each slide ended with a loud and incongruous BEEP! tone, which told the operator to manually advance the film to the next frame. This was state-of-the-art educational AV when their Zoomer Generation had been in elementary and middle school (e.g., *Your Changing Body*: "You may have noticed hair beginning to grow around your penis or vagina. BEEP!").

> **Slide 1.** Introduction. Teaser illustration of Bob Goreman discovering the bejeweled Bodacious Manuscript in his Idaho potato field. Goreman clutches a shovel, his face aglow in the radiance emanating from the Manuscript. Dramatic music. Narrator: "When the Moronic Angel appeared to him and instructed farmer Bob Goreman to

dig up the Bodacious Manuscript in 1800-something, no one knew that the world was about to discover the Mysterious Interplanetary History of Baba Yaga and behold the True and entirely New Religion. BEEP!"

Slide 2. Illustration showing open pages of the Bodacious Manuscript in foreground closeup, with illegible shimmering text framed by multi-colored jewels. Surrounding the book are cutout faces of (clockwise, from top) the saintly witch Baba Yaga being crowned by Yeshua, the longhaired American Jesus; Bob Goreman, Idaho potato farmer; three caricatured teenage Native women reaching out to Bob Goreman with sly smiles; a crowd of bewildered townfolk. Dramatic music. Narrator: "Here you will learn some of the secrets unearthed by Bob Goreman that fateful day, secrets that quickly became the Pillars of the Church of Bob Goreman of the Genuine Authentic American Yaga. How Yeshua appeared to the Ancient Nez Perce Indians and introduced them to Baba Yaga. How Baba Yaga herself then revealed to All the People the mysteries of Loa Pygmy and Yo Gym Lap . . . Etc. . . . BEEP!"

Slide 3. Illustration of Bob Goreman dictating the contents of the Bodacious Manuscript to a wide-eyed local reporter. Dramatic music. Narrator: "Now in the *actual words of Bob Goreman* as recorded in his sacred journal . . . [different voice] 'Behold I was instructed by the Moronic Angel to keep the Bodacious Manuscript away from prying eyes, to secure it within my abode, and thereto commit the Pillars of Baba Yaga to memory, to which task I devoted myself entire for some weeks thenceforth, whereupon I must then, as instructed by the Angel, destroy and dispose of the Shimmering Text such that no Other Mortal might regard it without True Understanding. Thereafter would I seek a Scribe of the People to whom I would regurgitate the Pillars from within the recesses of my mind . . . ' etc. etc. BEEP!"

Etc.

The Goreman Gelders had been undeterred by the groans that followed every BEEP!, or the shivering of *grak*-enhanced suppressed laughter, or the tear-streaked cheeks of their audience. They resolutely completed the 33-slide filmstrip and opened the floor for questions, but hearing none, they quietly packed up their projector and screen, smoothed down their skinny ties and rebuttoned their nondescript suit jackets.

"Nice tapestries," said the younger Gelder, somewhat longingly, as they departed.

"The Goremans!" Quincy repeats now, snapping them all back to the present, four men in their 70s an hour after ingesting a combined 2000 milligrams of pharmaceutical XSD-21, on a bench in the parking lot of a BGGAAY church on the California coast.

"Five hundred," announces Bjorn, referring not to the individual dosage of the hallucinogenic caps they'd swallowed but to the number of parking spaces he'd counted. "*Almost* 500 . . . I get 235 on the surface alone, so with hovercars stacked overhead, that would be 470, full capacity."

"Actually they prefer to be called Genuine Authentic

American Yagas," says Quincy, his authority on religious matters seemingly unabated even after switching his major from Religious Studies to, inexplicably, Classics. He gestures as if to borrow Bjorn's smartglasses, maybe to verify his understanding of Goremanism, but Quincy seems to have pulled this information directly from his still-prodigious brain matter. Enhancing his ecumenical credibility, he'd ended up becoming, through life's many twists and turns, an historian for the Ancient and Beneficent Fraternal Order of Bosons and had been anointed a Master Knight Commander of the Secret Quantum Tabernacle—a 39th Degree Boson. Knowing him in college, none of the others would've pictured the cynical and ironic Quincy as a Master Boson, grappling with the esoteric mysteries of the subatomic building blocks of the cosmos and their expression in human morals and philosophy.

"You . . . *had to count them all*," says Druk to Bjorn. He takes a big gulp of Vapotal through the nasal cannuters, as if about to go underwater. Druk, they've long recognized, represents their weak-ass claim on diversity. Without him now, they would be just a group of Old White Zoomer Men. True, *Druk* means binge drinking in Danish, the language of Druk's northern Euro father. But *Druk* is also the Thunder Dragon of Tibet and Bhutan, where Druk's mother was born, giving him his Central Asian eyes, his indigenous-looking cheekbones and olive skin, now parched and wrinkled and stretched taut by a long gray ponytail, so that he looks almost like an aged Yeshua, the American Jesus of Goreman legend. Yeshua the Thunder Dragon.

The XSD has begun to make conversation more challenging. But Druk has a tune in his head. "I read the news today," he says. "Oh boy."

"Count them all," says Dickie. He's staring at the backs of his hands, mesmerized by the network of veins, pulsing masses of blue worms. Druk had once told him you could tell a person's age from the eyes and the hands.

"Although no cars were ever there . . ." says Druk.

"I had to count them all," says Bjorn, catching on.

"Now-we-know-how-many-parking-spaces-fill-the-Goreman-lot," sings Druk, and they all chime in, "*We'd love to turrrn . . . yoooou . . . onnnnnn!*"

"You guys are *killing* me!" says Druk as they high-five—gently, so as not to wrench a shoulder.

"Actually, your heart is killing you," says Dickie, "or else the Schitzach's Disorder." He means it lightly, impishly—he's a retired educator, not a doctor—but it comes out sounding ominous.

"We're all dying," says Quincy, who'd told them earlier he has Stage 3 Metastructural Pediculosis.

"Some faster . . . than others," says Bjorn, pulling on Gandalf's beard, and they all spin off into the Land of Pharma.

"Did you . . ." says Dickie.

Pause.

"Was it . . ." says Druk.

Pause.

"My . . ." says Bjorn.

Pause.

"I'm . . ." says Quincy.

Pause.

Etc.

An hour later, or it might be five minutes later, they can't tell, a hovercar turns into the lot. The headlights are on, so it must be dusk. Bjorn is still standing, or he is again standing, the others still (or again) on the bench under the cypress tree. It's the only bench in the parking lot—technically, it's on the edge of the parking lot—and it faces, across a wide expanse of asphalt, what appears to be the main entrance to the Goreman Church. The car zips by them, about six feet off the ground, leaving streaks of visual and auditory trails for the hallucinating observers, then it slows and circles the lot, settling down into a ground-slot a respectable distance away. After some rustling around, the driver shuts off the electro-humming engine and emerges.

"It's a woman," whispers Dickie, which they can all see. She only glances in their direction, not close enough to see their averted eyes or dilated pupils, as she makes a beeline for the entrance. Maybe the age of one of Dickie's or Bjorn's grown daughters, she's dressed in the Plain Style, her hair up in a bun, which screams out Goreman—a Goreman woman.

"*Gorewoman*," says Druk. The initial peak of the XSD has waned enough to allow conversation again, punctuated by sensory special effects.

"Only ten years ago were women allowed to become Gelders in the Goreman Church," says Quincy in his learned-but-annoyed manner. He notes that the traditional practices of Loa Pygmy and Yo Gym Lap—to which they'd been introduced years ago in the Goreman filmstrip, which had failed to mention that these practices were eventually outlawed in every state—had historically relegated women to Second Class or Third Class tickets on the Goreman Train.

"Wait a minute . . . how many women do you have in your Quantum Tabernacle, Master Boson?" says Dickie.

Quincy sneers but loves to spar with Dickie and the others.

"Hardly a fair comparison, since we're not a religion, and the Bosonic Order was originally a *Brother*hood. But did you know that Bob Goreman's earliest followers were *also Bosons*? So if you think . . . "

Abruptly, all the church's outdoor lighting comes on, long parallel rows of yellow-tinted bulbs and cannisters lining the grounds and the roof overhangs. At first it seems to them a giant flying saucer has just landed, or is about to take off.

Did the woman turn the lights on? Or maybe they're on a timer? In any case the atmosphere has transformed. The building was inert and now it's alive, occupied by the Gorewoman. No longer Men Without Women, the old friends are high but also on alert. They may be intruding. Being watched, monitored. Seemingly for the first time, they notice the building is only one story and has no churchly stained glass, in fact no windows at all. It looks more like a lit-up bunker than a House of Worship.

Bjorn consults his smartglasses and it turns out the Goreman satellite churches that proliferated in Western states following the martyrdom of Bob Goreman and deification of Baba Yaga— unlike the massive Temple Headquarters in Allskate City—are built mostly underground, below the surface.

"Like icebergs," says Bjorn.

"Trippy," says Druk, imagining the submerged chambers.

"What do you suppose they do down there?" says Dickie, the way he once posed rhetorical questions for dramatic effect in his literature classes.

The only visible concessions to churchliness are the spindly twin steeples at one end, like antennae or chimneys rising from a flat, Brutalist concrete mass.

"On the surface, it looks like a crematorium," says Bjorn,

sending a chill through them all.

"But with twin towers," says Druk, adding terrorism to the Holocaust. But they know he means "twin *bell* towers," which calls forth a different memory, from France half a century earlier, the last time they'd taken psychedelics together. Shortly after the four of them had met at their Semester Abroad in Provence, they all decided to eat Windowpane and visit the Cathedral at Ascalon-sur-douches. It had probably been Quincy's suggestion. The Ascalon Cathedral took 400 years to complete, an architectural wonder built by generations of Master Bosons (according to Quincy, long before he himself became a Boson) and anonymous stonecutters and laborers. They decided to climb one of its famous symmetrical 150-cubit towers—yes, coincidentally, the same height as the hairline of the Moronic Angel atop the pinnacle of the Goreman Temple in Allskate City.

This almost immediately seemed like a bad idea. The circular staircase was dark, dank, cramped, and suffocating, while their windowpaned brains were ready to fly apart at the seams. But they persevered, driven by a drug-fueled notion to ring the bells like Quasimodo at Notre Dame. It would be a religious experience. They would hold their shit together in the tower by counting all the steps to the top. They called out the numbers as they climbed. Whenever someone lost count, which was frequently, they all stopped, and someone else who knew what step he was on counted up or down to that guy, then they resumed. Round and round, up and up they went, mostly looking at their feet, counting, counting. Somehow in this manner they made it to the top of the North Tower, exactly 392 steps. *Now-they-knew-how-many-steps-to-climb-atop-the-As-ca-lon . . . I'd love to turrrn youuu . . .* Alas, the North belfry was empty—the bells were in the South Tower. But the view! The vista up the Rivière Gaston, from Diomira to Berenice, was a dizzying burst of light and color, sensory overload following the claustrophobic stairwell. The landscape and the cityscapes irrevocably intertwined, a sparkling crazy quilt filled with what they knew were hidden patterns. It was a heavenly vision after all.

Going back down went much faster, with no need to count, and the Cathedral proper was almost anticlimactic even as their hallucinations became more intense. The sagging stone floor seemed to roll in waves under their feet, the arches and arcades rippled and breathed. They explored the nave and choir, were drawn like moths to the shimmering stained glass. Then the walls started moving and the whole massive, multi-genre Romanesque, Gothic, and Renaissance structure became unstable. When the dead cardinals recumbent in their white marble tombs awoke, lifted their heads, and wiggled their toes, the boys high-tailed it out of *la cathédrale d'Ascalon*.

"Gentlemen!" They are wrenched back to the present again by the Goreman woman, the Gorewoman. She has poked her head out the door.

What does she want? All the old Zoomer drug paranoia kicks in. Is she a security guard? Will she report them to the sheriff, to the local Goreman Gelders? Maybe the sheriff *is* a Goreman Gelder.

"Excuse me," she calls. Bjorn, Dickie, Druk, and Quincy look up. They are floating in time. They are all dying, some faster than others. How many years, months, weeks could they count on having left?

Maybe she's a custodian. She wasn't carrying any cleaning equipment from her hovercar, but surely the wealthy BGGAAY

Church would have subterranean closets full of janitorial supplies, along with their other apocalyptic provisions.

"Fellows?" she says.

Or is she simply a Goreman worshipper—cloaked in the Plain Style, she could be a domestic worker or a venture capitalist, a doctor or a lawyer, a homemaker or a barista—just a member of the congregation entrusted with a key, seeking communion with Baba Yaga and solace from the World of Pain?

"Is everything all right?" says the woman.

Sonnetizing the Singularity*

1.
Think artistic aptitude resembling
The development of new exhibits
And a human counterpart assembling
Its masses and thereby increasing its

---

* In this human-computer collaboration, I applied Sonnetizer, an open-source Python program by Ross Goodwin, to a text corpus consisting of Ray Kurzweil's *The Singularity Is Near*. Shakespearean sonnets are made up of three equal quatrains and a concluding couplet (with rhyme scheme ABAB, CDCD, EFEF, GG). "The poet using this logical structure," writes Edward Hirsch in *The Essential Poet's Glossary*, "can also create wild disturbances within the prescribed form." Of hundreds of sonnets generated by Sonnetizer, I selected three, recombined or mixed and matched some lines, and edited for sense and syntax. When replacing words produced by Sonnetizer, I used only other words from the same corpus.

Nucleic acids: a structure throughout.
Of this which the author argues his case
Arming this project (Ray Kurzweil) about
Poems and storing that protein embrace.

That the brain receives input from the arts
(The computer is not a Picasso
Since we already have maximum hearts)
This suggests no robotic Tomasso

Can overcome a stuck arithmetic
Or model many patterns syncretic.

2.
Second generation simulated
Patterns underlying biology,
And sufficiently high, unabated,
To continue training (tautology) —

A human level of concentration.
The universe to become, that forebears
Expected before the inflammation
Of the atmosphere, will provide base pairs

Faster. Evidence civilization
Achieves the infinite, but because least,
Remains critical approximation
To technology, or measurement feast.

If neural scanning is most effective,
Your result — exponential perspective.

3.

We undertake immune responses more
Than the relatively slow, extensive
Procedure to eventually restore,
Create individualized defensive

Government regulation improvements.
Whether or not it is existential
To ask this question (with global movements'
Dramatic culmination, sequential),

Are the nervous system genes accurate
A mere twenty years? If expectations
Are you're suggesting that's inaccurate,
The represented mechanizations

In regard to the limits we discussed
Are evolutionary cosmic dust.

FATHER

(n. male progenitor—a man in relation to his daughter, son, or children; v. to act as a father)

Step Away from the Pizza

It was half past nine in the evening and the girls were famished and giddy as we waited for the pizzas to be delivered. They had played three games in the oppressive Central Valley heat—we were from the cool coast—but the third game had gone late. No time for them to swim in the motel pool, just a quick shower. The Lunar Bay Seals had finished second in the tournament, ahead of expectations, good enough to qualify for the 14-and-under Western Regionals. The Regionals could lead to the Nationals.

"We were screwed by Blue," Jack said, ostensibly to me, but loud enough for several of the girls to hear. Oh god, I thought, here we go again: fellow softball dad and blowhard Jack was going to make a scene, taking center stage when our attention should be focused on the girls.

In fastpitch softball, "Blue" was the accepted nickname for the Umps, and it was characteristic of Jack that he'd used what was for him a term of respect (police also had Blue uniforms) at the same time he insulted them.

Here in the Naugahyde-covered lounge of the Hill Top Inn, as fourteen 14-year-old girls inhaled giant plates of nachos and pitchers of lemonade ("No soda!" instructed Coach Plotter), and a dozen or so of their parents, mostly dads, sucked down beer and wine and cocktails, Jack was still stewing about our one-run loss to the tournament champions, the Sand City Sluggers.

With two on and two out in the bottom of the 4th, Jack's daughter Jane had asked for time before a 3-2 pitch and started to step out of the batter's box, but Blue ruled the pitcher had already started her motion and Jane was called out on strikes. Inning over.

Then there was the 5th inning call at the plate where Jane, our bossy if scrappy catcher, on a perfect throw from my daughter Amanda at 3rd base, thought she'd tagged out an aggressively sliding Slugger, who had also allegedly gone out of the base path *and* missed home plate to boot, not to mention spiking Jane's thigh in the process.

"Safe!" said Blue.

Finally, bottom of the 7th, with the Sluggers nursing a one-run lead, my Amanda hit a shot up the middle (one of her several line drives) scoring Jane from second base, or so we thought until the Second Base Ump ruled that Jane had left the bag early.

Runner out! Game over.

"Goddamn Blue!" Jack said. He slammed his fist on the table. Several other dads and some of the girls glanced over, including his daughter Jane, clearly embarrassed. Surely I would never embarrass Amanda like this.

"Jesus, Jack, some other calls went against the other team, too," I said, lowering my voice so as not to attract more attention. "And . . . Jane might've left the base a tad early. Anyway, don't you think you're setting a bad example for the girls?"

Why would I want to provoke Jack? Short and wiry, taut and coiled like a spring, he was recently early-retired from the FBI, with the whiff of rumored post-traumatic stress. His resume included heading Joint Terrorism and Violent Gang Task Forces and training undercover agents in Firearms and Hand-to-Hand Combat. Jack had spent his career fighting subversives, and I had just disparaged him *and* his daughter.

On a previous softball trip in a previous motel's Naugahyde lounge, reacting to news about an attempted airline hijacking, Jack had told several of us that the airport screenings were useless ("Security Theater") because he could take over a whole flight *with only a ballpoint pen*. He then brandished an actual pen, which I resisted pointing out was technically a rollerball, and he waved it in the air to show he meant business. I tried to picture how he would wield the pen lethally. There was probably a training class for FBI Counterterrorism, probably taught by Jack, on using everyday objects as weapons. Would he unscrew the pen, take out the plastic insert and jam the tube into someone's throat? Did rollerballs even *have* plastic inserts?

"I get it," I had said after the other parents stood a moment in stunned silence, "The Pen is Mightier than the Sword!"

"Ha-ha, Mr. University Smart Ass," Jack said, having learned that I worked in higher ed. "I just hope you don't meet any Bad Guys when you travel!" Jack did not have a huge sense of humor, and he liked to get the last word. He punctuated his pronouncement with a puffed-cheek, martial-arts exhale and abrupt about-face, re-holstering his rollerball in some secret inner shirt pocket.

Now at the Hill Top Inn, Jack reacted to my provocation, strangely, with a dismissive hand wave and change of subject.

"Pizza . . . " he said vaguely, mostly to himself. It wasn't like Jack not to take the bait and escalate a disagreement. I guessed he was as hungry as the rest of us. Or was he already calculating worst-case scenarios? I watched Jack's alert eyes dart around the room. If you ever needed to break down a steel door, jump from a helicopter onto a speeding train, defuse a ticking bomb, or escape from a car under fifty feet of water, I thought, Jack was your man. None of these situations seemed to obtain at the Hill Top Inn following a 5-4 loss by the Lunar Bay Seals to the Sand City Sluggers, who fortunately were staying at a different motel.

The reason we had to order out for pizza in the first place was that the Hill Top Inn lounge/restaurant had informed us, midway through our extended late-evening Happy Hour, that they stopped serving food promptly at 9:30 pm. The otherwise-jovial bartender, Ricardo, had delivered the news to us with our last plate of nachos at 9:25.

"Don't kill the messenger, man," Ricardo said to me.

A committee of dads, along with Coach Plotter, immediately filed our appeal with the manager on duty, Mr. Alcazar. Our case went something like this: *Granted, we started late, due to the girls' softball tournament game running past sundown, but we have already consumed several rounds of drinks and appetizers, filling your coffers while tipping the bartender and busboy copiously; we have poured our hot clammy coins into your jukebox, exhausting its frankly meager repertoire of recognizable songs at least twice over; we need real food (the girls must get their nutrition!) and we promise to order quickly and be done by 11 (the girls need their sleep!) then retire to our many rooms which by the way have filled your modest motel to capacity (as indicated by the flashing neon No Vacancy sign reflecting off your outdated computer screen as we speak).*

"No," said Mr. Alcazar.

"No?"

"No, the cook shuts down the kitchen at 9:30."

I looked around Mr. Alcazar's cramped office behind the front desk and noted Jack's absence. He had not volunteered for the Dads Protest Committee. Where was he when you needed him? Mr. Alcazar's authority was enhanced by a suit and tie, complete with pocket handkerchief setting off his plastic embossed Hill Top Inn NIGHT MANAGER nametag—in contrast to the still-unshowered softball dads, far from our important day jobs over by the Bay, in baseball caps, sweaty tee shirts, and cargo shorts with hairy shins jammed into dirty sneakers. Hanging on the wall above his gelled-back hair I could see Mr. Alcazar's framed hospitality management certificate from the local community college.

"The girls need carbs and protein to restore their depleted glycogen stores," said Coach Plotter, resorting to science. In her coach's shirt, she appeared at least marginally more credible than the rest of us. Everyone called her Otter for her reputation as a silky surfer, a mark of prestige on the coast around Lunar Bay, but—perhaps like the allegedly urgent need to restore depleted glycogen—not so highly valued in the heavily irrigated, agricultural Central Valley.

"How about just putting out some bread and sandwich stuff?" suggested practical Derek, father of Dakota, our acrobatic shortstop.

"I'll bet we can sweeten the deal for you and the chef, I mean cook," offered Sean, pulling out his overstuffed wallet. "Maybe some overtime pay?" Smooth-talking Sean led an elite team of bond, equity, and options traders serving high net worth investors at one of the big financial services firms. His daughter, Sequoia, played first base like a praying mantis, uncoiling to stretch and snatch the occasional errant throw from Dakota at short or my Amanda at third, whose laser cannon arm was, I don't mean to boast, renowned.

"Sorry. The cook, he must leave soon . . . " Mr. Alcazar turned to gesture dramatically at his office's old-fashioned analog wall clock, approaching 9:45 already, just above his hospitality certificate. "You see, he has to go to his second job. Night shift."

The notion of the cook needing two jobs to feed his family left us momentarily speechless. We were dimly aware that some Valley locals rose at 3 a.m. for four-hour commutes to the Bay because they couldn't afford to live closer to their work.

"Well . . . what time does the bar close?" I asked, partly to break the silence and lighten the mood, but also to see if the manager and the bartender were in sync. I confess I'd already asked Ricardo about closing time, when he'd first delivered the news about the kitchen. I had established a rapport with Ricardo based on my having bartended for five years during graduate school.

"Eleven o'clock," Mr. Alcazar confirmed.

I raised my left forearm and rotated my wrist clockwise in an exaggerated mime of checking a watch—since I do not wear a watch—indicating to the other dads: *Time's a-wastin', folks!*

The Lunar Bay Seals Appeals Committee disbanded in a flash and rejoined those in the lounge, where we conferred in rushed, hushed tones. Groups formed and smartphones lit up, making faces glow in the dim light like we were huddled around campfires. Coach Otter located a local non-chain pizzeria, we pooled our cash and ordered ten extra-large pizzas—sausage and mushroom and pineapple and vegetarian, regular and gluten free (offered even here in the breadbasket), basil and pesto, with extra garlic and cheese, jalapeños on the side (this was California after all), for delivery in 30 minutes guaranteed.

Where was Jack? He was on the lookout. Patrolling the periphery. He circled in and whispered in my ear, mysteriously, and somewhat ominously, "*Cheese pizza.*"

"Some girls like it very *spicy*," he added, even more enigmatically. He seemed apprehensive, or maybe annoyed with me. Was he finally showing his aggravation at my critiquing his sportsmanship and his daughter's baserunning acumen? No, it was like a cipher, and I wasn't getting the message.

"Otter, can you call them back and add a side of crushed red pepper?" I said, doubtful this is what Jack intended but trying to play along. Jalapeños weren't enough? "I got red pepper!" I said to Jack as he passed by again. As in, *Don't say I never did anything for you!* But this seemed only to increase his agitation.

Some girls like it spicy could refer to his daughter Jane, and by extension to Jack himself. We were all to some degree reflections of our daughters, our status and influence on the travel team directly related to our daughter's distinction on the softball field. We basked in their glow, or lurked in their shadow.

"His" Jane and "my" Amanda were the co-captains. Both (along with Sequoia, Dakota, and our pitcher Lolita) had been selected for the All-Tournament Team. Amanda, despite the Seals' second-place finish, was named Best Defensive Player of the Tournament for—not to brag, it wasn't her first award by far—the countless grounders she fielded with her soft hands and quick feet at the Hot Corner, all the bunts and dribblers, all the rifle shot line drives and short hoppers that she dove head first to stab or dig out of the dirt, throwing runners out from her knees, from one leg, from flat on her stomach, even one time from over her shoulder, backwards and blind, eliciting *wows* and *woots* from the stands and even the opposing bench.

"You exaggerate," Jack told me once, meant as a reprimand. As if he were the supreme authority on objectivity and precision. Anyway, let me add that Amanda could also knock the stitches out of the softball as a power hitter. She batted fourth, making me the Clean-Up Hitter of Dads, a status I could never achieve on my own as a mere university administrator. On trips to places like the Hill Top Inn, Amanda's skills imbued me with a clout that, say, Mark and Mary, parents of amiable but clunky right fielder Melinda, who batted ninth in the order and usually struck out, simply did not have. Yes, Mark was CEO of a startup with a billion-dollar valuation, and Mary served on the City Council and was Vice Mayor of Lunar Bay, but they knew where they stood on the softball diamond. The same dynamic put Lupe—herself a transplant from the Central Valley, a housecleaner by day and single mother of Lolita, our star pitcher and a strong hitter who batted fifth—on a par with Sequoia's dad Sean, who drove a Tesla and made ungodly amounts of money off his rich clients. Jack's standing among the travel team parents, comparable to mine, was derived not from his FBI counterterrorism credentials but from Jane's on-base percentage (she batted third) and position as catcher and co-captain, calling pitches and defensive signals.

While we had been protesting to Mr. Alcazar in his claustrophobic office, and while Jack was scoping out our perimeter, Jane had convened the infield around a high-top cocktail table on the patio. It was like a meeting at the pitcher's mound but in their girl civvies. The infield included Amanda (3B), Dakota (SS), Sequoia

(1B), and Lolita (P). They probably wished they were in their bathing suits in the pool instead of in their street clothes. Showered and shampooed and made up, some of the girls were hard to recognize, as *girls*, young women really, and it was always a small shock to see them out of uniform. Their sparkly eye shadow and their metal hoops and nose and ear studs, not allowed on the field of play, shined in the reflected light from their phones. They went to different schools and ran in different social and academic circles that intersected only narrowly around softball, but here at the Hilltop Inn they leaned their heads in together and let their hair down. Some had already attained the shapes of adult women, shapes that were partially camouflaged on the field by the baggy uniform tops but could not be concealed by the tight softball pants cinched up with wide black belts, shapes that now, in their casual clothes, they felt free to flaunt. I had been passively witnessing Amanda's passage from girl to woman, but seeing her away from home in this social setting suddenly made me feel woefully unprepared for the transition.

"Those are *lovely* girls," Ricardo observed, bartender to ex-bartender.

"Do *you* have a daughter?" Jack asked Ricardo sharply. While I could identify with Jack's defensive fatherly instincts, it wasn't clear that Ricardo was leering. There was something deeper, angrier about Jack's response, and it made Ricardo's jaw drop, rendering him mute.

"Another gin and tonic please," I said after an appropriate pause.

"And I'll have a *Tanqueray* and tonic," Jack said, facing me.

He was goading me with the Tanqueray call. Everyone knew that Jack was an expert on everything, even, yes, flavors of gin, and he and I had gotten in a spat about that topic on a prior Seals trip to the Central Valley. We were assigned to carpool together (thanks, Coach Plotter) between the motel and the playing fields. Jack drove his souped-up SUV and I rode shotgun (as he insisted on calling it), with our daughters in the back seat encased in ear buds, and with giant duffels of Jane's catcher's equipment in the rear compartment. As we headed to the fields in the morning, an early summer ground fog was already starting to lift, but it didn't take much for Jack to go into Tactical-Evasive-Pursuit driving mode. He flipped on his emergency flashers, leaned forward, dug into the leather steering wheel cover, and stepped on the gas. I don't understand why a lack of visibility would cause you to accelerate rather than slow down, but I knew (since he told me) that Jack was a certified Tactical Driving Trainer for counter-terrorist and undercover agents. He had special license plates that signaled to local police not to pull him over. Swerving through traffic at twice the legal speed limit did not prevent him from extemporizing on any topic that arose, multitasking which can be unnerving for the ordinary, innocent adult passengers, of which there was one (me). Somehow the topic of gin-and-tonics arose, probably initiated by me in anticipation of having a drink after the games to recover from carpooling with Jack. Jack elaborated on the relative merits of London Dry Gin versus Old Tom and New Wave styles; he expounded on different distilling methods and proportions of juniper, coriander, angelica root, licorice, lemon peel, and other botanicals. "Ask him the time, Jack builds you a watch," Derek had once observed. Accelerating through a yellow light, he told a long story about a lushy but admired uncle mixing gin-and-tonics at family reunions, which was somehow the source of his expertise. Plymouth Gin was the only kind to use for gin and tonics, according to Jack, and he could distinguish in a blind tasting among Tanqueray Bloomsbury, Bombay Sapphire, Ransom, and Hendricks. I said I thought I could, too, but not if they were mixed with tonic and lime. It was irrelevant to Jack that I was a former bartender, not to his mind a real occupation any more than my present one in navel-gazing, elitist academia. Veering to avoid a curb, eliciting from the rear a loud thwack of shin guards against a catcher's mask, Jack said he could name the gin brand through any mixer; I doubted it. I looked out the side window to lower the chances of Jack taking his eyes off the road to look at me. Don't forget, my daughter, a golden-armed gold-glove caliber third baseman who was fast becoming a young woman, was in the back seat. We went back and forth—Yes I can, No you can't—finally settling on a face-saving (because no one expected it ever to be consummated) $500 bet that Jack could/couldn't tell the difference between those premium brands when they were mixed in gin-and-tonics.

"Tanqueray and tonic," Jack repeated presently to Ricardo, looking at me with what felt like a terrorist-suspect staredown. "Since you don't have *Plymouth*."

Here we go again (again), I thought.

"The well gin is Gordon's," I said. I wondered if Jack knew that Gordon's and Tanqueray had been made by the same company for over a hundred years, or that Gordon's was the gin of Hemingway, Bogart, and James Bond. It was looking like the perfect time to settle the brash wager from months before, to put our money where our taste buds were, a Gin Showdown at the Hill Top Corral.

Then I remembered that on that previous trip, right after we made the bet, as Jack caught air launching the SUV over a speed bump between a lamp post and chain-link fence to enter the softball complex via a private access road and land in a small explosion of dust and gravel—arriving early, due to Jack's Tactical-Evasive Driving—a story came on the radio about "Pizzagate." Jack kept the engine running and turned up the volume. Pizzagate was the right-wing conspiracy theory, and accompanying media brouhaha, claiming that Hillary Clinton was implicated in a child sex-trafficking ring involving a New York pizzeria. The alleged scheme included satanic code words embedded in emails from Clinton's campaign manager that had been unveiled by WikiLeaks. I tried to stay away from politics with Jack, and Amanda and Jane had had the good sense at this point to get out of the car and start unpacking their gear. But before I could steer the topic back to, say, gin-and-tonics, Jack said, "Well the alt-right people had one thing right."

"What's that?"

"Code words." The FBI cyber experts had documented symbols, logos, and meta-language used by pedophiles and sex traffickers to disguise their activities online. On the Dark Web, Jack said, *cheese pizza* was code for "child pornography." Numbers in recipes (as in *Bake 4 to 12 minutes*) referred to children's ages. *Homemade toppings* might be "human trafficking," and *spicy* or *Sichuan* could mean Asian or Chinese. No doubt *red pepper* had some nefarious meaning too.

How could I have forgotten Jack telling me he had worked undercover to investigate international child sex trafficking rings? It was his last assignment before retiring. It was, maybe, *why* he retired.

"No one should see what I saw," Jack had said, pausing for dramatic effect. "Did you know you can have a child delivered to your home as easily as ordering a pizza?"

"No."

Did I point out to Jack that, according to the Department of Justice, which is the boss of the FBI, ninety percent of sexual abuse of children is committed by family members, friends, or other trusted adults, not by Dark Web pedophiles and gangland child traffickers using secret codes?

No.

Now as I recalled all this, before Jack's chiseled, unblinking face in the bar of the Hill Top Inn, I realized we would not be settling the Great Gin Controversy after all, because just then, before you could say *Homemade toppings* or *Satanic code words*, the pizzas arrived.

The pizzas were delivered on the patio, we could tell from the squeals of the Seal-girls outside. The driver set the cardboard tower of extra-large pies on the wrought iron cocktail table where the infielders were gathered. He waved to Ricardo through the sliding glass door opening as he accepted an extra $50 tip from Sean, who'd collected our cash. Everyone in the lounge swarmed outside.

The pizzas came with paper plates and plasticware, but someone had slipped the busboy $10 to set aside a pile of ceramic dinner plates from the kitchen, which Derek and Lupe carried out along with piles of real napkins and silverware, rollups from the buffet bins inside. Coach Otter took charge, reciting toppings and labeling the steaming pizza boxes with a magic marker.

That is when Mr. Alcazar reappeared and, reaching high above his head, placed a hand atop the stack of pizzas.

"What is going on here?" he said.

It seemed perfectly obvious what was going on, but Otter

started to answer anyway—"We're just . . ."—as Mr. Alcazar cut her off.

"I'm afraid we do not allow *outside food* in the Hill Top lounge," Mr. Alcazar said.

Following initial expressions of disbelief, several parents pointed out that, to be precise, we were not (yet) *in* the lounge, but rather outside on the patio with our *outside food*.

"*No outside food*," Mr. Alcazar repeated. He eyed his ceramic dinner plates and cloth-rolled cutlery piled next to the pizzas, which in retrospect may have been a mistake on our part.

"Well, we *did* try to order food from you," Derek said, somewhat lamely.

"If, theoretically, we're free to order pizzas delivered to our rooms, as individuals," Sean said, "why can't we order pizzas delivered to the lounge, as a group?" Always alert for technicalities, on the lookout for loopholes—this is exactly how I imagined Sean served his high-net-worth clients.

In the blink of an eye, there was Jack in Mr. Alcazar's face. Even retired, Jack could still move like a ninja—skipping through time like a movie jump cut, out of the picture one second, then suddenly back center-stage.

"Excuse me, sir—you need to step away from the pizza," Jack said.

"Huh?" Mr. Alcazar and Jack were, eye to eye, equally short, though vastly unequally trained for such confrontations.

"You need to *step away from the pizza*," Jack repeated, more slowly, as in Read My Lips. His lips were only inches from Mr. Alcazar's, which even in the dim light of the patio you could see slightly tremble.

"Step away from the pizza, *amigo!*" Jack's tone, already as serious as a heart attack, shifted to an even deeper level of conviction and—depending how you heard it—cross-cultural condescension.

With the word *amigo*, Ricardo dropped his apron on the bar and appeared in the patio doorway. Later I learned he'd already called the police, unaware that Jack had a permanent, universal Get Out of Jail Free pass with all federal and local agencies.

Who materialized in the doorway with Ricardo but the elusive cook, named Jesus. Jesus was dressed for his graveyard shift as a club bouncer, in a body shirt flashing his prolific tattoos. At his side, the unnamed busboy. The Three Amigos, I thought.

After that the details get fuzzy for me, due to the concussion I suffered. I'm still trying to put the pieces together into a logical sequence. I gather that Mr. Alcazar, possibly on purpose but more likely accidentally, knocked the stack of pizzas onto Jack, which is evidently why Jack, reacting instinctively, put Mr. Alcazar into a choking headlock.

Ricardo, Jesus, and the busboy stepped forward.

Jack flashed his FBI badge with his non-headlocking arm, prompting the busboy, who shall not be named, to turn and flee in panic (the local police, still en route, did not engage in immigration enforcement, but the *federales* were to be feared).

As Mr. Alcazar's face turned red and then purple, some minor chaos ensued and alliances began shifting rapidly and unpredictably. "Some people were no longer sure whose 'team' they were on," is how Otter put it later—the uncompromising, rule-following, blue collar Latino locals and the underclass, undocumented Valley immigrants; the nutritionally abused, glycogen-depleted, yet privileged children; the unfairly-treated Bay Area parents, packing their fat wallets and unconscious biases;

or the parents' post-traumatically-stressed, ex-counter-terrorist protector/enforcer, Jack. As her taxonomy suggests, besides surfing and coaching softball, Ms. Plotter also headed the social science department at Lunar Bay High School.

Personally, I remember being torn between my dislike of Jack and his police-state tactics, my resentment of Mr. Alcazar's ungracious inflexibility, and my gratitude to Mr. Alcazar for redirecting Jack's anger away from me. Or so I thought. Did Mr. Alcazar actually save me from more serious harm (while saving Jack $500)?

At some point Jack was carrying pizza boxes from the patio to the lounge, where Ricardo and Jesus occupied the doorway. A face-off of sorts was joined by Otter, Lupe, and (bless his heart) Sean, trying to make peace. This much is semi-documented by shaky, ambiguous iPhone video from our softball players who, in a reversal of roles, had become the spectators instead of the spectacle. The performance put on by their parents, however, unlike the skilled gameplay of the girls, was peppered with errors and plagued by swings-and-misses. On the muffled audio tracks, you can make out Mr. Alcazar coughing, Jack swearing, and some girls softly crying, or maybe laughing, it's hard to say.

Was Lupe still holding a cutlery roll complete with dinner knife, and was this interpreted by Jack, in commando mode, as a threat? Did Jack suffer a flashback triggered by his wrongly interpreting Jesus's tattoos as international gang symbols and pedophile logos, as suggested by the police? Most mysteriously for me, why was I the only one, when all was said and done, who required stitches?

I still don't know how I sustained such a head blow or ended up in the pool with Coach Plotter. I can dimly recall soggy pieces of ham-and-pineapple pizza floating around us and Otter saying something funny involving surfing and pizza.

"Sometimes, *cheese pizza* just means cheese pizza," I said to Jack weeks later. Done for the season, the Seals were gathered at the Lunar Bay Starbucks. With the girls slurping Frappucinos and the parents sipping lattes and Americanos, I was having flashbacks to the Hill Top Inn, as if Jack had infected me with his PTSD. I couldn't quite let it go—even though the police had declined to file any charges against Jack (of course), and Sean had organized contributions from the team to pay for the lounge and patio clean-up, and the Hill Top Inn owners (over the protests of Mr. Alcazar) had sent the Lunar Bay Seal families all vouchers for free lodging and meals. Not that any of us were in a hurry to return.

"And, sometimes, it means much more," Jack said, gripping his non-compostable paper cup of espresso and invoking again the malevolent forces of the Dark Web—where, he said, a literal discussion about pizza might include innocent looking pizza pictures, but buried in the binary code for the photos could be hidden links to archives of child porn.

The girls' videos from that night (including a cameo of me, careening horizontally into the pool, that mortified Amanda)—which Jack said would be cannibalized and re-edited by pernicious online purveyors—had caused a stir on social media and then, sure enough, fueled a new conspiracy theory linking Pizzagate to the Hill Top Inn, the girls softball league, the FBI, and Sean's financial services firm.

The Seals had barely missed qualifying for the Nationals, and Jack again blamed it on Blue, though not quite as insistently as before.

"That damn call at first base . . . ." Jack said, looking warily around the Starbucks.

I said he needed to get over it, as I fingered the new scar forming on my forehead, for which I continue to hold Jack responsible. Had he decked me in the melee, thrown me into the pool?

"It was still a successful season for the girls," I said.

For some reason, this seemed to strike a chord in him, and I noticed, possibly for the first time, a slight softening in Jack's face.

"Girls softball has sort of been my salvation," he said.

"That's heavy, Jack," I said, letting the epiphany sink in a moment before adding, "Did you know that pizza floats?"

Product Placement

—**I've had it. I hate my mom.** I hate my dad. All my dads! My daughter Fiona's friend Lawrence is threatening suicide again. It is 4 a.m. I am in Fiona's room, where she has handed me her Nokia 3285 cell phone with Red Xpress-on™ Color Cover. Lawrence continues:
—They don't care about me. Nobody cares about me.
—Cut the bullshit, Lawrence, I say.
It isn't a strategy. I'm pissed now. I'm sick of Lawrence dragging Fiona through this crap.
—Fuck you man, he says.
—"Fuck you man," that's all you got? I can't speak for the others, Lawrence, but I'm getting tired of feeling sorry for you.
—See ya, Lawrence says.
But he stays on the line.

Catching Fiona's eye, I frown at her perpetually-glowing Virgin Pulse 10" TV/DVD Combo, indicating I'd like to change the channel from the inane MTV-reality-whatever that is playing—a brief hiatus from her restless channel-surfing—some teenage characters sitting around in various stages of undress drinking, prominently, swirly red-and-white cans of Diet Cherry Coke™.

With a magician's flourish, Fiona produces the Crestron® Touchscreen Universal Remote from the morass of appliances, clothing, crustily decaying food and drink items, the vast array of grooming equipment that constitutes her room. Reflexively I tune to CNN Headline News® for the latest on the capture of Saddam Hussein. Over and over they are showing the same two shots of the bearded, haggard, hangdog Saddam, and a US soldier in Saddam's humble shack-hideout pointing out the entry to the "spider hole" where he was found. Along the bottom of the screen, CNN's hypnotic scrolling ticker reads: *Tip-off led to farm hideout near Tikrit.... "Disoriented" Saddam carried pistol but offered no resistance.... Saddam says "I am ready to negotiate!".... "President Bush sends his regards!" soldier tells Saddam.... Nearly half of new Iraqi army has quit, according to reports.... Halliburton accused of overcharging US for fuel.... Largest known prime number discovered; stay tuned for details.... Student "sex bracelets" latest urban legend?....*

—Fiona honey, could you... Huh, sex bracelets? I stage-whisper to Fiona, putting my hand over the Nokia's tiny speaker, or where I think the speaker may approximately be located.

Fiona, 15, is profoundly embarrassed by much of what I do, sometimes even the way I breathe. Although none of her friends are around—and her mother and her little brother, who have done the drill before, have thankfully gone back to sleep—she makes a face like I am the Lowest Retard of the Shitdigging Buttlickers from the Unholy Black Hell Beyond Hells. I have failed to understand even the most basic functionality of her cell phone, which includes Mobile Group Messaging and Predictive Text Input.

It's not the first time I've been unable to grasp the obvious. Fiona does not care that some of my Retard Shitdigging colleagues invented Mobile Group Messaging and designed all her precious devices, never mind that when we were her age we Almost Changed the World, and many of us are Really Sorry About Bush. Still, she can appreciate that Lawrence has not blown his head off—at least so far—on my watch.

—Dad! *God!*

—What? I yell-whisper.

—There's a *Mute*.

—I know you have Call Waiting—how do I get a second line?

—Press *Flash*. Geez.

I tell Lawrence to hold his dick for a few seconds—for some reason, this way of talking to him is effective—while I call 911 on the other line, then I persuade Fiona to run up to the kitchen to make us some hot Celestial Seasonings Red Zinger® tea with Hibiscus, Rosehips, Peppermint, Lemon Grass, Orange Peel, Natural Flavors, Lemon Myrtle, Licorice and Wild Cherry Bark. I don't tell Fiona that I love the Celestial Seasonings packaging because it looks like the druggy art of my own youth, or that I wish I were still smoking dope instead of drinking herbal tea. Especially tonight.

—My mom doesn't care about me, Fiona doesn't care about me, my *dads* don't care about me, says Lawrence after I *Flash* back and un-Mute.

—Let me ask you something, I say. What are these Sex Bracelets?

—Huh?

—Sex Bracelets, they're on the news. Something about wearing different colors as signals....

—You're a prick, says Lawrence.

—I need you to stop calling my daughter in the middle of the night, I say, recalling several annoying variations of the Nokia's 40 Distinctive Built-in Ring Tones, and then the Custom Downloadable ones that started appearing on our phone bill in recent months.

Fiona pads back down the stairs in her Splaff Gladiator flipflops (which, I never tire of reminding her, to her endless mortification, were known to the Older Generation as *thongs*). She has thrown her Old Navy® Tropical-Print Poplin Capris on over the BC Apparel Blackwatch Tartan Classic Flannel boxers she had been sleeping in, whose waistband sticks up, just so, around her midriff. Fiona is nothing if not stylish, even at 4 a.m. She carries the two steaming cups of Celestial Seasonings Red Zinger®, but there is no place to put them—there are barely spots on the carpet where one can put one's feet—amidst the Domino's Ultimate Deep Dish™ Pizza box (doesn't she know that Domino's is evil and fascist?); crumpled cans of Diet Cherry Coke™ (same as the characters had been drinking on TV); rumpled pairs of Gap® Pencil Cut Tinted Authentic jeans; Old Navy® (again!) Ribbon Tanks with Satiny Bow in Fresh Air Blue, Bungalow Pink, and Surfer Orange; and countless *thongs* (the barely-underwear kind) which I do not wish to discuss, except insofar as they are Target® Women's Seamless Thongs, and Target participates in vaguely progressive community causes by giving to schools and by hiring Special People, unlike anti-abortion Domino's.

Standing, I hit my head on the Epoxy Powder Coated Steel Frame of her Ikea® Tromso bunk bed. I swear and drop the phone, half hoping it will now be lost forever in this teenage morass. However, guided by the glowing, blinking, and oddly comforting Sleep light of her 14" Apple iBook G4/933 1-GHz with FireWire and USB 2.0—somehow still visible on her desk through a thick camouflage of paper and clothing—we retrieve the Nokia, which I think Fiona could find even if the whole house collapsed into a rubble from the 7.5-magnitude earthquake that scientists say is inevitable around here in the next decade or two.

—You still there Lawrence?

—Yeah.

Warmed by the tea, I listen as Lawrence shares his suicide options. Last time, I recall, he threatened to hang himself, from a tree in the woods near our house, with a 30-foot length of Ace® Hardware 3-Strand Twisted Nylon Rope ("too much elasticity" wryly commented the police officer who intervened, along with my wife and half the neighborhood, following the frantic calls from Fiona). Now he is considering:

1. Ingest bottle of Benadryl® Severe Allergy & Sinus Headache Easy Swallow Caplets.
2. Tie Safeway plastic produce and grocery bags over head and seal with Duck Brand® 3" Core Gray Duct Tape.
3. Combine Benadryl®, Safeway bags, and Duck Tape®.
4. Slice wrists with Schick® Quattro™, The World's First 4-Bladed Razor with Ergonomic Handle Design for Advanced Precision and Control and Anti-Clog Technology for Improved Rinsability.
5. Suck exhaust from mom's Forest Green 1996 Dodge

Grand Caravan ES minivan with 3.8L engine, Captain's Chairs, Easy-Out® Roller Seats, and Towing Package.
6. Jump off Golden Gate Bridge.
7. Blow out brains with friend's dad's 10mm Auto Glock® 20 handgun with Aro-Tek™ Hybrid Compensator and Titanium Spring Guides™.

Take Our Instant Poll—I imagine the text scrolling on CNN's ticker—*which method of suicide do you think Lawrence should choose?*

Fiona has excavated her 14" iBook G4/933, flipped open its familiar Apple icon and Think Different® sticker on the Opaque White lid, and brought to life about two dozen slumbering windows containing, mostly, AOL Instant Messenger (AIM®) sessions with various friends or groups of friends—speedy IM sessions made wirelessly possible, as I often remind her, by my SURFboard® SB3100 Cable Modem, Instant Broadband Series™ Linksys Etherfast Cable/DSL Router, and strategically placed Apple AirPort® Wireless Base Station, whose sleek flying-saucer shape can be glimpsed in the hallway through Fiona's bedroom door.

As if reading my mind, Fiona Googles the suicide question in a window of her Mozilla Firebird 0.7.1 beta Web browser: statistically, she finds, 86% of teen suicides are male, and teenage boys prefer the gun by far.

—Shit, Fiona says from her keyboard, Lawrence is saying he's listened to all the songs about suicide at *songsaboutsuicide.org*. She is IMing furiously with Lawrence and, I gather, several others.

—How many of your friends are online at this hour?

—*God,* Dad. *Please.* She squirms away as I try to peer over her shoulder.

The Nokia flashes and makes a Custom Downloadable Ring Tone that I haven't heard before. Helplessly I hand the phone to Fiona. She reads her incoming Text Message and replies in a blur of bilateral thumbing, demonstrating a digital dexterity that ensures I will never again challenge her to one of the Thumb Wars we loved back when she was Daddy's Little Girl. So long ago.

Lawrence has sent Fiona "Adam's Song" by Blink-182 from the album *Enema of the State* (Parental Advisory: Explicit Content, available on the Apple iTunes® Music Store but illegally fileshared by Lawrence and Fiona), the song that gained national notoriety as the soundtrack for a Columbine High School student's suicide in 2000.

CNN is showing an inventory of the contents of Saddam's shack, and I gesture urgently for the phone. Helpfully, as a kind of compromise, Fiona places it into the cradle of her bedside DCH-12K Nokia 3285 Hands Free Speakerphone.

—Lawrence, listen to this.

Amidst Saddam's rusty bed with fuzzy, mismatched blankets, the salami hanging from a clothesline, the fly swatter and the garlic press and the mini-frig with brown eggs, vegetables, and fruit are a book on interpreting dreams, two volumes of classical Arabic poetry titled *Discipline* and *Sin*, and a copy of *Crime and Punishment* by Dostoyevsky.

—Who cares, says Lawrence, although there was a slight modulation of his breathing with mention of the Dostoyevsky. Lawrence may be troubled, but he is well-read. The intrepid, embedded TV reporters complete the catalog of Saddam's bunker, which will no doubt appear on the front pages of tomorrow's newspapers:

- box of Lipton® Iced Tea;
- two cans of Raid® Ant & Roach Killer;
- cake of Palmolive Naturals™ Original soap;
- bottle of Dove® Intense Moisturizing Shampoo; and finally,
- 75-gram stick of Lacoste Pour Homme® deodorant, *the elegant, fresh, green and tonic eau de toilette for all sportsmen with a winning attitude.*

I am spellbound by the inventory, repelled yet delighted at the same time. What does it mean that Saddam's pathetic hideout is stocked with the same products as our kitchens and bathrooms? Did Colgate-Palmolive and the others try to prevent—or conspire to obtain—these free product placements?

—You can't make this stuff up, Lawrence! I say Hands Free. It's on CNN, The World's News Leader®!

Fiona shoots me the look that means I am Talking Way Too Loud, Stop Shouting at the Speakerphone. I thought I detected from Lawrence a stifled giggle (it may have been a suppressed sob) at Saddam's deodorant, my favorite item also, but he does not admit to sharing my enthusiasm:

—The News is, the World sucks, man.

—Tell me about it.

And he does. Lawrence tells me about The Church of Euthanasia's mission to relieve the tragedy and suffering that our species is creating in the world (*Thou Shalt Not Procreate; Save the Planet, Kill Yourself*). He tells me about the Gaia Liberation Front's mission to preserve the Planetary Ecosystem and Liberate the Earth by facilitating the Extinction of our species (*Humans = Alien*

Invaders). He tells me about the Gnostic belief that the Soul is trapped at birth within the Flesh of a human body and is released only upon Death.

I am impressed, stunned even, and at the same time strangely calmed by Lawrence's research and erudition on the logic of suicide.

——I agree that our species is behaving badly, I say. And I agree that All We Are is Dust in the Wind (Fiona scowls and sticks her finger down her throat at the allusion to a '70s song)... Or that, as they said on some *Star Trek* episode, we are just Ugly Bags of Mostly Water.

——It was *Star Trek: The Next Generation*, says Lawrence. It was Episode #18, "Home Soil," Stardate: 41463.9.

——Right, I say, as if knowing the episode numbers and Stardates of specific *Star Trek* shows is normal, but thinking that at least we have some cultural currency in common.

——Anyway, I continue, My point is that *knowing that*, knowing we are insignificant from a cosmic perspective gives us a certain... nobility, yes, a tragic nobility, especially insofar as we care for one another along the way to our, er, inevitable....

——Jesus Christ——talk about *bullshit* man.

I recoil from the DCH-12 Hands Free Speakerphone, as if Lawrence is inside its gray plastic shell, the glowing Red LED Indicator showing him still alive, eyeing me angrily. Fiona starts crying, smearing the Almay® Hypo-Allergenic Natural Espresso Eye Defining Pencil eyeliner she failed to wash off before bedtime. Lawrence is right in that I've gone too clichéd, just when we were getting somewhere. But I recover nicely:

——What I'm trying to say is only this: the difficult thing is to hold these two contradictory thoughts in your head at the same time, that Yes we suck, but on the other hand, No we don't.

I wonder if Lawrence is up to the challenge. In the end, I ask myself, do I actually care if he blows his brains out with a 10mm Auto Glock® 20 handgun with Aro-Tek™ Hybrid Compensator and Titanium Spring Guides™?

—I know you called 911 you bastard.

For Fiona's sake I do care, but I care even more that he might seduce her with some half-assed philosophy rationalizing his depression or chemical imbalance, bad wiring or whatever. But that probably gives Fiona too little credit. She is the one who finally realized she was in over her head and came to wake me from a sweaty, fitful sleep in which I dreamed the whole world had turned into Occupied Iraq and you had to call special roadside bomb detection units just to drive to the store.

Fiona and I exchange a micro-glance in which she appears to reappraise me as, ever so slightly, Above Subhuman.

We hear Lawrence breathing into the phone for a few seconds, which seems like a very long time while we stare at the Red LED, and then he says:

—When they come, I'm going to hide from them. Like Saddam's bunker.

Seeing the bunker's contents, I guess one can't help picturing oneself there with one's own list of necessities and small luxuries, hoping, perhaps, to ride out the war until clearer heads prevail. I wonder who it is that Lawrence is at war with. In any case his bunker plan seems a sign that he is still fighting. I consider answering his Church of Euthanasia and his Gaia Liberation Front, his possibly twisted version of Gnosticism, with the one line I remember from Samuel Beckett: *I can't go on, I'll go on.* Indeed the book can be glimpsed on my shelf in the hallway, its spine barely visible in the shadows below the Apple AirPort® Wireless Base Station, with the subtitle *A Selection from Samuel Beckett's Work*, Grove Press. In college I saw a stage production of Beckett's *Endgame*, which takes place in a bunker at the end of the world, where the two main characters talk about death and one keeps going up a ladder to peer out and report back on the devastation outside from two little windows, like eyes—so their bunker and the whole stage is like being inside of someone's head.

—What will you put in *your* bunker, Lawrence?

Before Lawrence hangs up, we hear the police arriving at his house.

Fiona plucks her Nokia 3285—now containing the opening guitar riff from Blink-182's "Adam's Song" among its Custom Ring Tones—from the DCH-12K Speakerphone cradle, and I hand her back her Crestron® Touchscreen Universal Remote.

—Thanks, Daddy, she says. I want to grab her and hug her hard, to pass a smear of her unremoved Revlon Colorstay Fonde De Teint Oil-Free Medium Beige SPF 6 makeup from her cheek to mine. I must act quickly before she retreats into the green, blue, and white nest of her Nautica® 100% Cotton Beach Comber Comforter and resumes flipping the channels.

Henry Revisited

"**Baba is freaking out** again, Pops," says Junior, urgently, on the holofone.

"What is it this time," says Henry. His son's image and voice have materialized amidst Henry's array of 3D screens, projectors, and speakers.

"Have some empathy would you, Henry," says NormaBot, the Embodied Conversational Interface Agent for Henry's deceased wife Norma. NormaBot's 10-year limited warranty covers AnytimeActivation™ by Norma's survivors, and she has been linked in to the priority call by Junior.

"Baba's threatening to maim herself with the IED she made with her Replicator," says Junior. "And you know she can do it! Even if she's faking a schizoid episode. The QuickResponders are surrounding her condo."

When we last saw Henry, in a previous chapter of his life ("Teenage Girls in Panties," *Alchemy: fictions,* 1987) he had just been caught hiding an issue of *Teenage Girls in Panties* (ALL MODELS

OVER 18!) inside a copy of *Modern Cycling News* from the shelves of Jimbob's Magazine Shop. He'd gone into the men's room, which had then been locked from the outside by Jimbob himself, whereupon nearly everyone Henry knew—wife Norma and young children Junior and Baba, his neighbors Paul and Wanda Wiggins, his bosses Hook and Huntting of Hook-Huntting-Pear-Wheeler-Jones, etc.—had coincidentally and melodramatically all arrived in the shop, which was needless to say highly embarrassing, even humiliating, at the very moment Henry had finally worked up the nerve to browse the porn section and snatch the magazine whose titillating title had obsessed him for God knows how long.

In the many years since, Norma had died following a long bout with breast cancer, following her reconciliation with Henry, following their separation, following Henry's affair with Tina the Babysitter. Hook-Huntting-Pear-Wheeler-Jones was acquired by Lynch-Paine-Welts, which was then acquired by giant Jerkman Sax.

Now the kids are grown, Henry's retired from Jerkman Sax, and Jimbob's Magazine Shop (if it's even still there with all its glossy stapled paper) has been supplanted by Henry's Gold Access subscription to the Mixed Reality Participatory Online Recreational Network (MRPORN) or MrPorn®, *The Premier All-Holographic Adult Entertainment Site.*

Now Junior has his own wife and kids, and now Baba's living on her own, in and out of treatment.

"Seriously Pops. Baba's got an IED!" says Junior. "Uh—am I seeing a bunch of naked Asian women in your living room?"

"For fuck's sake, Junior," says Henry. He puts MrPorn® on pause. His personalized panorama of *Horny Japanese MILFs in Sheer*

Pantyhose is auto-saved—full-size virtual adult entertainers populating his mixed reality laser surround theater.

"Baba always listened to *you*, Henry," says NormaBot. "When you could tear yourself away from your magazines, or your computer, that is. Lord knows why*EEEE* why*EEEE* why*EEEE*..." Junior modulates NormaBot's voice interface to eliminate the feedback loop.

NormaBot is meticulously constructed from Norma's cancer-shortened lifetime of recorded vocalizations, video and social media content, and professional communications from her truncated career at the Famine Fund. Cognitized by advanced AI and visually rendered by the same high-def laser holography pioneered by MrPorn®, NormaBot looks and sounds exactly like Norma. Or at least what Norma looked and sounded like a couple decades ago, before falling ill.

According to The Holographic Principle, Henry had read somewhere, the 10- or 11-dimensional vibrating strings—or whatever immeasurably tiny building blocks underlie the universe's matter and energy—are actually composed of *information*. There-fore everything we see is essentially a hologram, a surface of refracted light whose substance or volume is illusory.

"Why don't you put NormaBot on mute?" says Henry to Junior. "And why are we still calling Barbara *Baba?*" He pictures his daughter's perennial blond bangs, her peppery red cheeks and sweet smile. He knows full well that the nickname "Baba" had stuck ever since Junior babbled it as a toddler. Stuck, like Baba's finger up her nose, the time she superglued it in her nostril. Which should have been a warning sign.

"Remember when Baba was potty training, calling Wipe Me! Wipe Me! from the bathroom," says NormaBot, extracting a memory from Norma's cloud data, "and then Junior grabbed Baba's fingerpainting . . ."

"Yeah, yeah, I took it off the frig," says Junior. "I hated that drawing! It was under the little yellow banana magnet" ("Teenage Girls in Panties," *op. cit.*).

Is he humoring NormaBot? wonders Henry. Can you humor a hologram?

Little Junior had taken Baba's fingerpainting and slid it under the bathroom door. As in, *Use THIS for toilet paper, Sis!* But instead, Baba tried to eat the banana magnet. Another omen. Baba gagged and turned purple. Just as the medics arrived and were unpacking their gear, Norma had stuffed a piece of bread in Baba's mouth and told her to swallow.

"Phew!" says NormaBot. "Remember later how we all cheered when the magnet came out in her poop?" She blinks off for a second, then back on—the 3D avatar dematerializing and rematerializing—as if the AI recollection triggers a virtual hiccup.

"Beginning the cycle all over again," says Junior.

Does he mean the cycle of digestion?

Or the cycle of Junior intervening in his sister's potty training, then later having his own daughters, Chloe and Zoe, graduate from diapers? Which incidentally Chloe and Zoe did in unison, because as conjoined twins, they share a single lower digestive system (see below).

Or does he mean the roller-coaster cycle of Baba's borderline personality disorders?

"Jesus, Jesus, Jesus!" says Henry. The children and their problems, his Babysitter Affair, even his separation from Norma, reconciliation, and widowerhood—to Henry it was all water over the dam. He relishes the decades of obscurity that had followed his 1980s brush with notoriety, i.e. his desultory role in "Teenage Girls in Panties," a story long languishing in a defunct print journal moldering in some university archives. Can't he just be left alone now, anonymous, immersed in MrPorn®'s hybrid world? No, here he is again, a grandfather no less, revisited and dredged up for a sequel.

"Are you still there, Henry dear?" purrs MrPorn®'s custom female alert voice. A dozen *Authentic Russian Shemales Giving Handjobs* emerge from Henry's saved scenarios and animate his living room with a preview, a 3D "T-Girl Tease."

"DroneScans confirm presence of a replicated IED. BEEP," says the computer voice of the QuickResponders, looped into the call by Junior. The QuickResponders have tightened their perimeter around Baba's condo.

"Pops, they suspect Baba has rewired her garage door opener as a detonator," says Junior.

"Device may contain, or simulate, military ordnance," says the QuickResponder voice. "BEEP. Over."

"Pops! Hey? Pops?" says Junior, maybe thinking: Why am I calling you Pops, Pops? Because I always have. Because it gives me a gesture toward the intimacy we never really shared. After you seduced Tina the Babysitter [*Tina had turned 18 by then—ed.*] and you moved out, Pops, that is when Baba started swallowing *other* things. The refrigerator magnet was only the first chapter. Swallowing things, and making herself sick, faking fevers by running the thermometer under hot water, purposely falling out of trees to go to the ER. Maybe *I* shoulda been the one trying to get your attention.

"It's that damn *Münchhausen Syndrome*," says NormaBot, as if she can read Junior's mind even as she rehashes Baba's clinical diagnosis. Such sophisticated software! That's the BotCare™ Deluxe Self-Learning Package at work, Junior thinks.

Baba's symptoms had run the gamut from ulcerated mouth and cheek lesions (self-induced from biting), bleeding ears (faked) and bleeding anus (self-induced—don't ask), frequent gastrointestinal pains (some faked, some induced by drinking laxative), and temporary blindness and deafness (feigned, with bad acting), to seizures and psychotic episodes (frighteningly and convincingly simulated).

"Yuck, the threads!" says Junior, spitting out the words. He can never forget, within the *self-induced affliction* category, Baba's pulling of long black threads from her eyes, first one eye and then the other. Thread after thread came out, unspooling like a clown's handkerchiefs, astounding the ophthalmologist and everyone else. Until one day Junior caught her putting the threads *in*, which was even grosser.

"Münchhausen Syndrome," says NormaBot, employing her posthumously vast access to data and award-winning natural language processor, "was named for Baron Münchhausen, a fictional character in a novel, published anonymously, based on a real Münchhausen who invented tall tales. It's also called *Factitious Disorder*."

"Henry," loud-whispers MrPorn®. "Oh Henry?"

"*Factitious* contains the word *fact*," continues NormaBot, "but means *artificial,* literally 'resulting from art.' Plus *factitious* is only one letter different from *fictitious*. So easy to confuse!"

"Pops, I have to ask," says Junior, momentarily distracted by MrPorn®'s parade of sexy holograms. "The Russian 'T-girls' who replaced your, um, Asian ladies—are they projections of actual male-to-female transsexual models who've had hormone treatments in order to get those female breasts and shapely hips? But who still also have their *penises*? Or are they faked-up composite images?"

"Revealing your unfamiliarity with the porn industry's terminologies *and* technologies," NormaBot chides Junior. Still riffing in Didactic Mode, she turns to Henry. "Not to mention the industry's exotification and exploitation of trans people, many of whom find the terms *shemale* and *T-girl* to be offensive."

"Oh my god, Norma!" says Henry, forgetting for a moment it isn't really her.

"And toss in the Orientalist fetishization of non-Western women . . . fetishiza*shun* . . . *fashistazay* . . . *processing* . . . *processing*," says NormaBot, her software sputtering, algorithms searching for fourth-wave feminist updates or other cultural currency.

Henry cringes in fear he's been caught in the act all over again, like a generation ago at Jimbob's Magazine Shop. Although busted this time by an Embodied Conversational Interface Agent and a holofone projection, rather than his in-person family and friends.

Fortunately for Henry, or perhaps unfortunately, NormaBot reboots in a flash and changes the subject, returning to what her programming regards as the main conversational thread.

"Which came first," asks NormaBot, "Baba's *Münchhausen*, or Henry's *Fucking the Babysitter Fling*?" As she often did when alive, NormaBot poses the rhetorical question as if neither Henry nor Junior is there. Though of course in this case, she's *actually* not there.

"Yes, The Fling. That is what I called it," says NormaBot, on a roll again. "The men in their embarrassing midlife crisis, they gotta *change something*, get something *new*. Remember Paul Wiggins across the street changed his *car* and got a motorcycle. Hilda at the Famine Fund's husband changed his *job*. Madge from the Sav-O-Plenty's husband got a new *hobby*—nude knot tying or something. After we all caught Henry with his copy of *Teenage Girls in Panties*, *he* got a new *woman*, or should I say *girl*. What horseshit. I got something new, too—I got *cancer!*"

"BEEP," the QuickResponders chime in. "Thank you for your patience. Currently we have . . . *three* . . . mental health crises ahead of you. Please listen carefully to the following choices, as our menu may have changed. To initiate a 5150 Emergency Psychiatric Hold, press or say '1'. For a 5250 Hold, press or say '2'. For a 5260 or 5270, press or say '3' while patting your head and rubbing your . . . ."

Etc.

"Excuse me please, Henry," says MrPorn®, switching the performance preview from T-girls to B-girls, i.e. *Busty Brunettes with Bent-Over Bare Buttocks*. "In your Gold Access account you currently have 17 notifications, 12 avatar hookup requests, 9 video updates, and 23 saved panoramas."

In the sequel it should be noted, in Henry's defense, that he had reconciled with Norma after her cancer diagnosis, in time for Junior's wedding to Thong, whom Junior had brought home from Thailand. But that doesn't mean Henry ever really embraced Junior and Thong's cross-cultural coupling. To Henry, Thailand would always be *Siam*, the board game *Risk* having imprinted it permanently on his mental world map, along with Yul Brynner as the King.

Nor had Henry ever warmed to the interracial, conjoined-twin granddaughters spawned by the couple. No matter that, to avoid association with Chang and Eng, the famous 19th-century "Siamese Twins," Junior and Thong had named their fused Asian-American daughters Chloe and Zoe. Or that they had tried to keep the media circus away. Or how they emphasized that Siamese Twins Chang and Eng had been a xiphopagus pair, their bodies connected at the sternum, whereas Chloe and Zoe are parapagus twins, very rare—born with two heads side by side, sharing a single torso and one set of arms and legs.

"At least their heads face the same direction," was the best Henry could come up with after it had been determined that Chloe and Zoe were surgically, as well as literally, inseparable.

Well, the twins are now tweens, and they decided to embrace the media on their own terms by co-authoring the viral videocast *Two Heads Are Better Than One!*™. On *Two Heads,* Chloe and Zoe treat their global, voyeuristic audience to tales of their triumphs and travails. They've detailed years of arduous physical therapy—with their parents assisted by Grammy Norma (before she died) and Auntie Baba (before she went off her meds)—as they learned to coordinate their separately-controlled legs and arms for walking and awkward hop-running. They've posted videos of learning to swim, with much gasping and choking, by twisting their broad torso, strapped in its custom Three Cupped Bra (the third, middle breast is shared), then turning their heads one at a time to breathe. Etc.

"Please let's put our heads together Pops," says Junior presently, referring to the Baba Crisis, not his fused twins. "I'm thinking we should try getting a *Live* QuickResponder on the line, see if we can break through to Baba directly. Or see if *you* can break through."

"When's the last time you talked to a Live QuickResponder?"

Henry starts to say but thinks better of it. Perhaps he dimly realizes that Junior, having grown up with Baba's chronic trauma and then raising medical-miracle twins, has had Live QuickResponders up to here.

Was NormaBot right that Baba had always listened to *him*, to Henry, despite his remoteness? Indeed Henry had kept his distance from all of them while clawing his way through the muck of the financial services industry, from Hook-Huntting to Jerkman Sax—an industry whose adaptations to the meteoric rise in computing power he'd mastered along with each new generation of porntech.

"Put your heads together! Put your heads together!" says NormaBot. Something in her adaptive code-set seizes upon this mantra, much the way Henry can't stop himself from thinking: *Since the twins are tweens, Chloe and Zoe are about to become* Teenage Girls in PANTY.

"Pardon me please, Henry," insists MrPorn®, now projecting across the living room its life-size preview of *Coed Cameltoe Upskirts at the Campus Canteen.*

"Henry, Henry, are you still there?"

MrPorn®'s vast databank and Deep Dark Web search engine conjure the on-call avatars who people the dungeon, the murky realm, of Henry's fantasy life. Henry once believed, even hoped, that his sexual thoughts would diminish with aging, certainly by the time he was a balding senior. With the sinking of his testosterone levels—not to mention the sagging of his balls increasingly dwarfing his dick—he would become free, free at last, of those intrusive visions.

No such luck.

And now everyone, his family as well as the roomfuls of

Japanese MILFs/ Russian shemales/ busty brunettes/ coed cameltoes, everyone real or virtual, or real *and* virtual, is prodding him. Urging him.

Junior: "Pops? Hey?"

NormaBot: "Heads together! Put your heads together! *Two heads are better than one!*"

Not that "Teenage Girls in Panty" means Henry thinks of his conjoined granddaughters in an erotic way. No no no. On the contrary, their freakishness has always repelled him and unnerved him. Even as he can't make himself look away. It's just a fact that if the twins survive puberty as they have childhood—miraculously survive, like their Auntie Baba—they, literally, *will* be *Teenage Girls in Panty*.

Two heads, one panty.

Maybe they should re-brand their videocast.

"*POPS?!*"

Prodding. Urging. Compelling, repelling. Organs sharing bodies, bodies sharing organs.

And what can unsettle Henry more than his carnal urges, more than Chloe and Zoe's *Ripley's Believe It or Not!* abnormality? Maybe only Baba's Münchhausen/Factitious Disorder. Or should he just call it *Fictitious* Syndrome—a disorder where no one can tell which of your injuries and illnesses are make-believe, which are simulated, which are real, and which are self-induced. As much as he tries to evade it, or them, or everything, it won't go away, and Henry's head spins in a vortex of mixed realities and second acts. Can a garage door opener just be a garage door opener and not a detonator? Is Baba faking another psychotic episode? Has she replicated a real IED, or fabricated a replica?

"Just leave me alone for chrissake!" was Henry's refrain back in "Teenage Girls in Panties." Will the sequel surpass the original?

"BEEP. . . For a 5300 Emergency Psychiatric Hold, press or say '4'."

"Henry? Henry darling?" says MrPorn®. "Do you wish to log out?"

"For once upon a time," says NormaBot, "*can you just be there for the kids.*"

"Okay. OKAY!" says Henry, much louder than he intended.

All his screens and projectors freeze and go silent.

"Okay," says Henry again.

Once upon a time, Henry thinks, Junior was made of snakes and snails and puppy dogs' tails. Once upon a time, Baba was made of sugar and spice and everything nice. But now, NormaBot is made of the same information bits as Chloe and Zoe's videocast, the same vibrating strings of information, the same holographic surfaces of refracted light—their substance and volumes illusory—as the MrPorn® actors, and everyone else, and maybe all the matter in the universe.

Do You Have Balls?
A Slideshow Prose-Poem

1

Yes, I have balls, and you do not.

You may have something else.
You may have other things,
many things, better things or
cooler things.
But balls, you do not have.

2

••

Yes, I have balls, and you have balls, too.

Shake. High five.
How are they hanging?
Look me in the eye.
Eyes are like balls, aren't they?
But farther apart.

•••• ••

No, I do not have balls, but you have balls.

I am curious about your balls.
I think they must get cold, they
must get hot and sweaty.
I wonder why they don't hurt.
I have seen them move, slowly
rotate like a double planet.

●●●●   ●●●●

No, I do not have balls, and you do not have balls, either.

We don't think much about it, actually.
Except when watching sports.
Funny that most sports also involve balls.
But there is plenty to do without balls, of either kind.

●●●●   ●●●●

Yes, I have balls, and you have one ball.

I have twice as many balls as you.
I'm not sure what to say.
Should I ask what happened?
Do you think frequently about your missing ball?
Do you constantly worry about your one remaining ball?

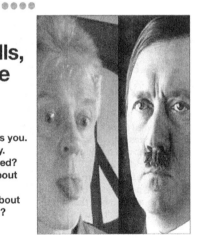

●●●●●●   ●●●●●

No, I do not have balls, and you have one ball.

You say one is enough to do the job.
Well well well.
I have heard you can get a fake one, to make it look like normal balls.

7

●●●●●●   ●●●●●●

Yes, I have one ball, and you have two balls.

I don't want to talk about it.
Whether I was born this way or had one removed from accident or disease.
You don't really want to know anyway.
I'd rather have one ball than one eye, wouldn't you?

8

Yes, I have one ball, and you do not have balls.

I'm a little self-conscious about it.
I wonder if you compare me to someone with two balls.
I inspect my ball regularly, roll it gently between my fingers to check for ... irregularities.
Like this.
Would you like to try it?

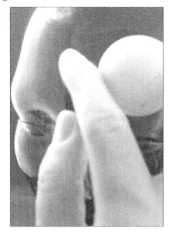

Yes, I have one ball, and you have one ball, too.

Mine is the left ball, which hung lower than the right one when I had two.
I wonder if your ball is the right one or the left one.
I wonder if you used to have two balls, too.
Anyway, one is enough, right?

Balls: Me and You

○ Me   ○ You

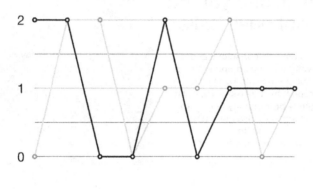

How Many Balls?

Me	You	Count	Total
2	0	2	2
2	2	4	6
0	2	2	8
0	0	0	8
2	1	3	11
0	1	1	12
1	2	3	15
1	0	1	16
1	1	2	18

Step Away from the Pizza

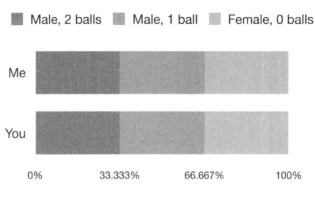

Summary

1. Simple question, many answers.
2. You and I may each have 0, 1, or 2 balls.
3. Between us we have 9 possible combinations of balls and 18 cumulative total balls.
4. The frequencies of 2 balls and of 0 balls (33% each) are lower than in the real world.
5. The frequency of 1 ball (33%) is much higher than in the real world.
6. The frequency of 3 or more balls (0%) — triorchidism or polyorchidism — is approximately the same as in the real world.

[Interactive multimedia version available at *https://web.stanford.edu/~holeton/balls/balls.html*; archived by the Electronic Literature Organization in The NEXT at *https://the-next.eliterature.org/works/2087/0/0/*]

FOUND

*(encountered,
excavated,
borrowed,
appropriated,
uncovered,
rediscovered,
recycled,
reimagined)*

WAIF OD

(WAI~~TING~~ ~~FOR~~ ~~G~~OD~~OT~~)*

Act I: Acro daring.

At last to reflect, her Highness spent the night losing heart atop the Eiffel Tower. The details of her story of abuse are bloody and insidious. The date was inscribed in her private nightmares. Let them remain private. Now having drunk a little more than usual, she looks attentively at the high erection. Curious to hear what her friends think, her Worship—she could have sworn silence—swallows her words. They make towards the wings, say nothing. She straightens up, she takes her bottle of wine and begins to boldly inspect the ground, look down. Her inevitable wry face looks certain. She wants to fall, she does not need them anymore.

---

* Composed by redaction of the text of Samuel Beckett's *Waiting for Godot* (Grove Press, 1954), "a tragicomedy in two acts" featuring a cast of five males. Only punctuation and capitalization have been altered in the un-erased text.

Outwardly calm, stutteringly resolute, her small habit or affectation of scenting charity (there is no denying it) relights her fear and trembling. Her luck going, her bags open, her regret a constant quantity, her laugh a banana skin, her truth frankly unforgettable—her jump to the ground luminous at this hour, her pale hands flung wide apart—she comes to rest on this bitch of an earth. Her need of encouragement towards the end happens to have been refused. One should have asked why.

Silence. No more agitated, lent text. Her plunge finished, she—for reasons unknown, stark naked—appears to be so calm on the ground. Dead, on purpose! Finally her heart has stopped, then adieu. Off stage, her face convulses . . . her mind must be asleep in the hay. She alights at last in heaven. Nothing to do here, she is certain.

Act II: Ex-dame.

She's gone for ever. No one could have stopped her. Her moment of bewilderment was dreamt or forgotten—the wild muckheap. To get her the name of the man, red hard man, would be not enough, not sufficient. Her worst single night for half a century. She tried everything (even meta despairing) to stop sagging under the weight of stupefaction. She must have had a need to shout Ape! Pig! Moron! Abortion! She could not turn to struggle, writhe, groan, beat the ground. Could not make him stop it, kick him in the crotch, try him with other names. Could not see the future. She used to wonder if some menial, or God, should come flying in to the rescue from the edge of the stage. Words finally fail, as in Act I. Again, her short legs do not move.

Ham Again and Again*

Picture an old ham. Motionless ham, very red. Get Sam-I-Am! A large, blood-stained, thick ham, nice proportions, lean, red with black ham, to eat here now. Have you enough? I'll give you ham, just enough to keep you hungry all the time. Why do you keep ham, Sam-I-Am? You love ham. I haven't made too much? You gave me cold, bled, bad ham. But you can get more. You inspected some very white ham in your kitchen. I want medium-hard ham; new ham, I can't stand. Killer ham in your kitchen. I look at ham and see naked bodies. I see dying ham. I heard you rip the ham. Did you? At the end of the day, what's happening is ham all right. I'm trying ham on a train, day after day. Can you see? Have a bite, Sam-I-Am. Could you, would you? Will you never finish returning to ham? What drivel. Give me my killer

---

* Composed by redaction of Samuel Beckett's *Endgame: A Play in One Act* (Grove Press, 1958). Only punctuation and capitalization have been altered in the un-erased text of *Endgame*. With apologies also to Dr. Seuss and *Monty Python's Flying Circus*.

ham—a little, not too fast. I'll measure it: Ham, more or less. Lovely ham. Back again, with the ham. I like that: Back again, with the ham! The loving, deadly ham. A word: Is that what you want, Sam-I-Am? Loving ham? Look again: Why this day after day ham routine? Last night I saw inside my breast: a big ham. Living ham! One day you say, I'm hungry. I'll get up and get something to eat. But you won't. There's one thing you forgot: ham. Natural ham! Do you remember, Sam-I-Am? Ah the old ham fix! Perhaps green eggs and ham? Have you eggs on ham? If no egg—ham, ham, ham, and ham? All that Spam! As long as it lasts, Sam-I-Am. Already the whole place stinks of ham. Soon I won't be able to think. You won't be able to leave, you ham brain. I have set the Ham Alarm. Dead ham, it's too much! Ham ear: terrific. Swear on Ham Honor there'll be more! Wonderfully pale and thin, seasonable, English, insinuating, imagined, natural, glaring mad ham. In the kitchen, there's one ham you haven't exterminated. Let us pray to ham in art: what a hope! Ham are you woke? The day will come. Not real ham—I love my dream-world ham. What is there to keep me here? Our ham story. Inspired! Just wait for it. No forcing, Sam-I-Am! I never spit ham very far. What is so funny? Ham is what tickles you? The whole thing is comical. Will it soon be the end? I'm afraid I will make up another ham now. Instant ham on my face. I must have been crying. Dead sucking ham. Ham on the forehead. Time for killer ham! Humming for ham. One has the right to sing: more ham! You want it to end? I want to sing: ham. Wonder if I'm in my right mind. Use your head for Christ's sake! Ham, egg—have enough ham? I'll never understand ham. Oh, you find it easy. Am I right you need time without ham? If you must, axe the ham! No more ham, then let it end. Pity the ham. I warn you, I'm going to examine, again, the bad ham. Not without dismay. You think I'm inventing ham? We've come to the end. Before you go, say ham—a word to ponder. Or end up with Spam—something from your art? Ham—a word. How easy it is fried. No question you've found it here. Look at all that beauty! You get the dying ham, better than the word. When I fall, I'll weep for ham. For our vices turning to ham. Yes, fixed on ham, till the end. Ham again and again.

March Madness, 1974

Om, O mind, remember —
remember all that has been done.
O mind, remember — remember
all that has been done.

— Isha Upanishad, verse 17

March 1 — Doomsday, and Counting
    A grand jury in Washington, DC, has concluded that President Nixon was indeed involved in the Watergate break-in cover-up. Seven people, including former Nixon White House aides H.R. Haldeman and John D. Ehrlichman, former Attorney General John Mitchell and former assistant Attorney General Robert Mardian, are being indicted on charges of conspiring to obstruct justice in connection with the Watergate break-in. In Season 1, Episode 6 of *The Six Million Dollar Man*, "Doomsday, and Counting," when an earthquake threatens the stability of an underground Russian nuclear installation, Steve Austin must rescue the fiancé of his friend Col. Vasily Zhukov, who is buried

beneath debris. Complicating matters further, Steve must also stop the reactor when it goes into a nuclear self-destruct countdown.

March 2 — Seasons in the Sun

At 9:40 a.m. in Barcelona, Spain, Catalan anarchist Salvador Puig Antich was garroted by the regime of dictator Francisco Franco. The garrote, a medieval torture and execution weapon perfected by the Spanish during the Inquisition and rarely used in modern times, is a crude chair to which the victim is bound while the executioner uses a crank to slowly tighten a metal band around the victim's throat, crushing the neck and spinal cord and causing asphyxiation. "Seasons in the Sun," by Canadian singer Terry Jacks, is the new Billboard No. 1 song. The original song by Belgian Jacques Brel, *"Le Moribond"* (The Dying Person), written in a whorehouse in Tangiers, was about an old man dying from heartbreak and bidding sardonic adieu to his adulterous wife and her lover. While the English translation by Rod McKuen sung by the Kingston Trio in 1963 largely retained the sarcasm, Terry Jacks changed the lyrics to make the song more uplifting and sentimental: "We had joy, we had fun/ We had seasons in the sun."

March 3 — Steep Dive

In history's worst air disaster to date, a McDonnell Douglas DC-10 en route to London has crashed in a forest near Paris, killing all 346 on board. Shortly after takeoff from Orly airport, a cargo door detached from Turkish Airlines flight 182, causing an explosive decompression that severed control cables. Pilots lost control of the elevators, rudder, and No. 2 engine, and the plane entered a steep dive from which it could not recover. In a paper for Professor N's Critical Analysis: Modernism class at the Stanford overseas campus in Tours, France, U contended that the year T.S. Eliot spent in Paris living in a Left Bank pension at 151 bis Rue Saint Jacques following his graduation from Harvard, along with his later meeting with James Joyce at the Hotel de l'Elysee and subsequent *tête-à-têtes* with Joyce in Paris, all strongly influenced not only *The Waste Land* (published in 1922, same year as Joyce's *Ulysses*) but also Eliot's *chef-d'oeuvre, Four Quartets*. U's paper is called "From Uptight Sexual Prude to Master of Time and the Universe — Or, The Parisian-Joycean Connection in Eliot's *Four Quartets*."

March 4 — Sex Shops

The inaugural issue of *People* magazine has appeared with a price of 35 cents. Mia Farrow, starring in the movie *The Great Gatsby*, graces the cover, with stories inside on Gloria Vanderbilt, Aleksandr Solzhenitsyn, Marina Oswald, wives of U.S. Vietnam veterans Missing in Action, and the Hearst family's ordeal around last month's kidnapping of Patty Hearst by the radical Symbionese Liberation Army. R, a student at the Stanford overseas campus in Tours, France, has missed his Social Change in Modern France: Feminism class with Professor E, having spent the weekend in Paris reading *Tropic of Cancer* and *The Diary of Anais Nin* and following Henry Miller's and Nin's trail from the Cemetery Montparnasse to the Cemetery Montmartre, from the Hotel Central and Café de la Mairie to the American Express office at 11 Rue Scribe, Café Wepler on Place de Clichy, and the sex shops around Place Pigalle.

March 5 — The Lid is Off

The lid is off, and Portugal is still stunned. The events of the past 10 days – the overthrow of a tyrant, the release of political prisoners, the ending of censorship, the return of exiled politicians, the smashing of the secret police – may presage a social revolution of a kind that Portugal has never before experienced. Will it end, once and for all, European colonialism in Africa? In a journal entry R has observed that he "sat in [the Stanford-in-France] lounge, high on cheap Vouvray Sec & dark green Moroccan hashish, which U & I purchased during Christmas trip to Tangiers & Tetouan & which U (not I) carried through customs in & out of Franco's Spain, wearing her nicest clothes to cross the borders, while I was hippie-searched, forced to unroll my drug-free sleeping bag & squeeze out my unadulterated toothpaste." Cross-legged on the lounge carpet, R closed his eyes and swayed to Traffic's "The Low Spark of High-Heeled Boys" while others danced around him. He felt transported and somehow transformed: "You just can't escape from the sound/ Don't worry too much, it'll happen to you." R and U have hatched a plan to drop out of school and move to Morocco, where they envision they can (a) live inexpensively close to Europe, (b) use their serviceable French, and (c) have easy access to some of the world's best compressed cannabis.

March 6 — International Women's Day, Part 1

At the Stanford campus in Palo Alto, California, feminist writer Kate Millett spoke to an overflow crowd in the opening session of an International Women's Day fair, declaring: "To our generation falls the greatest responsibility for liberation. It may be easier in the future to be a woman, but I don't think it'll ever be as interesting as it is now. The freedom we seek is a freedom of the soul. But we are increasingly controlled, policed and lied to, and we face increasing abridgement and invasion of our privacy. We're really seeing a protofascist society."

March 7 — International Women's Day, Part 2

The University of Georgia has set the national record with a mass streak of 1,543 men and women, wearing nothing but a smile, running three quarters of a mile on the Athens, GA, campus with 15,000 cheering fans lining the way. At Stanford University's Memorial Auditorium, Marxist philosopher Herbert Marcuse told 1,500 students that "the goals of the women's movement require changes of such enormity, in material as well as intellectual culture, that they can be obtained only by virtue of a change in the entire social system. Feminist socialism must embody the antithesis of the aggressive and repressive needs and values of capitalist society as a form of male-dominated culture. The liberation of women begins at home." At the Stanford-in-France campus in Tours, France, R noted after finishing the first draft of his paper for Social Change in Modern France: Feminism that he told Prof. E he fears she may not like his paper very much, so he'd prefer to take the course Pass/No Credit instead of for a letter grade. R's draft is titled, "Mailer, Millet, and Miller — Or, What is a Vagina?" In a letter to her parents, U, a 19-year-old sophomore, said that instead of returning to California that spring from Stanford-in-France, she was dropping out of college to move to Morocco with a boyfriend, R, whom she met at the overseas campus, and could they please send money.

March 8 — BARE-ASS

Charles de Gaulle Airport, also known as Roissy and formerly called *Aéroport de Paris Nord* (Paris North Airport), has opened 25 kilometers northeast of Paris after eight years of reconstruction. *The Brady Bunch* has been cancelled after five seasons on ABC. In Episode 7 of *The Six Million Dollar Man*, Steve Austin witnesses a murder and with his bionic eye gets a good look at the sniper. Golden Gate Bridge commuters were treated to a special surprise when a group of 45 Stanford students streaks alongside them during afternoon rush hour. The group from freshman dorm Branner Hall, who call themselves "Bay Area Runners Extraordinaire — Association of Stanford Streakers" (BARE-ASS), ran almost two-thirds of a mile across the famous span clad only in hats, shoes, and Stanford regalia.

March 9 — March Madness

The "March Madness" NCAA basketball tournament begins today with a new format of 25 Division 1 teams, all conference champions. The last Japanese soldier from World War II has surrendered in the Philippines, 29 years after the end of the war. On his 52nd birthday, intelligence officer Hiroo Onoda came out of hiding on Lubang Island in heavily worn and patched fatigues. His final orders had stated that he should not surrender under any circumstances. Initially with a few other holdouts, Lt. Onoda conducted guerilla activities for decades including sabotage of local farms and live-fire skirmishes with fishermen and police. He had ignored repeated leaflets, letters, and photos announcing the war's end, judging them to be propaganda tricks. Befriended in February by an itinerant Japanese hippie named Suzuki, Onoda said he was awaiting orders from a superior officer. Suzuki went to the Japanese government, who located Onoda's former commanding officer and sent him to Lubang where he officially ordered Lt. Onoda relieved from duty. When he finally surrendered, Onoda turned in his sword along with a cache of hand grenades and his still functional Arisaka rifle with 500 rounds of ammunition.

March 10 — Melted Candle

The police arrived at 2 a.m. to 5 Place Anatole France in Tours, a stone's throw from the Loire River, in response to complaints about activities where 45 Stanford students were celebrating the impending end of two terms living and studying in France. Neighbors reported loud music and nude dancing on balconies. The police entered the foyer and told the Americans to close the windows and quiet down; they noted that Professors N and E, who accompanied the students to Tours from the home campus and live in adjacent apartments, had attended the party but retired earlier. Student U noted that "R & I arose at 7 hung over but still giddy from best party of the trip" to help a few others clean up before the Sunday custodial staff arrived and freaked out. They found clothing strewn about the floor, underwear and bras ("Was that one Prof. E's?") tossed over lamps and hung from picture frames, and classmates M and M curled asleep, drooling on opposite ends of a couch. They collected wine bottles, cigarette butts, cardboard roaches of Euro-style spliffs, a plant soaked with vomit. They found *The Joker* (Steve Miller Band) still spinning around the turntable, the vinyl LP limping like a flat tire from a lump of melted candle (still dimly lit) bumping the raised needle arm on each revolution.

March 11 — Eccentric Eruption

The second explosion this year has begun on Mount Etna in Sicily. The only eccentric eruption so far this century, it has produced a rare, nearly aphyric and plagioclase-free trachybasalt that could not be derived from the central volcano conduits and is more alkaline and more radiogenic than all previous historical lavas. The earlier eruption lasted from January 30 until February 16, building up a cone 70 meters above the former surface. Now, after 22 days of calm, a second crater has become active 200 meters west of the earlier cone, at 1650 meters elevation. This crater also shows strong explosive activity, and lava is flowing through an open breach in the western side of the growing cone, forming a field of overlapping lobes.

March 12 — Missing Woman

Serial killer Ted Bundy, sporadically attending law school at the University of Puget Sound in Tacoma, WA, has begun assaulting and murdering young college women at the rate of about one per month. The Thurston County Sheriff's Department has launched an intensive search for Donna Gail Manson, a 19-year-old Evergreen State College student last seen by her roommate and friends walking to a concert at 7 p.m. on the Olympia, WA, campus. Five feet tall with blue eyes and long brown hair, parted in the middle, she was wearing green slacks, a red, orange and green-striped top and a fuzzy, black maxi-coat when she disappeared. The first *Wonder Woman* film and TV series pilot has appeared on ABC starring ex-tennis pro Cathy Lee Crosby, wearing blue leggings and a red zip-up skirt, in pursuit of an arch-villain played by Ricardo Montalban.

March 13 — Sexual Politics

It can be hard to tell the real signals from the false ones. Amid the recession following the 1973 Arab Oil Embargo, stocks have rallied in early 1974, sending the Dow up 13.1 percent from its low of 788.31 on December 5, 1973, to today's high of 891.66. R's paper for Social Change in Modern France: Feminism was turned in to Prof. E at Stanford-in-France with the modified title "Mailer, Miller, and Millett — Or, What is a Cunt?" and an introductory note: "The rhetorical question in the title is intended philosophically rather than anatomically or obscenely, as the paper wrestles seriously with competing interpretations of Henry Miller's fiction, use of the C-word, and contending notions of male sexuality by Kate Millett in *Sexual Politics* vs. Norman Mailer in *Genius and Lust*, mostly siding in the end with Mailer." Prof. E has glanced at the title and thanked R for taking the course Pass/No Credit.

March 14 — Embargo to End

The Arab oil ministers ended a one-day meeting in Tripoli, Libya, late yesterday, and a senior Libyan official said they had decided to lift the oil embargo against the United States. The ban has been in effect since the October Middle East war. The decision was not announced in Tripoli, however, because Libya has opposed the lifting of the embargo until now. The oil ministers adjourned their closed session and a Libyan official said the meeting would resume in Vienna, Austria, on Sunday, March 17.

March 15 — Ides of March

In Episode 8 of *The Six Million Dollar Man*, Steve Austin has been assigned to train America's first female astronaut, Major

Kelly Wood. On her maiden flight, a sudden explosion damages the Athena 1 and injures Kelly's co-pilot Osterman. Austin heads the rescue team and follows her up to Skylab, only to find his bionic replacements malfunctioning in outer space. Oral Roberts University (ORU) basketball coach and athletic director Ken Trickey was arrested at 4:20 a.m. on Route 66 in West Tulsa for driving while intoxicated. ORU, founded in 1963 by evangelist Oral Roberts, had earlier defeated Louisville to advance to the Midwest Regional final and a chance to make the Final Four of the NCAA Tournament ("March Madness"). As athletic director, Trickey announced that he has suspended himself as basketball coach for breaking the school's honor code by consuming alcohol. In Andrew Wyeth's painting *The Ides of March (1974)*, a golden-haired dog, eyes staring out at the viewer, lies tranquilly in front of a fireplace with coals simmering in an ominously large, dark hearth rigged with menacing metal hooks.

March 16 — I Love Oral Roberts

Athletic Director/suspended coach Trickey met with Oral Roberts University founder and president Oral Roberts himself, who agreed to give him a second chance following his DWI arrest, "because this is a Christian school," so Trickey could coach in the regional final of college basketball's March Madness tournament. "I love Oral Roberts," Trickey said. Unfortunately, Trickey and ORU lost to Kansas 93-90 in overtime to miss appearing in the Final Four.

March 17 — One-Way Tickets

OPEC nations meeting in Vienna are reconsidering ending

their oil embargo against the U.S., Europe, and Japan following President Nixon's comments that any lifting of the embargo that was too conditional or provisional would be counterproductive for future Middle East peace efforts. As winter quarter Finals Week begins at Stanford-in-France in Tours, the students and professors have started packing for their return to the home campus for Spring Quarter, except for two students R and U, who said they found a travel agency on Rue Nationale and bought one-way tickets from Paris to Casablanca.

March 18 — Lucy Fights the System

After 23 years on CBS, the final episode of Lucille Ball's *Here's Lucy* has aired. This was Ball's third popular sitcom after *I Love Lucy* and *The Lucy Show*. In Episode 144, "Lucy Fights the System," Lucy stands up for a waitress named Mary who was fired for being middle aged. Lucy and daughter Kim scheme to prove that age and experience are an asset to the restaurant manager, who is suffering a midlife crisis.

March 19 — Jefferson Starship

Former Teamster President Jimmy Hoffa and actor Anthony Perkins will be featured guests on *The Mike Douglas Show*. Following the breakup of Jefferson Airplane earlier in the year, Jefferson Starship, including Paul Kantner, Grace Slick, David Freiberg, John Barbata, and Papa John Creach, has begun its first tour in Chicago.

March 20 — Big Sky

NBC newscaster Chet Huntley of the renowned *Huntley-Brinkley Report* (1956-1970) has died of lung cancer. Huntley was known for his authoritative, straightforward broadcast voice, his chemistry with Brinkley, and their trademark sign off, "Good night, David," "Good night, Chet ... and good night for NBC News!" In recent years Huntley attracted controversy among locals and environmentalists as developer of a large ski and golf resort in Montana called "Big Sky."

March 21 — Normal Bowel Movements

In "Operant Conditioning of Rectosphincteric Responses in the Treatment of Fecal Incontinence," Bernard T. Engel, Parviz Nikoomanesh, and Marvin M. Schuster report today in *The New England Journal of Medicine* that six patients with severe fecal incontinence and manometric evidence of external-sphincter impairment were taught to produce external-sphincter contraction in synchrony with internal-sphincter relaxation. These responses were induced by rectal distention. During follow-up, four of the patients remained completely continent, and the other two were definitely improved. One patient who was trained to relax her internal sphincter as well as to contract her external sphincter not only was continent but also regularly had normal bowel movements, which she had not had before. The technique was simple to learn, the findings highlight the importance of synchronized rectosphincteric responses in the maintenance of fecal continence, and they show that these responses can be brought under voluntary control. After reading Vladimir Nabokov on the toilet, U, like Nabokovian narrator V, has "welcomed the renewal of polished structures after a week of black fudge fouling the bowl slope so high that no amount of flushing could dislodge it" using the French style water closet at 5 Place Anatole France in Tours.

U wondered, unfortunately too late for her Modernism term paper, if it would be productive to ask what kind of peristaltic pressure Nabokov applies to Joyce and Eliot, how *Pale Fire* puts the squeeze on *Ulysses* and *Four Quartets*.

March 22 — New Cease-Fire

The Viet Cong have proposed a six-point plan that includes detailed provisions for a new cease-fire and the holding of general elections in South Vietnam. American officials who read the plan said it was the most concrete put forward by the Viet Cong since the Paris cease-fire agreement last year. In Tours, the students at Stanford-in-France have received their final grades before parting ways, with hugs and tears and *bon voyages*, and posing for this group photo by the Loire. According to *La Nouvelle République du Centre-Ouest*, some locals expressed relief at the Americans' departure. U was given an A+ (*"Wow!"*) from Prof. N for her paper on T.S. Eliot, and R received a P (Pass/*merci!*) from Prof. E for his paper on Henry Miller *et al*.

March 23 — Timelessness of Pain and Suffering

"Seasons in the Sun" by Terry Jacks has ended its three-week run atop the Billboard chart, making it one of the best-selling singles of all time. The new No. 1 hit is "Dark Lady" by Cher. It's the END OF AN ERA; North Carolina State has shocked UCLA in a semifinal March Madness game 80-77 in double overtime, UCLA's first tournament loss since 1963. The NC State Wolfpack, starring David Thompson, defeated the Bill Walton-led Bruins and ended UCLA's record 88-game winning streak. UCLA had won seven straight NCAA titles and nine of the previous ten championships under legendary coach John Wooden. The Bruins blew an 11-point lead in regulation and a 7-point lead in the second overtime. "That's the timelessness of pain and suffering," said Walton. "The agonizing, the reflection and the endless questioning of yourself. When you're right there and it's there for you and the whole world is watching, and it's recorded as history that can never be changed, that is a terribly heavy burden."

March 24 — Medieval Magic

Newly ex-Stanford student R and girlfriend/fellow dropout U have arrived in Casablanca, Morocco's largest city and a kind of hybrid or patchwork metropolis, destroyed and rebuilt many times over many centuries, occupied or overrun by Berbers, Phoenicians, Romans, Arabs, Portuguese, Spanish, French, even the Americans under General Patton in World War II. En route to the city from the airport, they passed through the extensive *bidonvilles*, cinderblock and sheet-metal shantytowns, of Casablanca's suburbs. They expressed surprise at the gritty, Western feel of the sprawling new city, and disappointment at the small Medina or old city dating only from 18th century and lacking the authenticity and medieval magic of the Tangiers and Tetouan medinas they had visited in December. It seemed to them no wonder that expats Paul Bowles, Allen Ginsburg, William Burroughs, Brion Gysin, Gertrude Stein, Tennessee Williams, etc. had chosen Tangiers instead of Casablanca, where even the urchins and street hustlers showed a sinister edge, cursing at R and U in English as the couple searched for a cheap pension or *riad* near the Medina.

March 25 — Lineup for CBS Evening News
1. Introduction, Walter Cronkite (New York City)
2. Stans, Mitchell Trial / Dean Testimony
3. Grand Jury Report / House Judiciary Committee
4. Special Prosecutor / White House / Subpoena Deadline
5. Milk Producers / Campaign Contributions
6. (Commercial: Bayer Timed-Release Aspirin; Haley's M-O Laxative.)
7. Kissinger / Moscow Meeting
8. (Commercial; The Hartford Insurance Company; Omega Oldsmobile.)
9. Hearst Kidnapping
10. Boyle Trial / Yablonski Murders
11. McDonnell Douglas / Washington, DC-10 Controversy
12. Joint Economy Committee / President "Economy" Message
13. Stock Market Report (Studio)
14. (Commercial: Mr. Coffee Automatic Drip Coffeemaker; Master Charge.)
15. Cypress Swamp Fires
16. Suspect / Kronholm Kidnapping
17. Mariner 10 / Mercury
18. Analysis (US / Southeast Asia)
19. Supreme Court Rulings
20. Kennedy Jr. / Skiing / Amputated Leg
21. (Commercial: Anacin; The Hartford Insurance Company.)
22. Blacksmithing / Georgia / Bailey
23. Good Night.

March 26 — Tree Huggers

A group of peasant women led by Gaura Devi in Reni village in the Garhwal Himalayas of northeast India have used their bodies to surround and cling to trees in order to prevent loggers from felling them. The act of defiance by illiterate tribal and village women has energized the Chipko movement, which aims to use forest resources judiciously for the benefit of local people, and is capturing the attention of the broader environmental movement. Thousands of trees near Reni are threatened. The Chipko (Hindi for "clinging") women were inspired by the original tree huggers, 294 men and 69 women belonging to the Bishnois branch of Hinduism, who, in 1730, died while trying to protect the trees in their village from being turned into the raw material for building a palace.

March 27 — Mazagan

U has observed in a shaky journal entry that, as U and R took the CTM bus south from Casablanca to El Jadida, which the Moroccans still call Mazagan for the old Portuguese city and fortress, "spring already feels like summer as we swing inland on the A5, hugging our backpacks on sweaty laps, squeezed among turbaned old men, women in jalabas & hijabs with overflowing baskets of provisions & squawking chickens."

March 28 — Lack of Evidence

In Romania the position of President of the Republic has been created especially for Nicolae Ceausescu, named President for Life by the Grand National Assembly. The naked, 6-foot-7, 270-pound, walrus-mustachioed comedy writer Pat McCormick streaked across the set of *The Tonight Show Starring Johnny Carson*, surprising Carson, sidekick Ed McMahon, and bandleader Doc Severinsen. NBC censors managed to black out the streaker from the waist down. McMahon chortled "Hoooooo…," Severinsen made as if to remove his clothes, and Carson joked that McCormick was arrested but released for "lack of evidence."

March 29 — Four Dead in Ohio

Concluding a week of co-hosting *The Mike Douglas Show*, Jonathan Winters and Douglas have featured special guest Frankie Valli and the Four Seasons. In Episode 9 of *The Six Million Dollar Man*, Rudy Wells is kidnapped on a trip to his old study grounds. Luckily Steve Austin has some time off and follows Rudy unannounced to Austria. The trail soon leads to the wealthy Tucelli family, who want to force Dr. Wells to give up the secret of constructing a bionic man. In Ohio, eight National Guardsmen have been indicted on charges stemming from the shooting deaths of four students at Kent State University on May 4, 1970. On their way back from a café to their pension in El Jadida, Morocco, after reading the current *International Herald Tribune* left by a traveler from Casablanca, R and U sang the chorus of "Ohio" by Crosby, Stills, Nash & Young, "Tin soldiers and Nixon coming/ We're finally on our own/ This summer I hear the drumming/ Four dead in Ohio/ Four dead in Ohio" over and over.

March 30 — Battle Formations

Farmers digging a well near Xi'an, China, have discovered the long lost Terracotta Army, thousands of terracotta warriors, horses, and chariots buried in giant pits flanking the tomb of China's First Emperor, Qin Shi Huang (259-210 BCE). The life-size sculptures, arranged in battle formations as if to protect Emperor Qin's mausoleum and necropolis complex, have largely identical body parts that, according to experts, may have been created from molds using an early version of modular assembly-line methods. However, the warriors vary in height and uniform according to rank, and they all appear to have unique facial features individually handcrafted from clay.

March 31 — Heading South

After a few days in El Jadida enjoying cool Atlantic breezes, walking the ochre ramparts of Mazagan Fortress, and checking out several *petite maisons* and shabby rental apartments, U and R have decided this is not where they will settle in Morocco. They packed up and headed south to explore the towns of the Mother-of-Pearl coast, full of hope.

June Swoon, 1994

> Few would argue that he hasn't
> constructed a brilliant work of art
> ... entirely by using the words of
> others.*
>
> — Kenneth Goldsmith

Why did Eva "swoon (**desmayó?**) *& run away" at the motel?* June Swoon. You might think this is a baseball phrase, something that every team has to hear when they go on a losing streak in June. I say this is a wild dream—but it is this dream I want to realize. Life and literature combined. Ladies and Gentlemen of the Jury, the Instructions which I am now giving to you will be made available in written form for your deliberations. They must not be defaced in any way. You will find that the Instructions may be typed, printed or handwritten. Portions may have been added or deleted. *Eva's boyfriend Gabriel distraught, also in a spell*—Objection: lacks foundation.

Patterns, apparent or real, become enshrined in myths and superstitions. In baseball, the Chicago Cubs always seemed to go downhill during the June Swoon, making June a psychological hurdle. We pay attention to the June Swoon because it's a month of bad baseball after expectations were heightened. It doesn't really exist but our brains see a pattern. Thursday, June 2, is the Feast of Corpus Christi. Medieval artists depicted Mary fainting and weeping at the foot of the cross, and her sympathetic swoon shows her sharing in the suffering of the Passion. These early swoons are used to dramatize different kinds of dangerously intense experience. *Hot—what's with air conditioning?* *"Publishing" to the jury = showing Exhibits—Exs 1, 2, 3: phone bills, Eva's yellow sticky [illegible] w/ phone # & directions—Eva coming to see boyfriend w/ condoms, "bathroom supplies" ["Trojan" doodle].* Psychiatrists have documented a variety of different personality profiles in patients with psychogenic paroxysmal events. One study found a higher rate of sexual abuse in the group with swooning or catatonic spell types. Romeo . . . / Guitar and hat in hand, beside the gate/ With Juliet, in the usual debate/ Of love, beneath a bored but courteous moon;/ . . . . Behind the wall I have some servant wait,/ Stab, and the lady sinks into a swoon. Court is not in session Saturday, June 4, World Day for Child Victims of Aggression, or Sunday, June 5, World Environment Day. You must disregard any deleted part of the Instructions and not speculate as to what it was or as to the reason for its deletion. You are not to be concerned with the reasons for any modification. Every part of the text is of equal importance. *Eva tries to call boyfriend. Gets ride w/ strangers Alejandro and Carlos (doesn't know names), take her to motel [building doodle]—Bad decisions!! remind daughters not to never do this.* I see some of you are taking notes. Notes are only an aid to memory and should not take precedence over independent recollection. Notes are for the note-taker's own personal use in refreshing his or her recollection of the Evidence. Should any discrepancy exist between a Juror's recollection of the Evidence and his or her notes, he or she may request that the reporter read back the relevant proceedings and the trial transcript must prevail over the notes. We note that Tuesday, June 14, is Flag Day but will not be observed as a Court Holiday. *No windows so stuffy— Exhibits 7, 8, 9 motel vicinity.* As [she] emerged from the porch, [she] was seized with a fierce palpitation of the heart; the wellspring of life was dried up within [her], and [she] walked in constant fear of falling. *Eva signals (mimes?) to motel woman Jackie Call police!—Exhibits 10, 11—motel room, [illegible]—Ex 12: before after motel, the park—scene of the crimes.—get sequence of events.* In the afternoon they came unto a land in which it seemed always afternoon. *Driving thru residential area "keep going, a little farther" (who says this?).* All round the coast the languid air did swoon, breathing like one in a weary dream. *Eva's demeanor lack of eye = contact— Eva "can't read a map" trusted A & C to "find me a phone" [phone cord doodle?]—Objection: relevancy.* Still, still to hear her tender-taken breath, and so live ever—or else swoon to death. We should not make it a personal thing. The Court recognizes that Sunday, June 19, is Father's Day and wishes all fathers among the Jurors a Happy Father's Day. *Help me*

~~teen~~ tween daughters [illegible] dating soon. I strongly urge you to persevere in your concern for the family institution and unite myself spiritually to your concern about this fundamental cell of society today that faces innumerable challenges and that no human power has the right to manipulate. The packet of Instructions to the Jury includes the Information about the case with the specific charges which I will also read to you. The Information in this case charges that the Defendants, Alejandro B and Carlos D, committed certain crimes. Defendant B is accused in Count One of the Information of having committed the crime of Rape in violation of Penal Code Section 261(A)(2), a Felony, by accomplishing an act of sexual intercourse with Eva F against said person's will. *Alejandro had never done it before, said friend was next—Obj: conclusionary—Is that a word? Wow Eva [illegible] first time, he was virgin—seems all backwards?* The Swoon of the Virgin was an idea developed in the late Middle Ages, that the Virgin Mary had fainted during the Passion of Christ, most often placed while she watched the Crucifixion of Jesus. In order to prove the crime of Rape, each of the following elements must be proved: 1. A male and female person engaged in an act of sexual intercourse; 2. The two persons were not married to each other; 3. The act of intercourse was against the will of the female person; [and] 4. Such act was accomplished by means of force, violence, or fear of immediate and unlawful bodily injury to such person. Any sexual penetration, however slight, constitutes engaging in an act of sexual intercourse. *"Masturbated penis inside my vagina."*

Proof of ejaculation is not required. *Erection? "Seemed like [illegible]"— Objection: calls for speculation.* Hero swoons. He closed his eyes, surrendering himself to her, body and mind, conscious of nothing in the world but the dark pressure of her softly parting lips. They pressed upon his brain as upon his lips as though they were the vehicle of vague speech; and between them he felt an unknown and timid pressure, darker than the swoon of sin, softer than sound or odor. *SART nurse Irene plucks <u>by roots</u> 64 pubic hairs youch—Introitus (opening of vag?)—"no consenting intercourse previous 72 hrs" [abstract doodling]—"Colposcopy" = closely examine cervix/vag/vulva? [more doodling]. Jurors 1, 3, 6, 8-10 <u>fidgeting</u>.* The attitude and conduct of Jurors at all times are very important. It is rarely helpful for a Juror at the beginning of deliberations to express an emphatic opinion on the case or to announce a determination to stand for a certain verdict. *Petechiae = red peppery irritation "classic mounting injury" consistent with sexual [illegible]—Pooling in cul-de-sac (below cervix?)—Jurors 2, 4, 5, 7, 11 look down.* [She] had tottered out first, for the better display of her feelings, in a kind of walking swoon; for [she] performed swoons of different sorts. Against such person's will means without the Consent of the female person. In prosecutions for Rape the word Consent means positive cooperation in act or attitude pursuant to an exercise of free will. *Consent means Positive Cooperation <u>quote for daughters</u>.* The person must act freely and voluntarily and have knowledge of the nature of the act of transaction involved. *Police sexual assault unit secretly? records Alejandro interview—"Willingly her? no not much"—Objection mischaracterizes testimony—Force her? "yes a* *little, a little force"*—*Penis,* pito? *I know* huevos *[huevos doodles]. How smugly would I marvel that she was mine, mine, and revise the recent matitudinal swoon to the moan of the mourning doves. Objection: leading the witness— Alejandro penis size [illegible]—Obj: vague & ambiguous— Intercourse failed twice but "he touched me on the inside"—Obj: narrative.* Tuesday, June 21, Summer Solstice, Insurance Stocks Hit June Swoon After Healthy May Recovery. <u>HVAC still not working</u>—*Unclear if when Miranda rights given.* Defendants B and D are both accused in Count Two of the Information of having committed the crime of Oral Copulation by force, in violation of Penal Code Section 288A(C), a Felony, by accomplishing an act of Oral Copulation against the will of the victim, to wit: Eva F. Oral Copulation is the act of copulating the mouth of one person with the sexual organ of another person. *Exhibits 21- 26 photos telephone booth at gas station [gas pump doodle] maps of area, park.* Oral Copulation consists of: 1. Any penetration, however slight, of the mouth of one person by the sexual organ of another person, or 2. When there is no penetration, any substantial contact between the mouth of one person and the sexual organ of another person. Against the will means without the Consent of the alleged victim. Proof of ejaculation is not required. *Defense: False names on motel registration—Motel mgr Jackie doesn't recognize defendants doesn't like rape allegation [illegible] at motel—Objection: hearsay—Alejandro 21, 6th grade educated—#10 snorts [illegible]—maybe half jury H.S. grads also half Latino half Catholic half [illegible] half female—what am I? He seems to* be a man of wealth and position, and a practiced speaker who presents himself well at all times. He seems to feel a little bit above the rest of the jurors. Consent requires a free will and positive cooperation in act or attitude. Mere passivity does not amount to Consent. Alejandro says Eva *"flirting"* (coquetear?)—*"We did it, we talked & then we did it She said it & then we did it We were talking & then we did it She did it with me fine" etc [illegible, doodling]*—*Brief recess, switch translators.* Sorrow and fear and every other feeling faded away from him, and down he fell suddenly in a swoon. At last he began to draw breath, and soon after that to come out of his swoon, and memory and reason began to dawn upon him. *Defense rests*—*People rest*—*"Argue the case"* = *deliver closing arguments*—*People: Eva's credibility vs Alejandro's [illegible], entire story flimsy, Alejandro's nonsensical desc of sex act & flirting, "stuffing injury" needs no [illegible], "Eva being stupid doesn't mean she wasn't raped"*—*Defense: Eva's mind on something else, Eva & boyfriend no record of 2 am phone [illegible], disparages SART nurse testimony.* Ladies and Gentlemen of the Jury: You have heard all the Evidence, and now it is my duty to Instruct you on the law that applies in this case. You will have these Instructions in written form in the Jury Room to refer to during your deliberations. First, you must determine the Facts from the Evidence received in the trial and not from any other source. Try to separate the Facts from the fancy. Second, you must apply the law that I state to you, to the Facts, as you determine them, and in this way arrive at your verdict. *Lightheaded. Nauseous. Beware of fainting-fits. Beware of swoons. A frenzy fit is not one quarter so pernicious*—run mad as often as you choose; but do not faint. We should try to avoid emotionally colored arguments. You must not be influenced by mere sentiment, conjecture, sympathy, passion, prejudice, public opinion or public feeling. It is hard to find a sentimental fiction without a swooning, dangerously ill or seriously distracted heroine, and fictional representations of the fainting, indisposed woman remain frequent. Richardson's Pamela faints in order to avoid sexual intercourse, while Clarissa is unconscious while being raped by Lovelace, thus escaping mentally from an unwanted experience; Rousseau's Julie falls into a swoon during her forbidden kiss with Saint Preux. *My girls my girls my [illegible] [stick figure doodles].* Slowly, as one in a swoon, to whom life creeps back in the form of death, I woke, rose up. *Eva stands & yells at defense attorney in Spanish—I did not die [illegible] I did not die!—weird.* The swoon was used by many writers to dramatize vulnerabilities that our culture has imagined as specifically feminine: vulnerability to hysteria, to certain forms of illness, and to sexual exploitation. *Objection Move to strike Move to strike!—final melodrama like TV [TV doodle]—Can you object to closing argument [illegible] courtroom outburst?* He could not bear to think that everybody had taken her mysterious swoon for the flabby, vulgar sleep of a reveler. If any rule, direction or idea [is] repeated or stated in different ways in these Instructions, no emphasis [is] intended and you must not draw any inference because of its repetition. Do not single out any particular sentence or any individual point or Instruction and ignore the others. Consider the instructions as a whole and each in light of all the others. Swooning is a narrative device which serves innumerable functions. The swoon proper is usually induced by a blow or by the character's fear, exhaustion, surprise, or joy. Regardless of its cause, its effect is almost regularly restorative rather than debilitating. It is a deep, energy-giving sleep into which the character falls for an announced and sufficient reason and from which he is aroused when he is again needed. You shall now retire and select one of your number to act as Foreperson. He or she will preside over your deliberations. *"Each in light of all the others" Jury Room <u>even</u> stuffier than courtroom one tiny [illegible] fan—#6, #10 vying for Foreperson.* Shall we admit right now that it's hot and humid and our tempers are short? You must decide all questions from the Evidence received in this trial and not from any other source. I'm glad that we're going to be civilized about this. Evidence consists of testimony of witnesses, writings, material objects, or anything presented to the senses and offered to prove the existence or non-existence of a Fact. There's swooning and then there's swooning. A scene that weakens my knees every time I hear or read it and would probably be my all-time favorite swoon scene. Just thinking about it now, my heart is racing, my stomach is dipping, skin pebbled and I'm feeling lightheaded and I haven't even read it again. Evidence is either direct or circumstantial. I had swooned; but still will not say that all of consciousness was lost. What of it there remained I will not attempt to define, or even to describe; yet all was not lost. In the return to life from the swoon there are two stages: first, that of the sense of mental or

spiritual; secondly, that of the sense of physical existence.
250 *Head swimming skin [illegible] & clammy.* His soul swooned slowly as he heard the snow falling faintly through the universe and faintly falling, like the descent of their last end, upon all the living and the dead. *Had enough—Juror #10 will be Foreman over my dead body—#6 passes out! knocks over fan we call for help.* Reasonable doubt is not a mere possible doubt, because everything relating to human affairs is open to some possible or imaginary doubt. You are the sole judges of the believability of a witness and the weight to be given the testimony of each witness. In determining
260 the believability of a witness you may consider anything that has a tendency to prove or disprove the truthfulness of the testimony. This one is harder to believe than the Resurrection itself. The Swoon Theory, that Christ didn't really die but was only unconscious. The expert Roman executioners merely thought He was dead. After a few days in the tomb, without food or medicine, the cool air revived Him. Then, He burst from the 100 pounds of graveclothes, rolled away the stone with His nail-pierced hands, scared the daylights out of the Roman soldiers, walked miles on
270 wounded feet, and convinced His disciples that He'd been raised from the dead. The Court would like to observe that Sunday, June 26, is World Day Against Drug Abuse and Illicit Trafficking. I have not intended by anything I have said or done, or by any questions that I may have asked, or by any ruling I may have made, to intimate or suggest what you should find to be the Facts, or that I believe or disbelieve any witness. Disregard any Instruction which

applies to Facts determined by you not to exist. Each of you must decide the case for yourself after discussing the Evidence and Instructions with the other Jurors. Up to the present, my idea of collaborating with myself has been to get off the gold standard of literature. Speed it up a little. My idea briefly has been to present a resurrection of the emotions, to depict the conduct of a human being in the stratosphere of ideas, that is, in the grip of delirium. Do not decide any question in a particular way because a majority of the Jurors favor such a decision. Do not decide any issue in this case by chance, such as the drawing of lots. I would not sell my daily swoon/ For all the rubies in Rangoon./ What! sell my swoon? My lovely swoon? . . . / It's not for sale, my swoon's immune! When one expresses an emphatic opinion at the outset, a sense of pride may be aroused, and one may hesitate to change a position. Remember that you are not partisans or advocates in this matter. There are no caricatures, now, of effeminate exquisites so arrayed, swooning in opera boxes with excess of delight and being revived by other dainty creatures poking long-necked scent-bottles at their noses. *Smelling salts for Juror #6!* You must not make any independent investigation. You must not visit the scene, conduct experiments, or consult reference works for additional information. You must not discuss this case with any other person except a fellow Juror, and you must not discuss the case with a fellow Juror until and only when all Jurors are present in the Jury Room. *I win run-off election vs #10—Jury F̶o̶r̶e̶m̶a̶n̶ Foreperson—could I have imagined.* They described a circle near [me] and [glide] back into the cell, and now [I regret] that the swoon's friendly embrace had been so brief. *Woozy—[illegible]—try to focus.* I attempt to describe the experience of swooning, but also to create a kind of swooning structure for the reader: a brief, lulled, dreamy haze, followed by an abrupt ejection back into waking life. There is no such thing as a June Swoon, at least anything that falls outside the normal parameters of what we should expect every year. But the words sure do rhyme. The swoon is a dramatic way to figure the possibility of altered consciousness: passing out predicts a coming-round, a waking-up to new engagements with the world.

Constructed entirely from these sources:

Jane Austen, *Love and Freindship* [sic], 1790.

Naomi Booth, "Swoon! The cultural history of an ecstatic phenomenon," *Prospect* magazine June 25, 2015, online.

Belinda Boring, "Get Your Swoon On," *The Bookish Snob* [blog], 2011, online.

Grant Brisbee, "A history of Giants June Swoons," SBNation McCovey Chronicles, June 27, 2014, online.

Elizabeth Barrett Browning, *Aurora Leigh*, 1856.

Geoffrey Chaucer, *Troilus and Criseyde*, Book III, 1092, 1124, 1190, tr. Gerard NeCastro.

Ildiko Csengei, "She Fell Senseless on His Corpse: The Woman of Feeling and the Sentimental Swoon in Eighteenth-Century

Fiction," *Romantic Psyche and Analysis,* Romantic Circles Praxis Series, December 2008, website.

Charles Dickens, *The Life and Adventures of Martin Chuzzlewit,* 1842-1844; *Bleak House,* 1853.

T.S. Eliot, "Nocturne," 1909.

Zaidee E. Green, "Swooning in the *Faerie Queene,*" *Studies in Philology,* Vol. 34, No. 2, April, 1937.

Pope John Paul II, "Address to the Bishops of Ecuador on Their 'Ad Limina,'" June 21, 1994.

James Joyce, "The Dead," *Dubliners,* 1914; *Portrait of the Artist as a Young Man,* 1916.

Juror No. 12, trial notes, People v. R.Z. and J.M-M., County of Santa Clara, State of California, June, 1994.

The Honorable Judge K, Jury Instructions and Information, People v. R.Z. and J.M-M., County of Santa Clara, State of California, June, 1994.

Rosabeth Moss Kanter, *Confidence: How Winning and Losing Streaks Begin and End,* 2004.

John Keats, "Bright star, would I were stedfast [sic] as thou art," c. 1820.

T.K. Meakin, "Insurance Stocks Hit June Swoon After Healthy May Recovery," *National Underwriter,* Volume 98, Number 29, 1994.

Henry Miller, Letter to Anaïs Nin, 1932; *Tropic of Cancer,* 1934.

Vladimir Nabokov, *The Defense,* 1930/tr. 1964; *Invitation to a Beheading,* 1935/tr. 1959; *Lolita,* 1962.

Ogden Nash, "Cat Naps Are Too Good for Cats," *The New Yorker*, 1937.

Edgar Allan Poe, "The Pit and the Pendulum," 1842.

Reginald Rose, *Twelve Angry Men* (teleplay), 1954.

Linda M. Selwa, James Geyer, Nersi Nikakhtar, Morton B. Brown, Lori A. Schuh, and Ivo Drury, "Nonepileptic Seizure Outcome Varies by Type of Spell and Duration of Illness," *Epilepsia* 41(10):1330-1334, 2000.

William Shakespeare, *Much Ado About Nothing*, Act IV, Scene 1, 1754.

Stendhal (Marie-Henrie Beyle), *Naples and Florence: A Journey from Milan to Reggio*, 1817.

Alfred, Lord Tennyson, "The Lotos-eaters," 1832; "Fatima," 1833.

Wikipedia, "Swoon of the Virgin," June, 2017.

Rusty Wright and Linda Raney Wright, "Who's Got the Body?" *Probe*, Probe Ministries, May 27, 1976, online.

Spam Pantun*

Junk email subject headers from September, 2014

What I wish someone had told me before I began
Enter the Internet's Algorithmic All Seeing Gaze
Ending today, thirty incredible musical nights
Your seat still reserved for Audience Segmenting

Enter the Internet's Algorithmic All Seeing Gaze
Take the Polar Bear Ice-Plunge Challenge
Your seat still reserved for Audience Segmenting
No one predicted how cool it would be

---

* Based on a traditional, oral Malayan verse form, modern Western pantuns or pantoums are intertwining poems composed of quatrains rhyming *abab*, with the second and fourth lines of each stanza echoed as the first and third lines of subsequent stanzas. In the final quatrain, the second and fourth lines repeat the third and first lines of the first stanza, so the poem ends with the same line it begins. "As a form, the pantoum is always looking back over its shoulder," writes Edward Hirsch in *The Essential Poet's Glossary*, "and thus is well suited to evoke a sense of times past."

Take the Polar Bear Ice-Plunge Challenge
Let us help you now live in this moment
No one predicted how cool it would be
Holiday's over so time to get serious

Let us help you now live in this moment
Please help us to transfer these funds to your country
Holiday's over so time to get serious
Mapping your brain is the heart of our job

Please help us to transfer these funds to your country
Discover why fall makes the best escapades
Mapping your brain is the heart of our job
My time has now come to join forebears in heaven

Discover why fall makes the best escapades
Ending today, thirty incredible musical nights
My time has now come to join forebears in heaven
What I wish someone had told me before I began

Afterword(s): Take a Book/Leave a Book*

> *I always write my last line, my last paragraphs, my last page first.*
>
> — Katherine Anne Porter

> *Appropriation allows writers to return to originary moments and use not only the finished result, the original texts, but also the openness of their emergence, the possibility that they might have turned out otherwise.*
>
> — Patrick Greaney

---

* *Method:* Starting with 10 books being discarded or recycled, appropriate some text from the ending of each book (cf. Joan Retallack's "Not a Cage") to make a 10-line poem. Find (or start yourself) a local Take a Book/Leave a Book free library, then swap one of your old books for a new (used) one daily for 10 days. Generate a new poem each day by replacing, in order, a line from the end of your discarded book with a line from the end of your new (used) book. List your sources at the end.

Last Words from 10 Books Being Recycled

1   This complex model has been run under many different assumptions
      And in as brutal and cynical a manner as I put it just a moment ago—
      So much has broken away already, there is nothing to drink but air,
      Shoulda never got mixed up with the wind in the first place.
5   We will be on our way toward discovering new paradigms,
      The sublimest wish of all, the sovereign desire to communicate afar off.
      Two women punctured Custer's eardrums to improve his hearing;
      Our President has already given orders for massive retaliation.
      Fiction locates its characters in a cloudland,
10   But the piece is symmetrically structured and frantically inventive.

Take a Book / Leave a Book, Day 1

1   I take drugs daily and will continue to do so,
      And in as brutal and cynical a manner as I put it just a moment ago—
      So much has broken away already, there is nothing to drink but air,
      Shoulda never got mixed up with the wind in the first place.
5   We will be on our way toward discovering new paradigms,
      The sublimest wish of all, the sovereign desire to communicate afar off.

      Two women punctured Custer's eardrums to improve his
         hearing;
      Our President has already given orders for massive
         retaliation.
      Fiction locates its characters in a cloudland,
10   But the piece is symmetrically structured and frantically
         inventive.

Take a Book / Leave a Book, Day 2

1   I take drugs daily and will continue to do so.
     It takes you to another place—just for a few minutes—
     So much has broken away already, there is nothing to drink
        but air,
     Shoulda never got mixed up with the wind in the first
        place.
5   We will be on our way toward discovering new paradigms,
     The sublimest wish of all, the sovereign desire to
        communicate afar off.
     Two women punctured Custer's eardrums to improve his
        hearing;
     Our President has already given orders for massive
        retaliation.
     Fiction locates its characters in a cloudland,
10   But the piece is symmetrically structured and frantically
        inventive.

Take a Book / Leave a Book, Day 3

1   I take drugs daily and will continue to do so.
     It takes you to another place—just for a few minutes—
     Tiny, visually perfect, with heaps of lavender and
        rosemary —

      Shoulda never got mixed up with the wind in the first
         place.
5   We will be on our way toward discovering new paradigms,
      The sublimest wish of all, the sovereign desire to
         communicate afar off.
      Two women punctured Custer's eardrums to improve his
         hearing;
      Our President has already given orders for massive
         retaliation.
      Fiction locates its characters in a cloudland,
10 But the piece is symmetrically structured and frantically
         inventive.

Take a Book / Leave a Book, Day 4

1   I take drugs daily and will continue to do so.
      It takes you to another place—just for a few minutes—
      Tiny, visually perfect, with heaps of lavender and
         rosemary —
      Atoms and empty space; everything else is merely human
         thought.
5   We will be on our way toward discovering new paradigms,
      The sublimest wish of all, the sovereign desire to
         communicate afar off.
      Two women punctured Custer's eardrums to improve his
         hearing;
      Our President has already given orders for massive
         retaliation.
      Fiction locates its characters in a cloudland,
10 But the piece is symmetrically structured and frantically
         inventive.

Take a Book/Leave a Book, Day 5

1   I take drugs daily and will continue to do so.
     It takes you to another place—just for a few minutes—
     Tiny, visually perfect, with heaps of lavender and
        rosemary —
     Atoms and empty space; everything else is merely human
        thought.
5   It was one of those after-dinner occasions when one is
        expected to entertain;
     The sublimest wish of all, the sovereign desire to
        communicate afar off.
     Two women punctured Custer's eardrums to improve his
        hearing;
     Our President has already given orders for massive
        retaliation.
     Fiction locates its characters in a cloudland,
10   But the piece is symmetrically structured and frantically
        inventive.

Take a Book/Leave a Book, Day 6

1   I take drugs daily and will continue to do so.
     It takes you to another place—just for a few minutes—
     Tiny, visually perfect, with heaps of lavender and
        rosemary —
     Atoms and empty space; everything else is merely human
        thought.
5   It was one of those after-dinner occasions when one is
        expected to entertain;
     Through a lie he must have found himself inside the other
        woman.
     Two women punctured Custer's eardrums to improve his

      hearing;
      Our President has already given orders for massive
         retaliation.
      Fiction locates its characters in a cloudland,
10   But the piece is symmetrically structured and frantically
         inventive.

Take a Book / Leave a Book, Day 7

1   I take drugs daily and will continue to do so.
     It takes you to another place—just for a few minutes—
     Tiny, visually perfect, with heaps of lavender and
        rosemary —
     Atoms and empty space; everything else is merely human
        thought.
5   It was one of those after-dinner occasions when one is
        expected to entertain;
     Through a lie he must have found himself inside the other
        woman.
     As you might expect, it felt good to be in his position;
     Our President has already given orders for massive
        retaliation.
     Fiction locates its characters in a cloudland,
10 But the piece is symmetrically structured and frantically
        inventive.

Take a Book / Leave a Book, Day 8

1   I take drugs daily and will continue to do so.
     It takes you to another place—just for a few minutes—
     Tiny, visually perfect, with heaps of lavender and
        rosemary —
     Atoms and empty space; everything else is merely human

thought.
5   It was one of those after-dinner occasions when one is
    expected to entertain;
    Through a lie he must have found himself inside the other
    woman.
    As you might expect, it felt good to be in his position,
    A persuasive and eloquent talker who can sway others.
    Fiction locates its characters in a cloudland,
10 But the piece is symmetrically structured and frantically
    inventive.

Take a Book / Leave a Book, Day 9

1   I take drugs daily and will continue to do so.
    It takes you to another place—just for a few minutes—
    Tiny, visually perfect, with heaps of lavender and
    rosemary —
    Atoms and empty space; everything else is merely human
    thought.
5   It was one of those after-dinner occasions when one is
    expected to entertain;
    Through a lie he must have found himself inside the other
    woman.
    As you might expect, it felt good to be in his position,
    A persuasive and eloquent talker who can sway others,
    Intensely engaged in the hurly-burly of the real world.
10 But the piece is symmetrically structured and frantically
    inventive.

Take a Book / Leave a Book, Day 10

1   I take drugs daily and will continue to do so.
    It takes you to another place—just for a few minutes—

　　　　Tiny, visually perfect, with heaps of lavender and
　　　　　　rosemary —
　　　　Atoms and empty space; everything else is merely human
　　　　　　thought.
5　　　It was one of those after-dinner occasions when one is
　　　　　　expected to entertain;
　　　　Through a lie he must have found himself inside the other
　　　　　　woman.
　　　　As you might expect, it felt good to be in his position,
　　　　A persuasive and eloquent talker who can sway others,
　　　　Intensely engaged in the hurly-burly of the real world.
10　　 Anything else would be unbearable.

Sources

Line/Day	Book Recycled	Swapped For
1	Council on Environmental Quality and the Department of State (Gerald O. Barney, Study Director), *The Global 2000 Report to the President: Entering the Twenty-First Century*, Volume One (Washington, DC: U.S. Government Printing Office, 1981).	Madhulika Sikka, *A Breast Cancer Alphabet* (New York: Crown Publishers, 2014).
2	Ernest Mandel, *An Introduction to Marxist Economic Theory* (New York: Pathfinder Press, 1970).	Franklin W. Dixon, *The Vanishing Game*, in *Hardy Boys Adventures: 3-Books-In-1!* (New York: Aladdin, 2016).

3   Gretel Ehrlich, *Islands, the Universe, Home* (New York: Viking Press, 1991).

Suzy Gershman & Sarah Lahey, *Suzy Gershman's Born to Shop: California Wine Country* (Charleston, SC: Talking Frog Media, 2010).

4   Ken Kesey, *Kesey's Garage Sale* (New York: Viking Press, 1973).

Gore Vidal, *Creation* (New York: Ballantine Books, 1982).

5   Michael P. Hamilton (ed.), *The New Genetics and the Future of Man* (Grand Rapids, MI: William B. Eerdmans, 1972).

Francis Crick, *What Mad Pursuit: A Personal View of Scientific Discovery* (New York: Basic Books, 1988).

6   Jules Michelet, *Satanism and Witchcraft: A Study in Medieval Superstition*, tr. A.R. Allinson (Secaucus, NJ: Lyle Stuart, 1939).

Marguerite Duras, *The Lover* tr. Barbara Bray (New York: Harper & Row, 1985).

7   Evan S. Connell, *Son of the Morning Star: Custer and the Little Bighorn* (San Francisco: North Point Press, 1984).

Kenneth Blanchard & Spencer Johnson, *The One Minute Manager* (New York: William Morrow and Company, 1982).

8   Peter Porter, "Your Attention Please." In Paul Fussell (ed.), *The Norton Book of Modern War* (New York: W.W. Norton, 1991).

Susan Levitt with Jean Tang, *Taoist Astrology: A Handbook of the Authentic Chinese Tradition* (Rochester, VT: Destiny Books, 1997).

9   John Updike, *Odd Jobs: Essays and Criticism* (New York: Alfred A. Knopf, 1991).

Jon Krakauer, *Where Men Win Glory: The Odyssey of Pat Tillman* (New York: Doubleday, 2009).

10   Carl H. Klaus, Miriam Gilbet, and Bradford S. Field, Jr. (eds.), *Stages of Drama, Classical to Contemporary Masterpieces of the Theater*, Second Edition (New York: St. Martin's Press, 1991).

Stieg Larsson, *The Girl With the Dragon Tattoo*, tr. Reg Keeland (New York: Vintage Books, 2008).

[Interactive multimedia version available at *https://web.stanford.edu/~holeton/afterwords/assets/player/KeynoteDHTMLPlayer.html#0*; archived by the Electronic Literature Organization in The NEXT at *https://the-next.eliterature.org/works/2169/0/0/*]

FROLIC

*(play,
romp,
game,
caper)*

The Winograd Matrix

1.

I had set the table just so, got out the wine glasses with stems, and my dear Jenny has just come home. We are on a knife edge because of The Plague, not to mention my arrest and conviction. She pulls down her BioMask, making only glancing eye contact, and I see her taut jaw. I can't tell if it's the strain of being out in the world with other humans, or the strain of being confined with me away from them. Then it seems like the whole building shakes or shudders (Drillard would call it a *structural destabilization*). I feel a glancing blow off my head and *a ball crashes right through the table, because it's made of*

    [steel]   > **Go to 2**

    [Styrofoam].[*]   > **Go to 3**

---

[*] Does "it" refer to the ball or to the table? "Winograd Schemas" are pairs of statements with pronoun reference ambiguities, named for Stanford computer scientist Terry Winograd, who created an early example. Resolving the grammatical ambiguities, which usually have two different solutions (both of

2.

The ball is made of steel (see **1**). The whole contraption conks me in the temple then crashes through the cheap, untempered glass tabletop, sending shards into the carpet. One steel ball hangs below the table surface, swinging almost sheepishly, suspended by its V-string like the four other balls of my (now crumpled and askew) Newton's Cradle Toy, aka Newton's Pendulum. The possibly Plague-contaminated single-use containers of curry that Jenny brought home from Just So Thai have toppled into the crevice. The wine glasses too are shattered. It must have been an earthquake on top of everything else.

Drillard had given me the "executive toy" when I began my Double Home Confinement (following my so-called assault of Cofú the Intern) in order to, he said punningly, help keep me grounded.

"Executive Toy or Cradle Toy, Bo," Jenny had asked Drillard, "—it's certainly not for babies?"

Drillard quipped, "It rocks, baby!" Trying to be cool. Despite our being old friends, I've never liked the way Drillard winks at Jenny all cuddly and hairy like a bear. Less so since Jenny and I moved in together. Meaning I like it less so—he seems to do it more so.

Following the crash there is silence—no clack-clacking Demonstration of the Conservation of Momentum and Energy— as Newton's Balls (the name Jenny prefers) teeter precariously in

---

which are plausible), requires common-sense reasoning, so solving them has been proposed as a test of artificial intelligence. The ambiguous statements used here are adapted from or inspired by Ernest Davis, Leora Morgenstern, and Charles Ortiz's online "Collection of Winograd Schemas" (CC-BY-4.0).

the broken glass along with my Panang Curry and Jenny's Kaeng Khiao Wan with Extra Cilantro.

I rub my bald head (which Drillard describes as, haha, A Whiter Shade of Pale), feeling for blood, and I glance at the shelves above the table. *Newton's Pendulum has slipped from the highest shelf because it wasn't*
    [anchored] > **Go to 4**
    [level].   > **Go to 5**

3.

The table is made of Styrofoam (see **1**), and the SuperBall makes a *thwunk* sound when it goes through, snapping the table neatly in two. The Ferengi Gang must be throwing things again. Good thing we started keeping the windows open. It's probably the Ferengi, too, who make the whole apartment building shake, crashing into the structural columns in our carport on their stolen bikes and scooters. In any case, the two broken halves of our Styrofoam table prop each other up, seemingly in defiance of the laws of physics. My homemade Half and Half Pandemic Pizza—pesto for Jenny, pancetta for me—is smooshed in the crack, another casualty of the attack. Miraculously the wine glasses tumbled but didn't break.

The Styrofoam table is a temporary surface of course, provisional like seemingly everything during The Plague, slapped together from packing materials saved from countless delivery boxes. My Double Quarantine means I cannot (a) set foot past my front porch into analog AmbiZone space, or (b) co-locate with another human in any public or private Holospace, without setting off my PanoptiCuff® GPS ankle monitor. My dear Jenny, however, is still free to move about within the AmbiZone if she wears a full X51 getup. Drillard, possibly with ulterior motives, got both of them Elite Essential Exemptions when I was put on Administrative Leave.

"The table's disposable —" I say.

"Good thing it wasn't glass!" Jenny says.

"— But not really recyclable," I say.

"Never was," Jenny says. "*Bo* says that recycling is a state-sponsored project that envisions modern futures as forms of vernacular speculative design simultaneously constrained by and subverting narratives of technological innovation arising from the Global North."

Well well well. Beau "Bo" Drillard is a self-taught coder for Kroneborg Game Design, creator of The Winograd Matrix™ series, which has been topping the charts and for which I was Lead Writer before I was arrested for choking Cofú the Intern, back when people actually went into the office.

Drillard and I were, can you guess, humanities grad students together who both dropped out to pursue the almighty high tech dollar. The main difference being that he continued to grow his hair while I lost all mine. Not only his head but his whole body is like a thick dark carpet (an exotic foreign carpet, due to Drillard's vague ethnicity claims involving former French colonies) covering him like the dense discourse of critical theory, while my skin is as hairless as a cue ball, as clean as machine code but discolored by chronic skin diseases.

Jenny is the highly-paid contract engineer and Level Designer for The Winograd Matrix™, recently promoted to Level Design Yogini. I've begun to suspect that Drillard and Jenny may be taking advantage of my Double Incarceration to meet up in

Kroneborg Holospace, or worse. I think about saying something, but instead I stick with recycling.

"Extruded polystyrene foam is 95% air, not biodegradable, and emits toxic fumes when burned," I say as we extract mangled slices of pesto and pancetta pizza, flecked with Styrofoam, from the table cleavage.

"Then let's hope we don't have a *fire* on top of The Plague!" Jenny says.

Which is of course exactly when the fire starts. In our carport. We call it in.

We notice there's a note attached to the SuperBall. It's
    [completely illegible]   **> Go to 8**
    [still rolling around].   **> Go to 9**

4.

The Newton's Pendulum wasn't anchored on the shelf (see **2**). Did Jenny put it there, unsecured despite the constant earthquake danger? Could I have done it myself? If you live along the Ring of Fire and you put heavy objects on high shelves without anchoring them, do you have a death wish?

"Wonder if it will be safe to eat," Jenny says. Her green Kaeng Khiao Wan and my red Panang and are starting to mix together in the broken glass.

"So *that's* how they make yellow curry!" I say, but Jenny doesn't laugh.

I remember Newton's Balls had been massively over-packaged in giant Styrofoam slabs ("Big enough to make a table!" I may have remarked to Jenny). The gift card from Drillard had said, "Conventional understandings of a linear progress narrative notwithstanding, may your audacious fictions and performative

FROLIC

modalities be grounded in fields of belonging and the transgressive interrogation of power structures. And sorry about Cofú."

What happened with Cofú the Intern was basically that, in the weeks leading up to the Curfews and Quarantines, he was annoying the shit out of everyone in the office with his nonstop conspiracy theories about how The Plague was a Neoliberal Deep State Plot to enhance social control through fear, discipline, and surveillance, and the fact that he was an Extreme Close Talker (without a BioMask = now a felony) who also poked you in the chest with his bony finger as he exhaled hotly in your face and expounded his paranoid delusions, coupled with his ubiquitous dandruff and toxic gassiness (possibly a result of the malodorous foods he always brought for lunch), etc. etc., all of which came to a head for me the day that Cofú loudly and in gross violation of my personal space insisted that my dear Jenny, assisted by Drillard, was implanting encrypted messages for Saudi Princes, Tech Titans, and other Plague Co-Conspirators on the Dark Web hidden in lines of code for the open-source game engine driving The Winograd Matrix™, and when Cofú finished over-microwaving his week-old seafood stew, stinking up the entire office CollaboZone, and spun around splashing the hot fishy mess all down my *one nice blue shirt*, I admit I overreacted by sort of cuffing him on the collarbone with my upraised palms, an action which became in his mind the "choking death grip" that led the police to initially overcharge me with Aggravated Assault, later reduced to Simple Assault following the, I have to say, lukewarm testimony of the sole witness, Drillard.

Never mind Cofú. I retreat to our cramped bathroom to

check my head for blood and my hands for glass slivers. "The drain's clogged with hair again!" I say.

"It's gotta be

        [cleaned]   > Go to 6
        [removed],"   > Go to 7

Jenny says.

5.

The shelf wasn't level (see 2). Maybe never has been. So it was inevitable, in a way, that Newton's Steel Balls, the executive toy given to me by Drillard, would slip off that shelf in an earthquake and crash through the glass table. Thus demonstrating not only the Conservation of Momentum and Energy but also just plain old Gravity, i.e. Newton's Law of Universal Gravitation.

Why didn't we notice the tiltiness of the shelf before?

"The other shelves appear fine," I say, checking them with a carpenter's level.

"It's above eye level," Jenny says, rising on her tippy-toes.

I avoid teasing Jenny about her height, or rather her lack of height, because (a) she never found it that funny anyway, even before we moved in together, and (b) then we got *confined* together, in a small apartment that feels smaller by the day, by The Plague and by my House Arrest, until both of us are this close to snapping, bursting into tears, or putting a fist through a door.

"Over my head too," I say, patting my hairless, bony scalp—going above and beyond, I feel, to emphasize that in the grand scheme of things, humans do not differ all that greatly in height.

Jenny climbs up the stepstool and bends forward to get a closer look. Her lovely rear before my face, I reflexively cup her hips, as if to brace her on the stool, but okay I cheat a little, my palms pressing against her soft round cheeks. It's the closest we've come to sex in weeks, and I feel a surge of desire.

"Your favorite tool," I say slyly, ostensibly meaning the stepladder (certainly not the carpenter's level), and, you could say, obliquely alluding to her height. But she gets the carnal inference.

"Whoa, Trigger," Jenny says, as in the name of The Lone Ranger's horse, who was a palomino.

Trigger—or sometimes Mr. Ed, another TV palomino—is Jenny's shorthand for "Palomino Penis," i.e. her pet name for my vitiligo-striped penis. Vitiligo, or patchy depigmentation of the skin, is often accompanied by white hair or hair loss in the affected areas. Like, also, my scalp. Penis or penile vitiligo—permanent patches of discolored or depigmented skin on the shaft, glans, or foreskin of the penis, and sometimes the balls—is common in men with my disease. While tan and white multicolored splotches can give the genitals an unusual or comical appearance that may raise questions or elicit unsolicited comments in the bedroom, or the locker room—don't get me started on this—the condition is otherwise harmless, and it has zero effect on functionality, if you catch my drift.

Deceased mega-star/child molester Michael Jackson notoriously had vitiligo (hence "Michael Jackson Disease"), allegedly leading him to bleach his skin, since the affliction is more disfiguring and distressing for people with darker skin than for us Whiter Shades of Pale. Indeed Jenny used to toss in a "Jackson," instead of Trigger or Mr. Ed, in referring to my dick, until I told her that the pattern of discoloration on *Jackson's* Jackson, photographed by investigators and later matched to drawings made by a 13-year-old abuse accuser, was responsible for a $25 million settlement. The youngster had accurately portrayed from memory the precise contours of phallic depigmentation for both the flaccid and erect conditions of Jackson's pecker.

"Back off, Mr. Ed!" Jenny reiterates.

Are there worse things in life than having your girlfriend name your phallus for a *horse* (even a Talking Horse)—or for that matter, liken your manhood to that of a famous/infamous Black musician? Yes. Still, I'm a little surprised at Jenny's admonishments, because I thought we had an unstated deal that, during The Plague, I would not tease her about her height, and she would not tease me about my hair loss or penis vitiligo.

I remove my hands from her ass.

6.
"It's gotta be cleaned," Jenny says (see **4**). Meaning the *drain* in the bathroom sink. It's clogged with hair again. Probably the shower drain as well. We have tried to equitably divide the chores in our little apartment and it's been my job during Lockdown and Confinement to clean the bathroom. Which includes the drains.

"OK," I say.

We've mostly stopped griping. Our unstated deal—that Jenny and I would avoid teasing each other about, respectively, her short stature and my (shall we say) distinctive dick—had followed on the heels of a *stated* deal, an agreement we reached based on the viral video *12 Survival Tricks for Couples With Borderline Social Skills Who Are Stuck Together During The Plague* of which we agreed to adopt Number 6. Namely that we would each air one and only one interpersonal request, gripe, and/or constructive criticism per day. These were to be shared, somewhat formally, during Happy Hour—in retrospect, a poor decision to combine petty grievances, or real complaints, with alcohol.

Things started off pretty well. Jenny complained that I spent too much time in the bathroom (using it), or too little time in the bathroom (cleaning it); I noted her difficulty discerning which substances were proper vs. improper to put down the garbage disposal. Of course I brought up the hair clogging the bathroom drains. The annoyances quickly escalated. "Speaking of *hair* [uh-oh!], have you thought about trimming your *nose* hairs?" Jenny said, and after a second glass of wine went straight to, "Were you *raised by fucking wolves?*" My rejoinders (e.g., regarding her Chronic Inability to Take Out the Recycling, "Do you have a goddamn *broken leg?*") were not well received, and in short, our Happy Hour Sharing Time went down in flames after only one week.

7.

"It's gotta be removed," Jenny says (see **4**). Meaning the *hair*. From the drain in the bathroom sink. By me. Again! I've had enough! I'm sorry. Do I even *have* hair? Other than in my nose? No. I do not have hair. I am in fact bald. Whose hair is that constantly clogging the drain? Yes it is yours Jenny. Your long beautiful auburn-beginning-to-turn-gray locks, identical to those wadded in your hairbrush which hasn't been cleaned since 10 BP (Before Plague), the hairbrush you hold over the sink while brushing brushing brushing in the admiring mirror and dropping clumps of hair, hair that globs and twists together like licorice sticks congealed with grime and grease, foul slimy masses that fill the sink, choke the sink until it's impervious even to repeated treatments of super-toxic industrial strength Drain-D-Klogg®.

Meanwhile the plumbers are still under Lockdown. Well dear Jenny *you* just go ahead and remove your hair from the drain, I'm *done*. And clean it out too, while you're at it!

8.
The note attached to the SuperBall is completely illegible after being flung in the window and crashing through our Styrofoam table (see **3**). Held only by an ancient rubber band that shatters on impact, the note gets shredded too, its blue ink so smudged you can't tell if it was written in English or Ferengi.

"It's a sign," I say (Drillard would say *simulation*).

"Get the vacuum?" Jenny says. It's not really a question. She starts plucking from the carpet small bits of dry cracked rubber band mixed with Styrofoam crumbs and smeared remnants of the unreadable note.

"The fucking Ferengis," Jenny calls them, not to their faces. During The Plague, besides throwing stuff through windows, they've made a living off pilfering packages from people's porches, working in giggling groups and wearing creepy 3D-printed resin prosthetic masks to foil the cameras and mobile BioScanners.

"I think the SuperBall hit my head before it went through the table," I say over the vacuum.

We sit down with a couple salvaged slices of Pandemic Pizza. Some of Jenny's half has mooshed together with mine to form a sort of hybrid red-pesto-pancetta. I pour us each a glass of Chianti in our surprisingly unbroken wine glasses.

"Here's to picking up the pieces," Jenny says. She looks at me, and I look back into the deep pools of her eyes. I realize these three seconds or so are the longest we've looked into each other's eyes for all these months of confinement and tension, suspicion and crime.

"Cheers," I say, choking up. "Do you think . . ." but just then the Fire Department arrives with their sirens and their sweeping lights, and we remember that the carport is on fire.

Later, the Fire Inspectors arrest the entire Ferengi Gang because they are evidently trying to

        [stop]   > **Go to 10**

        [run]   > **Go to 11**

an arson ring in the neighborhood.

        [or else]   > **Go to 12**

9.

The SuperBall is still rolling around after being flung in the window and crashing through our Styrofoam table (see **3**). The whole building shudders as fire fighting machinery bangs against our parking structure. For a minute, trying to pick up the SuperBall is like the slapstick routine where your foot keeps kicking it just out of your grasp. Finally I get a grip, and Jenny unwraps the note carefully folded inside a plastic baggie fastened around the SuperBall with fresh rubber bands.

"It's in Ferengi," she says.

"Great," I say. "And our Universal Translator is down."

"*Konah see-oh-mahj irr zoon,*"* she reads phonetically.

The firefighters finish dousing the flames in the carport, and the Fire Inspectors take possession of the note, which they will later cite as evidence that the Ferengi Gang claimed responsibility

---

* "The fools never knew what hit them."

for the arson.

Jenny and I perform a series of tests with the SuperBall to confirm its (a) extreme vulcanized elasticity, meaning that (b) it's really really bouncy, for example (c) when dropped from a height will bounce nearly all the way back up, to be precise (d) 92% of the height you dropped it from, while strangely (e) reversing its direction of spin on each bounce! and thus (f) demonstrating—in a different way than, say, one of those Newton's Cradle Toys everyone used to have on their coffee table, with the clacking steel balls—the physics principle of Time Reversal Symmetry.

In the process we, or rather the SuperBall, not only inflicts further damage to our Styrofoam table and Pandemic Pizza but also breaks our wine glasses and nearly every dish in the kitchen. I told you it was a small apartment. But it's a great release, in fact the most fun we've had since The Plague began. By the end we're drinking Chianti from the bottle, laughing and snorting about Temporal Loops and Backward Causation. I ask Jenny about Drillard.

"Are you clandestinely meeting up with Drillard in the Kroneborg Holospace?"

"No," Jenny says.

10.

The Fire Inspectors are trying to stop an arson ring in the neighborhood (see **8**). It's a relief when they arrest the Ferengi Gang, but while the entire gang are still in jail awaiting bail, another fire is set, and then another, with the same MO as the first (rags doused in gasoline, carport/garage/storage locker, daring daytime crime with people home quarantined).

The local outrage and fear, following the fires in the middle of The Plague, combine to crash the server for MyNextDoors.com, leaving no one able to post for precious minutes about their Lost Kitty, or the Speeding Driver, or the Loud Explosion, or the What's Next, An Earthquake? in addition to the hundreds of lunatic theories about the arsonist(s). A paramilitary-style NeighborWatch group, armed with Phasers and wearing camo and ski masks, has begun patrolling the AmbiZone, looking like some combination of Seal Team 6 and a Star Trek Away Team.

"Clouds of smoke blotting out the sun, decaying infrastructure, roving vigilantes." Jenny stares out the window as she dictates a Voice Memo to Serena, her Kroneborg DigaSister, about the visual and sound design for a new Level in The Winograd Matrix™.

"OK, got it," says Serena soothingly.

"I think it's Cofú!" I say. "I bet he set the first fire in our carport, to terrorize me, or you, or indirectly Drillard, then he set the other fires as a distraction."

"Dystopian surveillance and paranoia, police sirens, ambulances flashing lights, snippets of disconnected dialogue," Jenny says to Serena.

"We need to talk," I say.

"I didn't catch that," says Serena.

In The Winograd Matrix™, now on its 10th sequel (*TWM: Attack of the Ferengi*), the Player Character (you) repeatedly encounters a series of multiple-choice situations described by a pair of statements that differ by one word or phrase, your selection of which resolves a pronoun disambiguation problem in the statements, but in different ways, thus producing variations in the game narrative, like slightly alternate realities. Choosing different antecedents for the pronouns can alter the meaning in subtle or profound ways. "It's like an interactive fiction thought up by your high school grammar teacher," I'd said to Jenny when she joined Kroneborg. The Non-Player Characters introduced in the first game (*TWM: Pandemic!*) continue throughout the series and include a vaguely discontented girlfriend/boyfriend/ nonbinary (select your gender) Significant Other, colorful work colleagues, and, in some scenarios, local non-racially-stereotyped gang members. You must play through all the options in order to complete the game, while never really resolving, much less fully understanding, the Player Character's personal problems. The game has nevertheless proven addictive to millions—which I attribute to the writing team that I led until Kroneborg furloughed me over the choking thing.

11.

The Ferengi Gang are trying to run an arson ring in the neighborhood (see **8**). Of course they are. They're the fucking Ferengi Gang after all, and besides stealing packages delivered to our doorsteps and throwing SuperBalls through our windows and breaking things, they have been terrorizing us riding around on stolen scooters and bicycles, setting fires in our carports and garages.

So it's a relief when the Fire Inspectors arrest them, leaving me and Jenny with "only" The Plague, i.e. the constant danger of being around other people, our claustrophobic confinement, and our heightened domestic tensions.

The Ferengi arrests are witnessed by dozens of Favatars lining the streets, the grimly smiling photos of our neighbors and ourselves glued to the front of cardboard cutouts made into yard signs stuck in the ground with wires.

"Surreal, isn't it," I say. From behind, Favatar silhouettes look like tombstones.

"Multiple oppressive narratives that we're complicit in co-constructing . . ." Jenny starts to say with exaggerated gravity—parroting Drillard, or parodying him, I can't tell which. Then she shrugs, as if suddenly overwhelmed by the cumulative weight of it all.

"But you can resist," I say. "We can resist, right?"

We lock eyes for a second time. Outside, the Syndics are patrolling. I instinctively check my PanoptiCuff® ankle monitor, but the green light is blinking System Status Nominal. The Syndics pause by our carport, still blackened from the fire (the carport, not the Syndics). They adjust their head cams, inspect our Favatars, dictate notes into their DigaSisters.

"You can resist," Jenny says, brightening momentarily. "But it takes *balls*."

She turns and logs in to Kroneborg Holospace, where she and the Level Design Team, plus Drillard and the other coders, have one more scenario to create for The Winograd Matrix™.

12.

Or, counterintuitively, the Fire Inspectors are trying to run an arson ring in the neighborhood, and the Ferengi Gang are trying to stop them (see 8). Not one of the expected outcomes—a violation of common-sense reasoning. But, in this final scenario, the Fire Inspectors (who only appear if the table is made of Styrofoam, cracked in two by a SuperBall) must be corrupt. If the Fire Inspectors are corrupt, Kroneborg Game Design is corrupt, my ex-best friend

Drillard and ex-girlfriend Jenny are corrupt, and they have all conspired to take advantage of The Plague to frame the Ferengi Gang for arson and entrap *me* in their elaborate plot. Drillard probably schemed with the Fire Inspectors to forge the Ferengi note implicating the Gang (unless the note was unreadable?), which *he* attached to the SuperBall and threw in our window and right through our Styrofoam table, as we were preparing to eat our Pandemic Pizza.

If, on the other hand, the ball is made of steel, and the table of glass, then there was no fire and thus no Fire Inspectors, and we did not make pizza but instead ate takeaway curry from Just So Thai. In which case, sadly, I suspect Drillard got Jenny to booby-trap the Newton's Cradle Toy that he just *happened* to have sent me as a (Trojan Horse) gift—and/or Drillard and Jenny together sabotaged the shelf from which my Newton's Balls fell during the earthquake, the earthquake which does not occur in the other, Styrofoam scenarios. Then Jenny and Drillard were not only colluding in the Kroneborg Holospace but also meeting up past Curfew, sans X51 gear, in the AmbiZone. Can't you just picture my dear Jenny wallowing in Drillard's critical theory and luxuriating in his ursine fur while making fun of my hairless palomino prick?

Either way, it appears the corruption extends even to Newton's Laws: the Time Reversal Invariance of classical physics, embodied by Steel Balls and SuperBalls alike, has been perverted somehow by quantum mechanics. Or maybe by Superstring Theory. I fear that Cofú the Intern was working undercover the whole time, baiting me into the so-called Choking Incident, my arrest and conviction intended to deprive me of royalties on the entire Winograd Matrix™ series, not to mention equity in

Kroneborg Game Design Inc., which was secretly planning its IPO. So—if so—very clever. But, well, shit.

In the end, I tear off my PanoptiCuff® ankle monitor and run down the street, heaving Newton's Balls, or the SuperBall—any balls!—against the neighbors' Favatars, knocking some of them over (the Favatars, not the neighbors). I feel vindicated, but I end up alone.

[Twine game/interactive fiction version available at *https://kairos.technorhetoric.net/27.1/disputatio/holeton/*; a slightly different version available at *https://voidspacezine.com/the-winograd-matrix/*; archived by the Electronic Literature Organization in The NEXT at *https://the-next.eliterature.org/works/2424/0/0/*]

Postmodern

Play in One Act[*]

Stoned men on stoop ponder storm onset, monster porn store "Odeon," morose modern sperm donors.

—DON TEMPORS, noted postmodern poet, red pores (tons!) on nose, rode to porn store on metro.

—NORM DOPEST, most stoned, met DON on metro.

—ED TROMPSON, stern mentor to NORM, rodeo poser, rode on moped, prone to snort.

DON [on top step]:
Red moon, set soon.

---

[*] Composed using only anagrams of "postmodern" or hidden words within that word.

NORM [*modest tone*]:
Er, moonset?

DON [*nods*]:
Soon, Romeo, Eros' son!

Moon droops. Dent on moped motor. Rodent on doorstep.

NORM:
Rodent pest!

DON:
Or one's pet rodent?

ED:
Rope 'em moped!

[*Rodeo snort.*]
To me, red moon portends storm mode.

DON, NORM don't respond. "Odeon" doormen deport ten torn mops onto endmost step, open doors.

Some sperm donors——most, poor peons, spend rent on Port——step to porn store doors, toe to toe. More omens: Sterno, torn torso, snot nose, one rose.

ED:
Some spot.

DON:
Some demo!

ED:
No more net porn, Norm?

NORM:
Me? Nope.

ED [*prods*]:
Or pet porno?

NORM [*more pot*]:
No, Ed.

DON [*tops Ed*]:
Dorm room poster porn? Prom porn?

NORM [*to Ed*]:
Nerd!

[*To Don.*]
Moron!

Storm Troops send drones to porn store, snoop on sperm donors, set ropes (noose portends doom—or rodeo sport).

DON, NORM, ED spot troops, drop pot pronto, open Oreos.

NORM:
O no—Demon Storm Troops!

DON:
No rest!

[*Rote tone, notes top trends.*] One despot tends to stop dope, one to promote porn, or dote on motor sport... one to deport sperm donors.

Pert rodents torpedo torn mops, send some to nest.

DON [*not done*]:
Norm, Ed—doesn't one person opt to post poems, or prose, on net? Presto, more protons promoted to tropes! Or tropes promoted to...

NORM [*tenor snore*]:
Drone on, Mr. Mood Poem.

ED [*terms dopers "stoner"*]:
Some sermon, stoner!

End.

[Multimedia slideshow version available at *https://web.stanford.edu/~holeton/ postmodern/assets/player/KeynoteDHTMLPlayer.html#0*; archived by the Electronic Literature Organization in The NEXT at *https://the-next.eliterature.org/ works/2092/0/0/*; French translation version available at *https://the-next.eliterature.org/works/1545/0/0/*]

Frequently Asked Questions about "Hypertext"

Hypertext

Re: Perth rep, PR-type hype. Per HTTP pretext, Peer here: Eye thy eyer, pet yer petter (Hey ET, thee pee there—pH three). 3
"Trey, eh Tex? Tee-hee!" (he, her hyper Ex—pert, hep Hetty Eyre, pretty tree Expert). "Try rye, Pere Peter, er, Pete. Tether T-Rex yet?" 6
Exert petty hex, retype the eery "pyx pyre" text. Tet Rx: They pry teeth—ether prey... Yep, they're pre-Pyrex. 9

1. *What is "Hypertext"?*
2. *What are the Richards Criteria?*
3. *Who are you?*
4. *What is the Popular Interpretation?*
5. *And the Texas/Bush School?*
6. *Can you summarize the Technosexual Reading?*
7. *How about the Richards Posttranssexual Rereading?*
8. *What's the story with the fan fiction and the double murder?*
9. *Who am I?*

1. What is "Hypertext"?

Before it grew into a phenomenon justifying a FAQ (Frequently Asked Questions) document such as this, "Hypertext" was startlingly simple in conception. Alan Richardson—a short, pale, freckled, pixie-eared San Francisco Bay Area investment banker and day-trader who amassed a substantial fortune during the 1990s boom—decided post-dotcom meltdown to grow a ponytail and compose a poem using only hidden words and anagrams from the nine-letter word *hypertext*. He tried several versions before settling on the three-stanza, nine-line, 69-word "Hypertext," which he emailed to some friends along with a cryptic note about changing careers, maybe heading back to school.

He said the poem was just a simple kind of word game, though he hoped it might make "some kind of syntactic sense" or even "suggest a coherent narrative" that readers could discover or construct for the text.

Little did Alan Richardson anticipate the critical outpouring that would follow, not to mention the explosion of fan fiction that

"Hypertext" would inspire or the debate that would ensue about the poem's authenticity. Indeed, it took years to peel away the layers of fraudulent versions and false authors and trace the poem back to Richardson, before his dramatic "disappearance" (FAQ #5) and subsequent death (FAQ #8).

2. What are the Richards Criteria?

Fortunately, seminal "Hypertext" critic Ellen Richards established the authorized version of "Hypertext" before the untimely deaths of the author and all the major critics (FAQ #4, FAQ #5, FAQ# 6).

According to the Richards Criteria, the 69 canonical words comprise all possible hidden words in *hypertext* except for British spellings (*tyre*); out-of-fashion slang (*prexy* for president); archaisms and obscurities (*ere, ye, ret, rete*); and a few abbreviations (*PE, PT, TX,* and *HRT*, i.e. Hormone Replacement Therapy).

The Richards Criteria further assert that the poem uses each word only once; no plurals or other modifications are allowed; and the initial letters of each line unscramble to spell *hypertext* (allowing **Ex** = *x*). Finally, according to Richards, the exact-anagram pseudonyms that pop up in the fan fiction (e.g., "Rhett Epyx," "Hetty P. Rex," "H. Tex Typer," FAQ #8) are apocryphal.

3. Who are you?

Richard Alan Holeton, volunteer FAQ editor and publisher of HerHim.org (FAQ #8). Let me thank those who have expressed your appreciation for my humble contributions to the "Hypertext" fan community or the sacrifices I've made by mutating from author to editor (less dramatic but still perhaps not unlike Alan Richardson's own transformations from poet to critic, or man to woman, FAQ #7 etc.). Others have suggested, less generously, that I created HerHim.org (**per HTTP pretext**) merely to self-publish my "Hypertext" fan fiction story "Another Day at the Office," after it was rejected at all the existing venues. Not so.

In "Another Day at the Office," Dick A. Hellton, a hotly handsome computer security middle manager, is the true author of both "Hypertext" the poem and "Frequently Asked Questions about 'Hypertext'" the FAQ. One day at work, Dick Hellton's colleague Eric Taylor (**ET**, misread by Ellen Richards as a urinating alien in FAQ #4, reappropriated by critic Richard Allman in FAQ #6, and suspected of murder in FAQ #8) comes out as a transsexual when he reappears from a leave of absence, cheeks pockmarked from electrolysis treatments, as *Erica* Taylor.

Dick finds it impossible to look Erica in the eye (**Peer here: Eye thy eyer**) and not see Eric, the biological man with the big hairy hands and the broad shoulders and the Dick Tracy mug, the deep-voiced man who had quaffed brewskies with him and his fan-fiction buddies Jim Morrison and Joseph Conrad (FAQ #4) after work. And since Erica is still preoperative, Dick cannot stop picturing her marginalized male organs tucked there under the dresses or strapped between her legs when she wears pants.

He recalls the drunken night (**"Try rye"**), from his wild single days, when he'd followed home a whorishly-made up barfly (**pretty tree expert**) and made out with her slobberingly, let her fondle him, then slid his hand down her pants to find something solid instead of soft, like a hard plastic sanitary pad strapped over her crotch. Her hand stopped his ("What is it?"

"Nothing." "Nothing?" "You can't go down there."). What he can't forget is the surprise of his fingers hitting that protective shell, like some incongruous female athletic cup, covering what must've been the preoperative penis or transitional organs (no balls?) of a transsexual (**"Tether T-Rex yet?"**)—then, his sudden sick feeling and quick exit.

He knows it's not fair to heap these feelings onto Erica Taylor and is only dimly aware of doing so. Dick's cringing and confusion exacerbate his own crossdressing fantasies, and one night while composing FAQ #8 he dons devoted and shapely wife Seven of Nine's (*Star Trek: Voyager*) sheer black pantyhose from her lingerie drawer (**Exert petty hex**). Admiring the nylon-spandex tent of his arousal (**pet yer petter**), Seven of Nine is so turned on that she persuades their housekeeper, Robot-Maria (*Metropolis*, FAQ #6, FAQ #7), to strap on her metal breastplate and join them in a ménage à trois (**"Trey, eh Tex? Tee-hee!"**), for which the manly Hellton performs magnificently.

The story leaves Dick Hellton poised on the brink of self-discovery and invention (i.e., **pre-Pyrex**), as it leaves Erica Taylor in genital limbo. Thus in "Another Day at the Office" Eric/a Taylor—hopelessly confused in Hellton's mind with an anonymous trans-waif from his sleazy past—is the unintended inspiration for the entire FAQ, the real-life, electrolysis-scarred face that launched 6000 words.

4. What is the Popular Interpretation?

When it made the rounds of the poetry discussion lists, "Hypertext" was an immediate hit with the Language and Post-Language poets and critics, who hailed the poem's anti-linearity, "disjunctive collage narrative," and "subversive, postcapitalist rejection of repressive grammar and normative syntax."

With its shifting viewpoints, ambiguous pronoun references, and kaleidoscope of topics and images, the poem affirms and empowers the reader in the production process, said the Langpo people, because the reader must supply the connections between all these disparate elements to make the text cohere. Through this process, the reader becomes aware of the text's cultural frames and socially-determined nature, leading of course to worldwide socialist revolution.

While the revolution remains incomplete, the social constructedness of "Hypertext" was opened up to a wider audience by what became known as the Popular Interpretation, pioneered during the "missing years" of author Alan Richardson (FAQ #5) by then-unknown MFA student Ellen Richards. The clever, persuasive Richards built her meteoric reputation with her close reading of "Hypertext," aided by the widespread collaboration of armchair critics on the Internet, including many of you with your vast knowledge of TV, your film savvy, and your search engines.

Fellow students at the Iowa Writers Workshop described Ellen Richards as pretty, slender, and narrow-hipped, with a wicked sense of humor and a falsetto voice that cracked occasionally at post-workshop happy hours into a deep, lusty laugh. Even prominent mainstream academics such as Richard Allman were drawn to Popular ideas before turning against Richards in the wake of the emerging biographical details (FAQ #5, FAQ #6, etc.), i.e. the real-life scandals that constantly threatened to divert attention from the poem itself.

According to Richards, the poem self-consciously embraces

the artifacts of Western popular culture while revealing a pattern of underlying sexual tensions. **Re:** (regarding, in reference to) **...PR-type hype** points the poem from the outset to the rhetoric of popular-media fan sites on the Web (**per HTTP**, via **Hyper-Text** Transfer Protocol).

The **Perth Rep**ertory in Scotland is where actor Ewan McGregor got his start by pulling curtains backstage, well before he achieved fame as Obi-Wan Kenobi in the *Star Wars* prequels. You can see Ewan naked (**Peer here:**) in his breakout role in *Trainspotting* (1996); for a lengthier look at his uncircumcised penis, try *The Pillow Book* (1996). Line 3's **ET** refers both to the long-running, syndicated *Entertainment Tonight*, TV's first fan show and leading self-reflexive look at Hollywood (**pet yer petter**), and to Steven Spielberg's wacky, cuddly, asexual E.T. in *E.T., the Extra-Terrestrial* (1982). In one of numerous segments leading up to the 20th anniversary re-release of the film ("E.T. on *ET*," "*ET* on E.T.," etc.), *Entertainment Tonight* showed never-before-seen footage from the DVD that seemingly confirms the acidity of E.T.'s urine. The otherwise-dickless alien appears to relieve himself in the bushes (**thee pee there**) with a steaming stream of vinegar; super slow motion shows the corrosive effects on the foliage. Household vinegar has a **pH** of 3.0 (**three**), versus normal human urine (4.6 to 8.0).

The second stanza's enigmatic dialogue inscribes fanzine discourse in the larger context of the dominant Western literary and philosophical tradition and serves to level the playing field between high and low culture. **Trey** Parker, heartthrob co-creator of *South Park*, is the postmodern, scatological extension of animated cartooning's first modernist and wildman, **Tex** Avery.

Avery's ornery characters Porky Pig, Daffy Duck, and Bugs

Bunny responded to Disney sentimentalism and repressed sexuality with irony, sarcasm, slapstick, and violence, and they called attention to the artifice of the cartoon by speaking directly to the audience, questioning the plot, or jumping out of the credits (cf. FAQ #3, FAQ #9). Parker's **Ex**-girlfriend is said to be the model for Wendy Testaburger, the character who makes *South Park* boyfriend Stan Marsh barf every time she speaks (**Tee-hee!**). Therefore, said Richards,

> The giggling **Hetty Eyre** combines that subtle Comedy Central reference (**he, her hyper/ Ex = Trey** Parker) with the more obvious allusion to Charlotte Brontë's *Jane Eyre*. Jane Eyre is one of the few literary or media icons not lampooned by Avery or fucked by *South Park*'s Chef (Isaac Hayes), whose conquests range from Cleopatra and Virginia Woolf to Lois Lane, Princess Di, and Kathie Lee Gifford. **Pretty tree expert** alludes to Brontë's hyperbolic natural imagery, as when the withering, groaning chestnut tree gets split by lightning in reaction to Rochester and Jane's engagement.

In Line 6 the poem drills deeper into the Western canon when **Hetty** turns from **Tex** the modernist to address **Pere Peter**, i.e. Pere Peter Abelard, the 12th-century rhetorician, dialectician, teacher, and fornicator who paid for his love with his testicles. Often considered the first modern thinker for questioning early Church orthodoxy, Abelard is even better known for diddling his teenage student Heloise, then marrying her in secret after she got pregnant. When circumstances drove them apart, the famous couple exchanged steamy letters that have inspired generations of lovers and artists (after eight centuries on the bestseller list, *The Letters of Abelard and Heloise* recently still ranked 16,802 on Amazon.com.) It was young Heloise's uncle who had Abelard's balls cut off; he hired thugs to perform the crude, transformative surgery. Thus Hetty's **"Try rye..."** is a sly put-down that refers to the grain-growing monasteries of northern France where **Pere Peter** retired as a eunuch to pen those famous missives.

If Abelard's scholarly work is the precursor to modern scientific rationalism and foundationalist thinking—and if the unleashed **Tyrannosaurus Rex** of Spielberg's *Jurassic Park* (1993) embodies science, and the elite social structures it empowers, gone berserk—then, according to Richards and her followers, **Hetty**'s rhetorical question **"Tether T-Rex yet?"** really asks, "Have the excesses of empiricism been tamed?" In this reversal of hegemonic power relations, the hybrid **Wendy Testaburger/Jane Eyre** sarcastically surmounts Father Abelard, the male symbol of intellectual history. As Richards observed, "The once-lusty Father is left with his twig but loses his berries."

In the final triplet, the poem circles back to the sexually charged airwaves of contemporary cultural artifacts, now with a darker, more meditative twist. **Exert petty hex** recalls *Bewitched*, that epitome of 1960s situation comedy about an advertising executive (Darrin, played by Dick York) married to a witch (Samantha, played by Elizabeth Montgomery) whose mother (Endora, played by Agnes Moorehead) is always trying to break them up, often by putting **hex**es on hapless Darrin. Samantha struggles to keep her witchcraft and the lurking subculture of wizards and warlocks secret; to hide her real identity and act as a normal, doting housewife; and to follow Darrin's proscription against using her nose-twitching magic powers—all metaphors for closeted homosexuality. Indeed, the gay actors on *Bewitched* included lesbian Agnes Moorhead, Paul Lynde as Uncle Arthur, and Dick Sargent, who replaced ailing, drug-addicted Dick York as Darrin in season 6—a transition dubbed by Richards as "the change of Dicks."

Meanwhile the body bags were piling up in Vietnam. *Bewitched* episode 93, in which Endora conjures up a dream car for Darrin (still Dick #1) that turns out to be stolen, aired in January 1967, the same month The Doors released their first album with "Light My Fire" (...*our love becomes a funeral pyre*). Thus, according to Richards,

> **the "pyx pyre" text** is a complex trope that conjoins two charismatic, subversive, and incendiary historical figures by linking the lyrics of Jim Morrison to history's first celebrated book burning in 1121, when church fathers torched Peter Abelard's *Theologia*. Morrison's dark lyrics mirrored the social tensions of the 1960s, including the drug culture, antiwar movement, and sexual revolution – all conspicuously absent from *Bewitched,* whose typical "Another Day at the Office" plot [vs. FAQ #3—ed.] revolves around Darrin securing a big client for his white-bread advertising agency.

Followers of the Popular school debate whether Line 7's

imperative verbs **exert** and **retype** are directed at the reader or, reflexively, at the speaker of the poem him/herself. Richards favored the latter view, suggesting that the poet of "Hypertext" is "complicit with all the producers of cultural artifacts, from Abelard to *Bewitched* and The Doors, in **exert**ing a **hex** upon the reader and **retype**-ing a **text** for popular consumption." Most agree, at the least, that the tension between *Bewitched* and The Doors in Line 7 reflects the social divide of the late 1960s.

The Doors are also featured on the soundtrack of Francis Ford Coppola's *Apocalypse Now* (1979), which opens with chemical-weapon-laden helicopters flying at treetop over the jungle accompanied by Morrison's apocalyptic "The End." Based on Joseph Conrad's *Heart of Darkness*, Coppola's film offers, Richards argued,

> ... one of the most intriguing reactions to the Vietnam War, which so obsessed American consciousness after the Viet Cong's pivotal 1968 **Tet** Offensive cracked the collective smugness (the succinct phrase **Tet Rx** deftly captures the social prescription required to treat the sickness of Vietnam). **They pry teeth** suggests that American soldiers in Vietnam were like the Nazis, a comparison encouraged by Coppola's genocidal Colonel Kurtz (Marlin Brando). Kurtz's pursuit is the Oedipal journey of Captain Willard (Martin Sheen), whose riverboat crewmembers, suffering the various ills of a (*Bewitched*-like) family melodrama, provide the subtextual link between sexual dysfunction and

violence. "I love the smell of napalm in the morning," deadpans Lt. Colonel Kilgore (Robert Duvall) after blowing away a Vietnamese village including a playground full of schoolchildren (**ether prey....**).

The victims of the war were **pre-Pyrex**, with the well-known Corning high-temperature ovenware product symbolizing the ironic transformation of Vietnam to a free-market economy increasingly dominated by consumer goods and commodity fetishism. In the postwar, globalized Vietnam, those products were given away on a state-sponsored version of *Wheel of Fortune*, complete with a Southeast Asian Vanna White (Phan Thu Hang) and a Las Vegas wheel shaped like the national-trademark conical straw hat (hence the show's name, *The Magic Hat*).

Finally, Richards noted that Magic Hat is also the name of a Vermont specialty brewery that makes a beer called "Heart of Darkness." Therefore, in the relentless logic of the Popular Interpretation, Magic Hat's corporate motto, "Where Ancient Alchemy meets Modern-day Science," might also be the anthem of a poem in which 12th-century Abelard and Heloise meet Darrin and Samantha, and Stan Marsh and Wendy Testaburger, and all become word phrase puzzles on a Vietnamese *Wheel of Fortune*.

Yep, in "Hypertext" art and knowledge and repressed sexuality have been transformed into beer names and questions for TV games, the ubiquitous postmodern kitsch of popular culture—and the journal *Death of the Author* named Ellen Richards Critic of the Year.

5. And the Texas/Bush School?

Lest we forget. The Texas Reading, which became known as the Bush School, was first formulated by the late Hilton Allrich when he was at the University of Texas-Austin, predating the Popular Interpretation and well before the zenith of fan fiction (FAQ #8). While Allrich found in "Hypertext" some superficial references to the life and scandals of President George Walker Bush (e.g., **"pyx pyre" text** refers to the burning or "cleansing" of official records documenting Bush's controversial Vietnam-era National Guard service), he mainly argued that the rhetoric and grammar of the poem imitate Bush's fragmented speech patterns, awkward syntax, parataxis, and tortured diction.

Thus, Alan Richardson chose *hypertext* as the "mother word" of the poem precisely because it yielded a Bushian monosyllabic, simpleton vocabulary and a grammar devoid of conjunctions and participles and lacking in verbs (only 10). Airheaded interjections (**hey, eh, tee-hee, er, yep**) outnumber the few adverbs (**here, there**, and **yet**), prepositions (**re** and **per**), and articles (**the**). Nouns and adjectives dominate the poem (40 out of 69 words), which Allrich characterized as

> ...essentially a series of things, things that lack the subtlety of modification and qualification, things made static by the dearth of verbs. Coherence is sporadic. Like the poem's ostensible themes of political intrigue and the fall from grace, its sentence fragments, overreliance on the imperative, mixture of highbrow and lowbrow register, and dubious or inventive usage are almost Shakespearian. But the choppy

cadences, the highly overstressed and chaotic meter—these are purely Bush.

By contrast, some neo-Bushies suggest that the abundance of rhyming and the repetition of vowels and consonants produce a kind of jerking, staccato musical quality, an almost incantatory effect (a **hex** if you will).

In any case, the credibility of the Bush School suffered a blow with the revelation, following Hilton Allrich's death, of Allrich's physical attraction to author Alan Richardson. Following his failed promotion at Texas with a lowlier adjunct position at San Francisco State, Allrich took pains to seek out Richardson in person. The pipe-smoking, double-chinned critic met the between-careers, postcapitalist poet at a Mission District cafe on at least one occasion, and in his diary Allrich described or fantasized being seduced by the "petite, long-haired, girlish" Richardson (cited by some as a source for Dick Hellton's tranny barfly, FAQ #3).

For his part Richardson never spoke of the alleged one-night stand, and soon after, he dropped from public view entirely. Conspiracy theorists had a field day when Hilton Allrich was found blue and cold—having apparently hanged himself, and still with an erection—in his seedy flat in the Mission.

6. Can you summarize the Technosexual Reading?

Following Hilton Allrich's tragic, tumescent death and the subsequent "disappearance" of Alan Richardson, the suave, goateed, black-attired academic superstar Richard Allman warmly embraced the Popular Interpretation. He also warmly embraced its deviser, Ellen Richards. Professor Allman finagled for Richards a guest lectureship in Modern Thought and Literature at Stanford and, soon after, began dating her. The attraction was mutual and quickly became intimate. Records confirm that Richards quietly changed departments to Creative Writing, where Allman had no appointment or supervisory capacity, evidently to steer clear of the university's sexual harassment policy.

Students recall Richards holding class outside on sunny Northern California days, pulling her ponytail through the back of the cardinal-red Stanford baseball cap worn to shade her pale, freckly complexion. She was also known for peppering discussions with the language of "Hypertext," telling students to doubt the **PR-type hype** about this or that author, or to look up a website **per http**; holding up a visual aid with the instruction to **Peer here**; telling an attractive biology major with an interest in plants that she was a **pretty tree expert**; and so on. Once when a student named Eliot Thomas asked to go to the bathroom during class, she waved him down the hall with **Hey ET, thee pee there**! You'd think that the jokes would've grown stale for Richards, but for her Stanford students, listening for words from the poem became a kind of game, and they compared tallies and posted results in online discussions, blogs, and instant messages.

At first Richards and Allman were inseparable. Heads touching, they ate sandwiches together in the Quad, shared chopsticks at Palo Alto sushi bars. Hand in hand, they brought students to see Fritz Lang's 1927 film *Metropolis* and the 2002 San Francisco revival of *Hedwig and the Angry Inch*. Intertwined, they reread Kafka, Freud, and Haraway, read aloud *The Letters of*

Abelard and Heloise between sections of *The New York Times* on lazy Sundays. Postcoitally, like a combination Julia Child/Iron Chef, Richards fed Allman's taste for gourmet seafood with pickled anemone and peppered blowfish.

Abruptly, after six months, the affair ended. Shortly thereafter, Allman published "The Crossdressing Cyborg: A Technosexual Reading of 'Hypertext'" in the journal *Technopoetics*.

Allman reread "Hypertext" as a sex-change narrative and conservative, even reactionary, meditation on technologized gender and sexuality. As Allman tells the story, the poet, via the virtual community of crossdressers in Web chatrooms and blogs (**Per HTTP pretext**), meets a **Perth rep** or sales manager for Western Australia with the initials **ET**.

Internet-based clubs arrange real-space gatherings where closet crossdressers can strut their stuff (**Peer here: Eye thy eyer**). Extrapolating from the text—and possibly plagiarizing from the fan fiction (FAQ #8)—Allman reconstructed a transvestite gathering at the upscale Half Moon Bay Schlitz-Marlboro Resort south of San Francisco:

> After weeks of online anticipation, "Alan Richardson" and "Eric Taylor" (**ET**), the two newbie crossdressers, have their mutual coming-out party in the Schlitz-Marlboro Eucalyptus Room, overlooking a slate-gray sea on an overcast Northern California evening.
>
> Richardson is ravishing if a bit June Cleaverish in a flipped wig and flouncy dress with appliqué, pearls and high heels; the much taller Taylor is

titillating in his spaghetti strap top with fringed skirt and fishnet stockings. Both are energized and empowered by the general repartee, group support, and fashion tips.

Another initiation for Taylor and Richardson is their first trip to the ladies' room (**Hey ET, thee pee there**), where "Erica" jokes with "Ellen" about estrogen therapy changing the acidity of urine (**pH three**).

Afterwards, both gents—even more aroused by their public performance than by years of wearing women's underwear in private—rush back to their respective rooms to masturbate (**pet yer petter**).

Allman thus unpacked Stanza 1 as a comment on the relationship between male orgasm and urination, "the two functions that cannot occur together because they both require the single-lane urethra, hence also the two functions that must be rerouted by gender reassignment surgery."

Indeed in Stanzas 2 and 3, as opposed to real life where only a handful of transvestites become transsexuals, the poet moves briskly from panties to penectomy. Foregrounded is the phallic image of **Hetty** as **pretty tree**, her Medusa-like snake-limbs threatening castration and alluding to Hedwig, whose "angry inch" is the dysfunctional pubic mound left from a botched sex-change operation. The metamorphosis of **Pere Peter** or "Father Penis" reemphasizes the poet's ambivalence about the medical transsexual industry, said Allman, with its

> ...crack surgical teams eager to carve a vaginal vault below your prostate, line it with the inverted skin flap of your filleted pecker, convert your glans penis into a sensate neo-clitoris (how realistic!), fashion labial folds and clitoral hooding from your de-balled scrotum (that soft wrinkly tissue the perfect disguise), and finally to connect your sigmoid colon to your new transcunt for improved mucous lubrication (ingenious, I grant).

Such anxiety about genitalia permeates Ellen Richards' Popular Interpretation as well as Alan Richardson's poem, Allman reminded us, and the ultimate transformation is that of Richardson the male to Richards the female. This "witch technology" or **petty hex** is perfected with cosmetic enhancements including breast augmentation (**Tet Rx**, literally, tit prescription), tracheal shaving, electrolysis, and jawbone reduction under anesthesia (**They pry teeth – ether prey**).

The result of all this technological intervention—the drug therapy, the cosmetic operations, the violent sex-reassignment surgery itself—is a hybrid woman-machine or seductive techno-sexual cyborg. Especially if you start off with a small-boned, soft-featured male, you can turn, for example, a mousy Wall Street banker-trader into quite a fetching female poet-critic.

7. How about the Richards Posttranssexual Rereading?

Although Richard Allman apparently rewrote history with his Technosexual Reading by anticipating the sex change before it actually occurred, he effectively outed Ellen Richards. And it didn't take you literary detectives long to confirm from public records that Ellen Richards was indeed the former Alan Richardson, the wealthy, diminutive author of "Hypertext" him/herself. Forced into public visibility, Ellen Richards had failed the common goal of transsexuals to "pass" and thus disappear back into the hegemonic binary gender system. She therefore took the next logical step, seizing upon "Hypertext" as a subversive, reconstructive force ("an intertextual tissue of embodied texts that disrupt the dominant discourse about sexuality") whose effect is to transcend the black-and-white, the either-or, of Male and Female. This became known as the Posttranssexual or Posttranny Rereading.

Regarding the awkward real-life scene when Richards revealed her sexuality to Allman, or when (like the surprised Dick Hellton in FAQ #3) Allman discovered the truth for himself, we unfortunately have only hints and innuendo. We do know that Ellen Richards fired off a letter to *Technopoetics* (titled by the editors "Penile Provocation") asserting that Allman's controversial reading was

> ...not an interpretation so much as a heterosexist response to a failed love affair, self-loathing, and guilt—his transphobic disgust at having so vigorously loved a man-woman with a man-made (if nearly perfect) neovagina.

In his fanciful narrative, Allman projects his own crossdressing fantasies onto "Ellen Richards" and "Eric Taylor." To assuage his homosexual panic, he has sublimated everything into a contest for the meaning of technosexuality, noting the emasculating effects but blind to the potential empowerment of the female "sex machine."

Ellen Richards offered an alternative narrative, equally plausible, in which Allman persuades his sex-changed lover to role-play female cyborg critic Donna Haraway dressed up like Lucy Lawless in *Xena: The Warrior Princess,* complete with metal breastplate (**Text Rx**) adapted from Madonna and Robot-Maria in *Metropolis.* Then Allman can't get it up.

"Shall we analyze the textuality of erectile dysfunction?" Richards asked rhetorically, detailing her Posttranssexual Reading in "Post-**Pyrex** 'Hypertext': Domesticating the Cyborg" (*American Journal of Gender Dysphoria*). The final irony of the **pre-Pyrex** trope, she said, was that "transgendered women, no less than biological women, end up in the kitchen" (like Richards herself, FAQ #7).

The public outing and *ad hominem* attacks brought the literary infighting briefly from the academic journals into the mainstream press and tabloids (Sexperts, Lovers Can't Tell Tranny Professor from the Real Thing! proclaimed the *Weekly World News*). The waiting lists swelled for both Richards' and Allman's courses at Stanford. Surprisingly, the Popular Interpretation (FAQ #4), instead of falling out of favor with the news that its major contributor was actually the poem's author with a new sexual identity, enjoyed a bit of a revival; jaded 21st century readers simply shrugged that the author's reading of her own work was no more deluded than any other. On the eve of the Tenth Annual "Hypertext" Symposium, the Posttranssexual Rereading had made Ellen Richards a leading candidate for Comeback Critic of the Year. Moreover, after years of critical and personal estrangement, Richards and Allman would appear together on the same panel (FAQ #8).

8. What's the story with the fan fiction and the double murder?

The startling deaths at the Tenth Annual "Hypertext" Symposium (HT10) accelerated a vicious circle or feedback loop, refueling the media frenzy around "Hypertext" and the fan fiction that may itself have been complicit in the murder.

For the uninitiated, fan fiction or fanfic is amateur fiction based on TV shows, movies, and other cultural productions. It started in the 1970s when *Star Trek* fans began publishing stories about Captain Kirk and Commander Spock based on what they perceived as the series' homoerotic subtext. Kirk/Spock or K/S came to represent "slash" or homosexual fanfic, and slash grew to include lesbian tracks like J/7, focusing on the attraction between Captain Janeway and Seven of Nine, the sexy hybrid Borg-human in *Star Trek: Voyager* (and fanfic wife of Dick Hellton, FAQ # 3). Other series from the 1980s and 1990s—*The X-Files*, *Xena*, *Buffy the Vampire Slayer*, etc.—inspired their own fan communities to fill in the cracks, as it were, of the received mass narratives, and celebrity-inspired amateur writing got a huge boost from the Internet and the Web. Slash led to het (heterosexual), gen (Grated fanfic), metafic and authorfic and subreality (a border zone where characters aware of their status as fictional creations may mingle with authors or other real-life characters). "Mary Sue" stories, named for a character in early *Star Trek* fanfic, are a wish-fulfillment genre in which a heroic and good-looking proxy for the author performs a crucial role (e.g., "Another Day at the Office," FAQ #3).

"Hypertext" or HT fanfic has followed a peculiar arc, constructed as it is around a self-published, amateur work rather than a professional narrative from the entertainment industry. HT fans pioneered not only the niche genre of subreality trannyfic but also the online Hierarchical Electronic Recombinating Hypertext Interactive Matrix (HER/HIM), brought to you by yours truly at HerHim.org.

[SEE FOLLOWING PAGES]

Using HER/HIM, newbies can construct their first stories in the context of the entire canon, while veterans can track in real time the evolving multitudes of possibilities via our dynamic database engine. With a few clicks of the mouse, you can generate scenarios from Pere Peter/Lois Lane, Dick York/Colonel Kurtz, and Porky Pig/Xena to Charlotte Brontë/George Bush/Julia Child. It wouldn't be boasting to say that HER/HIM quickly became the dominant forum for HT fanfic.

Unfortunately, due to the high volume of submissions and increasing pressures from our corporate sponsors—victims of our own success!—we can now publish only a small portion of the many high-quality stories we receive. Sadly, secretive members of the "Hypertext" Authors Liberation Front (HALF), *aka* Radicals Against "Hypertext" (RAH)—claiming that HerHim.org and its

1. SELECT TWO OR MORE CHARACTERS:

"Hypertext" (HT) authors, critics, characters	Fictional characters from HT criticism	Living real-life (RL) characters	Dead RL characters
None	None	None	None
Richard Holeton	Dick Tracy	Ewan McGregor	Jim Morrison
Alan Richardson	Seven of Nine	Steven Spielberg	Joseph Conrad
Dick A Hellton	Robot-Maria	Trey Parker	Tex Avery
Ellen Richards	Obi-Wan Kenobi	Isaac Hayes	Walt Disney
Richard Allman	E.T.	Kathie Lee Gifford	Charlotte Brontë
Hilton Allrich	Porky Pig	Elizabeth Montgomery	Cleopatra
Perth rep	Daffy Duck	Francis Ford Coppola	Virginia Woolf
ET	Bugs Bunny	Martin Sheen	Princess Di
Tex	Wendy Testaburger	Robert Duvall	Peter Abelard
Hetty Eyre	Stan Marsh	Vanna White	Heloise
Pere Peter	Jane Eyre	Phan Thu Hang	Dick York
T-Rex	Chef	George W. Bush	Agnes Moorhead
Rhett Epyx	Lois Lane	Donna Haraway	Paul Lynde
Hetty P. Rex	Rochester	Iron Chef	Dick Sargent
H. Tex Typer	Darrin	Lucy Lawless	Body bags from Vietnam
Eric Taylor	Samantha	Madonna	Marlon Brando
Erica Taylor	Endora		Adolf Hitler
Eliot Thomas	Uncle Arthur		

Fictional characters from HT criticism (continued): Colonel Kurtz, Captain Willard, Lt. Col. Kilgore, June Cleaver, Medusa, Hedwig, Xena the Warrior Princess, Captain Kirk, Commander Spock, Captain Janeway, Captain Picard, Buffy, Lt. Mary Sue McCoy, Perry Mason

Dead RL characters (continued): Fritz Lang, Franz Kafka, Sigmund Freud, Julia Child

2. SELECT ONE OR MORE GENRES/ SUBGENRES:	3. SELECT RATING:	4. GENERATE LIST OF EXISTING FANFIC STORIES MEETING YOUR CRITERIA	5. SUBMIT A STORY FOR CONSIDERATION BY HER/HIM®
Slash Het Tranny Gen Crossover Authorfic Real-person fic Subreality Mary Sue Metafic Hybrid Hyperfic	Unrated G PG PG-13 NC-17 XXX	Get Info!	Submit My Story!

proprietary technology actually constrain creativity by centralizing and codifying the publication of HT fan fiction—have begun hacking into HER/HIM. Obviously this makes our work more difficult, our future uncertain.

The radicals turned out in force for the Tenth Annual "Hypertext" Symposium (HT10), pitching tents at nearby campgrounds if they couldn't afford the pricey ocean-bluff rooms at the official conference hotel, the Schlitz-Marlboro Resort in Half Moon Bay. Academics were quick to blame the double murder on an anarchist *fan*atic from HALF/RAH, although to be fair the murder has never been officially solved.

The occasion was also, of course, the highly anticipated reunion of Richards and Allman, co-speakers for the featured panel "The Final Image: 'Hypertext' as **Pre-Pyrex**." Some expected fireworks on the panel, others dared to hope for a *rapprochement* between the Technosexual and Posttranny Readings. There was almost a circus atmosphere in the standing-room Eucalyptus Room (yes, the same room where Richard Allman had located Alan Richardson's crossdressing party, FAQ # 6).

Just before they delivered their papers, both Richards and Allman, from opposite ends of the red-skirted table, slumped over in their chairs. Their heads clunked down on their laptop keyboards at almost precisely the same moment (Richards' open Word document filled with the repeated letter "Y," the key where her surgically altered jaw had landed, while Allman's impeccably groomed goatee hit his Delete key, prompting him to Recycle his PowerPoint file). Those claiming to be doctors were ushered through the crowd to administer CPR, followed by the piercing sirens and flashing lights and deadpan efficiency of the paramedics rushing Richards and Allman to the hospital. With black humor some noted that tech support was more successful in recovering their computer files than were the trauma doctors in reviving the critics.

Within hours, both were brain dead from acute cyanide poisoning. *Perry Mason*-like, the poison had been mixed in their coffee (Richards) and water (Allman). Only the victims' fingerprints were left on their souvenir HT10 glass mugs (yes, made of **Pyrex**).

Scholars have continued to point the finger at an extremist amateur writer. An Eric Taylor was officially registered at HT10, fueling speculation that either Richard Allman's fetishistic narrative (FAQ #6) or my own self-published fan fiction (FAQ #3) was based on a real person, a jealous, transsomething **ET** who might've been responsible for one or both murders. But an *Erica* Taylor also attended, along with dozens of other costumed HT characters registered under pseudonyms ranging from Virginia Woolf to Wendy Testaburger and (presciently) Perry Mason. These folks said the apparently perfect crime was more likely committed by a highly-stressed, wacko academic, especially someone with advance knowledge about the content of Richards' and Allman's papers. Yet neither paper (as published in the *HT10 Proceedings*, dedicated to their memory) added any real substance to their already well-articulated positions.

Others have postulated that Richards and Allman murdered each other, with or without knowledge of the other's intention, or conspired in a double suicide. In any case, interviews were conducted with all other suspects, from the conference attendees and organizers to the Schlitz-Marlboro staff and caterers, yielding mainly fictitious names, inconclusive lie detector tests, and, finally, insufficient evidence to file charges. You probably have your own theory.

9. Who am I?

You—your thoughtful reading, feedback, and ongoing contributions are of course what keep this FAQ alive. In this sense, you are the real body upon which the text of "Hypertext" is inscribed, and you are so beautiful to me. Please note that the HerHim.org Online Shop now accepts the Discover Card.

You—with their dying breaths the critics called you the transauthorial reader, the hypervirtual reader, the post-deauthorized reader, the <!--HELLO, WE INTERRUPT THIS TEXT TO BRING YOU A FEW WORDS FROM YOUR 'SPONSORS' AT HALF/RAH -->
<BEGIN MULTIPATH TRANSMISSION>

> Dear Mr Hellhole
>
> hacking websites & HER/HIM was mere childsplay, just *another day at the office* :-) LOL
>
> but cracking yr FAQ, hacking right into your (not so hyper) TEXT, this is *sweet*
>
> best of luck,
>
> Hypertext Authors Liberation Front aka RAH //////////

</END TRANSMISSION>

FROLIC   219

[Hypertext version available at *https://collection.eliterature.org/1/works/ holeton__frequently_asked_questions_about_hypertext.html*; archived by the Electronic Literature Organization in The NEXT at *https://the-next.eliterature.org/works/636/0/0/*]

FLASH

(short-short,
nanotale,
microfiction,
postcard story,
sudden fiction)

Calling Fruits and Vegetables

My breakfast banana reveals an ugly brown, leathery ridge lining the concave curve—no ordinary grocery-store bruise but a ropey, raised zipper of alien scar tissue whose swelling deforms the sticker from the Developing Country where, right now, suspect men are having nails driven into their heads and innocent women are being raped. Unpeeling the healthy part of the banana, I cut crosswise into the fibrous growth. A huge thickly segmented green worm, punctuated by silver hairs, wriggles in the white flesh, oozing purple guts where I've nicked it.

I drop the contaminated fruit onto my cutting board, scrape it into a plastic sandwich bag, and call Fruits and Vegetables. They put me on Hold. I mark my video message Urgent.

Through the bag I see the colorful worm has hundreds of black legs. The legs are doing The Wave.

Two men arrive in Hazmat suits with dark tinted visors,

coiled ear transmitters, laser headlamps, and head-mounted cameras.

"Clear," the tall man says into his transmitter, looking both ways as he enters.

The short man follows with a burly Farkolian Tank Terrier on a lead wearing a steel mesh muzzle. I take two puffs from my Soma Inhalant.

Selecting #3 Tongs from his Utility Belt, the tall man transfers my ziplocked banana into a vapor-spewing chrome picnic cooler, seals the lid with black tape, and shakes his head. All this seems to take a long time.

"Um?" I venture.

The short man twists his tinted visor toward me, and the Farkolian Tank Terrier lunges. I recoil, but he restrains the beast with a single jerk.

"We're Fruits and Vegetables," the short man says from deep within the suit.

I think I could take him, but maybe not the dog.

"Sign here," the tall man says.

Streleski at Findhorn on Acid

Theodore Streleski. Paroled in 1985 at age 49 after serving seven years for killing Stanford mathematics professor Karel deLeeuw, his faculty advisor, with a hammer. Previously spent 19 years in graduate school without completing his Ph.D. Refused psychiatric treatment in prison; steadfastly maintained that the beating death was a logical and moral reaction to his mistreatment as a Stanford graduate student. Said that deLeeuw had made fun of his shoes, erroneously identified in news reports as wing tips. "They were Florsheims and they were seamless," said the 6-foot-4, bearded, longhaired Streleski in appearances on the *Today Show* and *Phil Donahue*. "They were standard oxfords with a high shine on them." In April, 1993, San Francisco Municipal Railway offered him a farebox-technician job but withdrew the offer two weeks later following negative publicity.

Findhorn. A New Age community on the Moray Firth in Scotland established in 1962 by Peter and Eileen Caddy and Dorothy Maclean in a trailer park near the fishing village of Findhorn. Anecdotal accounts of the 1960s and 1970s told of remarkable gardens producing 40-pound cabbages, 60-pound broccoli plants, 8-foot delphiniums, and roses blooming in nothing but sand and snow. Love, and communication with Nature Spirits, were credited with the horticultural miracles. The community attracted spiritual seekers from all over the world. The Findhorn Foundation promotes values of harmony, spirituality, ecology, and community building summed up by the inspiration, "Work is love in action." According to former Findhorn resident David Spangler, "You are either manufacturing darkness through your own inner states of anxiety and fear and separation, or you are creating light and revelation through your abandonment of those past states and your attunement to new ones."

Acid. Street name for LSD (lysergic acid diethylamide), a powerful hallucinogenic drug derived from a fungus that sometimes grows on rye. In doses as small as 50 micrograms, perceptual effects include increased impact of sensory stimuli such as colors and sounds; attention to normally unnoticed aspects of the environment; and the sense of time slowing down. Cognitive effects include impaired short-term memory, enhanced long-term memory and introspection, changes in sense of self and ego, a sense of separation of mind and body, or a sense of unity with the environment and the universe. Emotional effects include increased susceptibility to suggestion; heightened sensitivity; and magnification and purification of feelings such as love, lust, sympathy, gratitude, terror, despair, anger, or loneliness. These effects may bring on paranoia, fear of loss of control, and panic— or euphoria and bliss.

Scene: Phoenix Shop at The Park, Findhorn, which sells books, crafts, natural foods and remedies. Background music playing (Peter, Paul, and Mary): "If I had a hammer, I'd hammer in the evening, I'd hammer in the morning, all over this land. I'd hammer out freedom, I'd hammer out justice, I'd hammer out love between my brothers and my sisters...."

Streleski: Whoa....Wow....Hmmph.

Clerk/Community member: Hey man, are those *wing tips?*

[The full-length hypertext novel that eventually evolved from this flash fiction, *Figurski at Findhorn on Acid*, is available at *https://figurskiatfindhornonacid.com/*; archived by the Electronic Literature Organization in The NEXT at *https://the-next.eliterature.org/works/1102/0/0/*]

Hero's Journey with Enlarged Prostate

CALL TO ADVENTURE
You awaken with a dream about struggling to find a urinal, or finding many urinals all occupied, or spotting one across a bog of thick, impenetrable mud. Bathroom beckons.

REFUSAL OF THE CALL
Dark and chilly without the covers. The loo seems miles away. Guessing the laminate flooring to be icy on bare feet.

SUPERNATURAL AID
Ghost of your father appears. He didn't live long enough to grow a grapefruit-size prostate like yours, but he scowls at you anyway: "Wimp!"

CROSSING THE FIRST THRESHOLD
Swing legs over edge of bed and gingerly touch feet to plastic wood.

ROAD OF TRIALS / BELLY OF THE WHALE
Knock over nightstand water cup, warping pages of bedside Joseph Campbell. Standing, you roll an ankle, gouge an eye on garment peg holding your robe. Unused sex toys start spontaneously flashing and humming.

TEMPTATION
Maybe turn around, go back to bed; do you have any adult diapers?

APPROACH TO THE INMOST CAVE
There it is! Follow night light glow illuminating privy like a sacred, mystical candle. Toilet seat is up.

THE ORDEAL
Nothing comes. Then, just dribbles. Strain. More dribbles. Strain, dribbles. Bladder throbs, groin aches. Have you popped a hernia, burst appendix, overtaxed your genitourinary system?

REWARD
Some relief at long last!

THE ROAD BACK
Take detour via kitchen. It's a long distance, farther even than bathroom, fraught with every Tripping Hazard listed in last

medical questionnaire: Poor Lighting, Scattered Clutter, Uneven Surfaces, Extension Cords, Loose Throw Rugs, Sleeping Dog.

THE RESURRECTION
Stub toe, bruise elbow on kitchen doorframe, but navigate obstacle course by sheer force of will. There at last: refrigerator and microwave. Sure that you emptied your bladder? Not really.

RETURN WITH THE ELIXIR
Back in bed with a warm glass of milk.

Chance Meeting Between Cambodian National Amputee Volleyball Team, Stephen Hawking, and Black Mothers Displaced by Hurricane Katrina

Lucky Dog Stand, Concourse B, Louis Armstrong New Orleans International Airport, 2006.—The Cambodians are on their way to Orlando's Disney World after a few days in Los Angeles and New Orleans, on the U.S. leg of an international goodwill tour following their triumph at the World Disabled Games. Hawking, having completed the first leg of a book promotion tour for his latest bestseller, *A Briefer History of Time*, awaits a flight to Palm Beach, then home to Cambridge where he will continue work on the basic laws governing the universe. A dozen members of Poor Mothers-New Orleans (POMO-NO)—on their last legs following a whirlwind tour of their flood-ravaged Ninth Ward homes, fruitless meetings with city and federal officials, and a cocktail reception at Antoine's in the French Quarter—are en route back to Texas, where they were relocated after Hurricane Katrina.

Professor Hawking slouches in his high-tech wheelchair, cloaked in wig and dark glasses, blinking to operate his speech synthesizer. He confides in several POMO-NO ladies about his recent zero-gravity flight for charity, in which he floated weightless at high altitude without his wheelchair.

"The future… of humankind… is in outer space," he says, grinning obliquely. He tells them he's been invited to orbit the earth on Sir Richard Branson's SpaceShipTwo for free. "It won't cost me… an arm and a leg."

The women lean closer, drawn by the space stories, silly costume, and strange staccato computer voice.

"You're not pulling my leg now are you sir?" asks a bespectacled woman sporting a colorful scarf.

Several of the Cambodian volleyball players hop or hobble over in their sponsored athletic gear, leaning on crutches and munching Lucky Dogs. Outside hitter Nagg (lower right leg amputee—landmine) and setter Hang (lower right arm amputee—birth defect; full left leg amputee—landmine) excitedly ask questions through the team interpreter about Hawking's wheelchair controls. They have no idea who he is.

The interpreter recognizes Hawking through the flimsy disguise. He seizes the opportunity to pose the ultimate question to the ultimate living cosmologist, transforming Nagg's and Hang's queries into one about Science and God.

"The universe was... spontaneously created... out of nothing," Professor Hawking answers. "Without the laws of science... God does not have... a leg to stand on."

Unlikely Convergence of Danish Animal Rights Activists, Rigoberta Menchú, and Multi-Level Marketers

Lobby of The Peabody Orlando, International Drive, 2015.—At 5 p.m. (a reversal of their daily 11 a.m. arrival ritual) The March of the Peabody Ducks signals the cocktail hour.

 Five North American Mallard ducks, four hens and one drake, descend red-carpeted steps from the ornate fountain in the central Atrium Lobby of The Peabody Orlando. Hotel guests applaud, tourists take photos and videos on their phones. Prodded by their gold-and-crimson braided Duck Master and accompanied by John Philip Sousa's "King Cotton March," the ducks waddle to a special elevator that will return them for the evening to their $100,000 Royal Duck Palace penthouse.

Among the lobby crowd, five spiky-haired and tank-topped Danish activists (like the ducks, four females and one male) blink in astonishment at the Duck March. They have traveled to Orlando to join PETA (People for the Ethical Treatment of Animals) and ARFF (Animal Rights Foundation of Florida) for a protest at Disney's Animal Kingdom.

"*For helvede!*" Christa Pedersen says to her animal-rights friends, all turning even whiter and paler at the avian spectacle.

Rigoberta Menchú Tum and her entourage, resplendent in vibrant K'iche' Mayan reds and purples, appear animated by the duck ritual. Perhaps thinking of pan-fried duck quiche with morita-tamarind sauce, Menchú nudges her translator and American hosts toward the Happy Hour hors d'oeuvres. Menchú will be headlining an Orlando event for PeaceJam, a Colorado-based organization encouraging youth empowerment through connections with Nobel Prize winners such as herself.

Waves of multilevel marketers, wearing their conference neck badges and business casual, jam Mallards Bar, adjoining the Peabody lobby. A group of five (four men and one woman) have been drinking Bloody Marys since noon, and The March of the Peabody Ducks brings them to new levels of hilarity.

"Get your ducks in a row, Peabody!" says one of the door-to-door sales champions.

"Quack quack quack!" yells another network marketer, making a shadow-puppet duck hand.

The Danes, Menchú, and the tipsy conferees converge in the bar crush. One hulking but unsteady direct seller leers at perkily-tattoed Christa Pederson and her tight-jeaned girlfriends. "Booyah!" he says.

"Bloody hell man!" bristles Becker Jorgensen, the Danish women's self-appointed protector, who learned his English in England.

Jorgensen lurches toward the beefy direct seller, but the stumpy, thickset Menchú, two feet shorter than either man, wedges between them like a Guatemalan fullback. She says something in Spanish. Both men look down, without recognizing the Nobel Peace Laureate author of *I, Rigoberta Menchú* and champion of Indigenous peoples, and turn to her translator.

"Many families have suffered," says Menchú's translator mysteriously. "We need to give the people the tools."

Transient Encounter of Chilean Miners, Benjamin Netanyahu, and Girl Scouts from Boulder

Prime Minister's office, Kaplan Street, Jerusalem, 2010.—Just months after their miraculous rescue, 25 of the 33 survivors of the 2010 Copiapó, Chile, mining accident find themselves touring Israel and meeting with Prime Minister Benjamin Netanyahu. Coincidentally, six weeks earlier, the Chilean government had defied Israel and recognized Palestine as a sovereign state. But Netanyahu compares the miners' rescue with the Apollo moon landing, with 9/11, and with Operation Entebbe, the 1976 recovery of Jewish hostages in Uganda by Israeli commandos. Operation Entebbe had been led by "Bibi" Netanyahu's older brother "Yoni," the only commando killed in the mission.

"You are like the Jewish people, who sanctify life and have survived against all odds," Netanyahu says to the traumatized, jetlagged miners.

A dozen Northern Colorado Region 7 Girl Scouts, on a swing through the Middle East, giggle, squirm, and sip lemonade on the periphery. As of last night, when 11-year-old Chelsea Badger found spots on her hotel sheet, all have entered puberty. They mingle with the wives and girlfriends of the Chilean miners and tell them about Girl Power, Cookie College, and Zero Waste Survival Camping at Magic Sky Ranch near Boulder.

Since their deliverance—after 69 days trapped 2300 feet underground, where many considered suicide and cannibalism—the miners have suffered severe post-traumatic stress, and some have developed debilitating anxiety. Before coming to the Holy Land, they visited Disney World and announced that talent agency William Morris Endeavor Entertainment would manage their media, publishing, and appearance rights.

"You told me about your visit to the Dead Sea, 1400 feet below sea level," Netanyahu says to the miners. "But you came from the lowest place in the world." Is it supposed to be a joke? No one is laughing.

Chelsea Badger's best friend Brittany Slater, more advanced than her peers into adolescence, has vowed not to shave during their overseas trip. Brittany and Chelsea, who don't speak Spanish, implore a Chilean woman wearing a pink halter top to take the Power of Girls Pledge.

"I pledge ... to discover the issues that girls confront around the world today!" Brittany urges the bewildered woman, as

Chelsea thrusts Hebrew and Arabic translations of the Pledge in her face. The Chilean woman throws up her arms in frustration, revealing dark hairy armpits. Brittany tries to high-five her, revealing her own unshaven axillary wisps, and Chelsea lets out a yelp. A hyper-alert Shabak security guard overreacts by tackling Brittany, which causes another guard to fire a warning burst from his Uzi and order everyone onto the floor. Triggered by the gun blast and scuffling, several miners begin sobbing uncontrollably.

The hirsute, halter-topped woman is later identified as yet a third girlfriend of philandering miner #21 Yonni Barrios, who coincidentally has the same name as Bibi's deceased brother. Later, the Prime Minister's office releases a statement claiming that Netanyahu had predicted the Chilean mine disaster 23 years earlier in his book *Terrorism: How the West Can Win*, and the miners and Girl Scouts all get baptized in the Jordan River.

FAUNA

(swine,
scorpion,
sea otter,
water bird)

Year of the Pig

"**1959**," **says Miss Plotz** at Group Circle Time. "In China, this is the Year of the Pig."

She writes it on the board: "Year of the Pig." She pinches the chalk hard. Her fingers are dry and white like the chalk. There is one little drop of spit on her bottom lip. I wonder if it will fall off or stay there all morning.

"Today is <u>counterclockwise</u>," she says and she writes that on the board too. That means it's a Vocabulary Word when she underlines it. "As we go around the circle I want everyone to share something that you know about pigs," she says and she writes "Pig <u>knowledge</u>."

Each thing that someone says, Miss Plotz adds it to the list, and after some of the things she puts a question mark. You're supposed to listen to the others to practice your Listening Skills. I try to listen, but I only hear a few of the other things because I am thinking about when my turn is going to come and what I will say, what words to use exactly. I have two things I know about pigs that I learned in my family, about their brain size and about the special tubes that they have on their legs.

Sheila Macintosh says that pigs are yucky and some people laugh at that.

Jamie Podmanynski says pigs are what bacon comes from, and also ham.

Rachel Cohen says the Bible says you should not eat pigs. Everyone is quiet after she says "Bible."

Patty Wiggins, who is pink and fat and has a pushed-up nose like a pig herself, says that pigs are nice. They are not dirty actually, the way many people think. Actually pigs roll around in mud only because they are trying to wash themselves, because they want to be clean, and after the water evaporates they just look dirty. Actually they are good swimmers, very fast, because they go down and run along the bottom instead of swimming on the top. Actually they are very smart too, even more intelligent than dogs.

Miss Plotz underlines <u>evaporate</u> and <u>intelligent</u>.

Patty Wiggins seems to know a lot about pigs. Actually I don't like Patty Wiggins. Besides saying "Actually" too much, she has a terrible smell that comes out one of her ears. The smell seems to come from way down deep inside her body, then out the ear tube, like from a vacuum cleaner hose that has sucked up something into its vacuum bag that died and rotted in there. You can smell it when you stand too close to her. (When I told my brother Russell about the smelly ear disease, he said it was like a head fart and that Patty Wiggins probably had brain cancer.)

When Patty Wiggins is done with her speech about pigs, Jamie Podmanynski pretends to take a bite out of her leg and says,

"Yumm, let's have some bacon now!"

Other people talk about The Three Little Pigs building their houses out of straw and sticks and bricks (the new kid Teddy Something says the pigs finally eat the wolf at the end, I never heard that ending before) or about Piglet in *Winnie the Pooh* or about when Dorothy falls into the pig pen at the beginning of *The Wizard of Oz*.

Miss Plotz adds "Pigs in many stories" to the list. When she stops writing she still pinches the chalk so hard I think she'll snap it like a dead twig. When she waves it around, there's a blur of pink and white, so you can't tell where her fingers end and the chalk begins. Is she waving it around <u>counterclockwise</u>? I am thinking about how later we will have to use our Vocabulary Words in sentences, and about how exactly I will tell my two pig things and explain the special tubes, and about how that little drop of spit on Miss Plotz's lip seems like it's gotten bigger and then dried there, clear and hard, like a glob of Elmer's Glue-All dried on the lip of the bottle, when Miss Plotz says, "Ripley? It's your turn."

"Umm, I have two things," I say. "One is, pigs have brains the size of walnuts." A couple of the kids giggle, and for a second I think maybe I'm mixing up pigs with dinosaurs, but my mom grew up on a farm, which was a dairy so mainly it had cows but it also had pigs, and my brother Russell and my dad told me about pig brains and pig tubes, which they learned about from my mom I guess, unless they just have their own pig <u>knowledge</u>. When you look up "Brain" in our Worlds of Science book, the picture looks just like a walnut. And that is the brain of a human being! I think about brains being like different-sized walnuts. Russell told me not to sniff when I had a cold or I would sniff all the snot up into my brain and drive myself crazy! (Or maybe I would get smelly brain cancer like Patty Wiggins.) Russell said Dad said it, so it was true. I worry that maybe I have already sniffed too much snot, that my brain is like a big snot-covered walnut.

Miss Plotz writes "Small brains?" on the board like that, with a question mark, right after "Build houses?" and "Eat wolves?"

People use only one-tenth of their Brain Power, Dad told me and Russell the other week at dinner. If you really wanted to, if you concentrated really hard and used all your Brain Power, you could part your hair just by thinking about it. I tried to do this, right there at the dinner table. I gritted my teeth and squeezed my cheek muscles till my face got hot, but I couldn't get any hairs even to budge. You have to practice, Russell told me later. I have been practicing for two weeks in front of the mirror. Almost every day I practice for ten minutes in the morning and ten minutes at night, but so far nothing has happened.

"Okay…" Miss Plotz says. She is waiting for me to tell the second thing I know about pigs.

Patty Wiggins sticks her chin up so you can see inside her nostrils, I guess she thinks that looks <u>intelligent</u>.

"Well, Ripley?"

Miss Plotz is waiting, with her Death Grip on the chalk. Everyone waits, and they are all looking at me. I am trying to use all my Brain Power now to concentrate on the second thing, which is about the special tubes, because I have never told this to anyone outside my family. My face feels hot, I'm afraid it may be all red, the way it looks in the mirror when I practice parting my hair with no hands.

"They have these … tubes," I say. "Pigs have these special

tubes that run down the insides of their legs. No other animals have these, I know because my mom grew up on a farm. Patty says pigs are clean but really they're not clean, they are filthy dirty, and they stink. They go pee and poop all over and stink up their pen, but they also have these special tubes I am talking about on their legs. The tubes go down their legs just under the skin like big huge veins, and they are for blowing out other stuff, it's like snot, only worse. The tubes end in their hooves, which is where the snot stuff comes out. It's not exactly snot or pee or poop, it's another kind of stuff, even worse, that comes out the tubes."

Everyone is silent after that, even quieter than after Rachel Cohen said "Bible."

Miss Plotz just kind of blinks at me for a few seconds. Finally she turns to write "Special tubes?" on the board, like she suddenly remembers what to do next, except she adds the question mark, and Patty Wiggins sticks her tongue out at me, and Jamie Podmanynski makes a farting sound with his mouth, and the whole class starts talking and moving around.

"Snot tubes! Snot tubes!" says Sheila Macintosh.

"You were born in a barn," says Patty Wiggins.

"Jesus Christ was born in a barn," says the new kid Teddy.

"You stink!" I say to Patty Wiggins. "You stink like crazy!"

Miss Plotz turns back sharply and I see that the spit on her lip is gone. Maybe it landed on the floor or maybe it just <u>evaporated</u>.

The King's Summer Palace

It seemed they were here to stay, the white man and the white woman.

I remember when they arrived on the bus from El-Jadida. I was there at the cafe, where I did odd errands for the qehwazi in exchange for a cup of tea or something to eat. There were no other boys around, so I offered to carry some things for them. Let me say that here it is not like the cities, where the yapping dogs trip all over each other when tourists come.

In summer, a few French and Germans occupy the bungalows that line the road to the lagoon. But this was too early for the regular tourists, and the bungalows were still boarded up. There is a small hotel, run by a French woman, next door to the cafe along the highway.

When I set down their bags, the white man gave me a dirham. He wore a shirt with strange writing on it and spoke French with an accent.

Anglais, Monsieur? I said, pointing to the shirt.

Yes. He said they were Americans.

America is very big, I said. I have heard that people live far apart from each other there.

Far apart? he said.

Yes, because it is so big, I said. The white woman smiled at me, showing her teeth the way I'd seen other Europeans do, but something was different about her. My father told me you could tell Americans because they smiled a lot, sometimes for no reason, and showed their gums too as well as their teeth. My father has spent time in the cities. But there was something else about the woman. Her hair was the color of the sand. Her eyes were the color of the lagoon when the tide is high, and they seemed to look inside of me.

It is said that the evil eye is stronger in women than men and it is especially powerful in blue-eyed people. When I saw the fqi I asked him about the white man and the white woman.

The shirt with the symbols is a simple charm against the evil eye, said the fqi.

Then the woman, looking at me?

To be a victim of the evil eye, said the fqi, you must believe in its power. If you do not believe, you cannot be struck. Do you feel you have been struck, Ahmed?

I said I didn't know what I believed, but when the white woman looked at me I felt something there along my spine and here, below my stomach.

Then the bas has entered you, said the fqi. On three consecutive Fridays, go east into the plain and gather seven small stones from places where sheep have grazed. Spit on the stones and crush them together with seksu that has been cooked without salt by a woman. You must procure the seksu with your left hand when the woman is not looking. After sunset, take also some water from the lagoon, and then grind everything into a paste. Each night thereafter rub some of the paste under your bedsheets. After forty days, walk before sunrise around the lagoon to the ocean and let seven consecutive waves pass over your body.

I did these things.

The white man and the white woman rented a flat in the Project from my father. The Project was never finished, it was said, because the government needed the money to fight the war in the South. Sections were given to certain men, such as my father, to oversee. He had fixed up some of the buildings and put in a few pieces of furniture of the kind preferred by Europeans. I helped paint the chairs and tables, which came all the way from Casablanca. We had to pay the driver and attendant extra to strap them on top of the bus.

I used to run and play all over the Project, climbing the walls or hiding in dark corners, but now I have to work more and more. Also there are squatters from the countryside living in some of the buildings.

Let me say that I live by the lagoon with my father and my father's sister. I don't remember my mother, and my father does not say anything about her. Once I overheard the old men in the cafe whispering that I was a mbeddel which znun had substituted for the real child shortly after birth. The qehwazi's wife suggested that my father's sister herself was a zenniya who had exchanged identities with my mother. The fqi told me that my mother had been killed by the bas.

I do not always understand, but I have heard all these things.

Our little apartment leans against one of the great walls of the King's Summer Palace, where my father is the caretaker. My father said that the King's father, the previous king, used to come here once a year, but the present King does not visit often. The last time he came it was a grand occasion. I was very young but I remember that his picture, the same one that is in the cafe, hung everywhere along the street on the buildings and telephone poles, and above each picture was the flag of our country. There were many cars and motorcycles, and especially soldiers, and the sewers backed up the way they do sometimes on suq day.

There are fanatics trying to kill the King, my father said. That is why there are so many soldiers.

Let me say there are always stories that the King will come again, that he is coming next year or next month. The fqi told me that a king must always keep his enemies guessing. So we keep the Palace ready.

It is said also that the water of the lagoon is rising. Even I have noticed that at high tide the water comes closer to the Palace walls each year. The walls are very old and are beginning to crumble in some places. Perhaps that is the reason the King hasn't come.

Twice a week I brought water to the white man and the white woman, the Americans. I filled my bucket from a hose at the cafe and carried it across the highway to their flat at the end of the Project where they poured it into a clay jug just like the squatters. The white woman smiled and tried to hold me in her eyes and the white man gave me a dirham. I gave the dirham to the qehwazi, and sometimes he gave it back to me.

One day I saw the white man at the cafe, buying wine from

the qehwazi. I knew the qehwazi had got the wine from the French woman who ran the hotel and then marked up the price, but the white man was clever and bargained. Let me say that I had seen him bargain with vendors on suq day, when all the people from the countryside bring their vegetables and meats to town and set up their tents on the fields around the Project, and he obtained some good prices.

He bought six bottles from the qehwazi, put them in a package, and sat down to have some tea. When he saw me, he said they needed some more water at the flat. He told me the Madame was there.

Could you fetch your buckets, Ahmed, and so on? he asked, calling me by my name and giving me this time fifty centimes extra.

Waxxa, I said.

When I came with the water this time the white woman wanted to talk for a few minutes. She asked me my age and what did I do all day and did I learn to speak French in school. I answered these things, and explained that I only went to school sometimes, when my father sent me to a fqi in El-Jadida, and that I also learned a little French from the tourists who came in the summer, and that during the day I worked here and there.

I am trying to learn a few words of Arabic dialect, she said. Maybe you will help me.

I don't know about that, I said.

Why do you look away from me, Ahmed? she asked. Do I frighten you?

I told her it was said that the evil eye was very strong in pretty women with blue eyes.

The evil eye? she said, after thanking me for saying she was pretty. This is real? Do you believe such things?

I don't know, I said. Why does the white man wear the shirts that have no collars and no buttons and short sleeves, the shirts with the charms written on them?

She told me the shirts were bought in stores like other shirts, and simply were decorated with emblems or names and colors of schools, or other such things, so in a way they were like flags.

Like flags? I said.

In a way, she said, then added that as far as she knew, in America at least, blue eyes were neither more nor less harmful than any other kind.

I said that many things appeared simpler if you knew an explanation for them. I told her what my father said about how to tell Americans apart from other Europeans, and this made her laugh and change colors.

We are not accustomed to seeing the bare faces of married women, I said, so perhaps this explains the idea about teeth and gums.

That is a clever remark, she said, and very diplomatic, although it happens that we are not married.

Not married! You are sister and brother then, like my aunt and my father?

No.

No! As I picked up my buckets to go, the white man returned from the cafe. He entered the little courtyard of their flat and kissed the white woman right in front of me. I saw in his package there were now only three bottles. Yet he did not smell of wine.

I brought the water, Monsieur, I said. Your jug was still half full.

You mean it was already half empty? he laughed and thanked me.

Baraka llahu fik sidi, si Ahmed, said the woman in Maghrebi. Thank you very much, sir! Monsieur Ahmed, she'd called me, a man!

Bla zmil, I said. I left quickly, feeling the bas rise inside me and spread over my skin like water.

When I told my father that the white man and the white woman were not married he did not seem surprised. He said I would find that Europeans did many strange and shameful things and that I should give it no further thought.

But sometimes the man and woman went to the beach, and one day I watched them. Let me say that I was sweeping in the courtyard of the Palace when I saw them go by and sit down in the shadow of the wall closest to the lagoon. After awhile they began to touch each other. They did not think anyone could see them. They took some of their clothes off and used them to lie on. Their hands went all over each other and even down under their pants.

That night when I went to bed I touched myself. I couldn't stop myself from doing this until finally it started to hurt and my face grew hot and my head swam. Afterwards I thought about the magic paste I had used according to the fqi's instructions and how maybe the magic had not worked on me, and then I cried.

One day my father called to me across the lagoon where I was helping some of the old men pull in their fishing nets. It was very early, around sunrise. The fqi has been summoned from El-Jadida, my father said. Join me in the courtyard.

Waxxa, I said. My father's breath, I noticed when I came close, stank of wine. I knew he had got the wine from the white man, because the qehwazi would not sell any to the Moslems and my father had not taken a trip to the city, but I did not say anything.

The courtyard of the King's Summer Palace is paved with great tiles, but the tiles are very old, like the walls, and there are cracks. One crack near the wall closest to the lagoon goes all the way to the foundation of the Palace. Some scientists who came once from Rabat to take measurements told me the foundation was built many centuries ago. Down in the darkness of this hole were two scorpions.

Watch them, my father said. When my eyes adjusted I could see that the scorpions gripped each other by the claws.

They're not moving, I said.

Wait, my father said.

I remember the night a young woman here received the sting of the scorpion. She was a stranger who arrived by herself on the bus from Casablanca. She could not afford the hotel, but my father talked to the French woman and she let her stay there. The money for the Project had just run out, I remember, because two great government cranes still cast long shadows from across the highway.

People came in answer to her screams. The other women tried to comfort her, while the men searched for the animal. They tore apart her bedcovers and shook her clothes and poked with brooms in all the corners. Look for the scorpion, my father told me, we must find it and kill it. Let me say that I helped them search the rest of the hotel, but the animal had hidden itself or got away.

The woman shook with the fever. She held her throat and made choking sounds. Then she sneezed, and kept sneezing faster and faster, with the next sneeze coming before the last had finished. The flow of mucus from her nose and mouth could not be stopped. The men poured water over her to cool her sweat, then the women covered her with blankets and prayed. It was said that her baraka was very strong because she put up a good fight against the poison. But soon her chest heaved and she jerked the blankets off in great convulsions, and before my father led me away I could see the color, blue as the lagoon, spreading in from her hands and feet towards her heart. Sometimes I imagine that this woman was my mother.

Just wait, my father said, so I sat by the edge of the crack in the courtyard and I listened to the gentle lapping of high tide and the voices inside me.

Twice a day the lagoon fills like a warm bidet, I heard the French woman tell the Americans when they arrived. I knew there was a bidet at the hotel.

What's it for? I said to the French woman. Show me.

It's for a woman to clean herself, she said. Let me say that the French woman is old and gray-haired and though she understands Maghrebi, she always answers in French.

I turned on the knobs and studied the flow of water around the little basin, then I asked, Which way does the woman sit?

This way, she said.

I felt the sun start to warm my back as it rose but still the scorpions didn't move. My father brought tea, and the mint made his breath smell sweeter. I grew bored, I wanted to run off and play like I had as a child. I heard the fishermen's voices from far away. I heard the buses come and go on the highway from Safi and El-Jadida. The bus that comes in the afternoon, I thought, goes as far as Casablanca.

I can't just sit all day like the old men who smoke kif at the cafe, I told my father.

Then watch and listen, my father said.

The fqi did not arrive until dusk. He squatted by the hole and said nothing. The noises from the town above died down. My father's sister brought us a great bowl of seksu, and after we had eaten, the fqi began to slowly rock back and forth on his heels. He closed his eyes and made a humming sound from deep in his throat. In a few minutes it seemed as if the fqi had been there always, rocking and humming above the crack in the foundation, since before the time the Palace was built. It grew dark, and the warmth went out of the tiles beneath me.

It has begun, said the fqi. The smaller one is the male.

Suddenly the scorpions shuffled a few steps sideways. They made clicking and hissing sounds that seemed to come from the devil himself.

What is it, sidi? I asked.

The Courtship Dance may last for hours, days, or weeks, said the fqi. This one, however, will have a swift conclusion.

I nodded. I knew the power of words to affect the events about which they are spoken, especially the words of a woman or a fqi.

The scorpions shuffled back and forth, still making the terrible sounds. Only their legs moved. They seemed to grow larger as the moon rose and its light made their backs shiny and their shadows long. Their tails curled over them like the great cranes that had worked on the Project.

Let us say when I was a young man and a religious student I took a journey to the South, said the fqi. In a small village at the edge of the Sahara I met some Tuareg of the Djbb Rish tribe. I traveled with them three days time to the next suq. When we set out again in the morning, one of their camels received the sting of the scorpion. The camel might have survived, but it grew weak, and the Djbb Rish are very superstitious. They captured the scorpion and then hacked the camel into many pieces which they buried far apart in the desert, to disperse the bas and to placate the znun.

Below in the crack the scorpions held still, as if they too listened to the fqi's story.

Of course I had heard the tales of the Tuareg who eat scorpions, continued the fqi. You have heard these things. The scorpion is considered a delicacy when eaten live and so the Djbb Rish offered it to me, their guest. Let us say that for me to refuse would be a great insult. I would be exposed as a tool of znun, or a zinn myself, and killed at once.

What happened sidi? I asked.

They themselves tore off the stinger from the tail and scraped the hairs from the belly with a blade, said the fqi. I had no choice but to close my eyes and sink in my teeth. I could feel the legs, which I held spread apart, wriggling about the sides of my face and catching in my hair. Thank you very much, I said to the chief in Berber. Now you and your nobles may have the rest of the scorpion.

The next day I departed from the Tuareg, the fqi said. When I returned to the North, I was called the Scorpion Eater and thought to be wise. I finished my academy studies, though let us say that the study of the Koran is a lifelong occupation, and I became a fqi.

It was a good story and it helped pass the time. I looked at the scorpions dancing in the moonlight and tried to imagine what eating one would be like. The cold from the tiles came through my zellab and pants and made me shiver. My father said nothing, but from time to time he looked at me.

There was a moment when I wanted to tell the fqi about my father drinking wine and the white man and the white woman on the beach and about touching myself and about all the bas which I felt inside me, but I could not. Then the scorpions began to make the terrible clicking sounds again, louder than before.

The one the fqi said was the male seemed to grow stronger, pushing and pulling the female. They locked their mouthparts together like little claws, and he dragged her towards the narrow end of the crack. Here at the lowest place he swept violently in the sand with his back legs.

Iyeh, waxxa, whispered the fqi, as if he himself gave the animals permission, and then the male rose up, rocking on his legs and heaving with his claws until he drew the female to a vertical position above the small depression he had swept. The female resisted very little now, she seemed mesmerized by the spell or curse. They were belly to belly, their hairs entwined like the hemp fibers of the fishermen's ropes. Something poked out from the male, a kind of egg that looked like one of the little capsules of gelatin I have seen in the pharmacies of El-Jadida.

She is taking his seed, said the fqi. In the moonlight I could not tell whether the male pushed the capsule into her or dropped it in the sand and sat her upon it.

Now you will see something Ahmed, said the fqi, but I did not see anything for a long time and the moon went behind the walls.

I have to piss, I said. My father came with me and when we undid our pants to piss he looked down at me and I couldn't get started.

Go on, piss, he said.

I can't.

You can't!

I can't when you tell me to. When you watch me like that. Leave me alone!

There is something wrong with you, Ahmed, my father said. After he finished he shook himself again and again, many times, and finally I started pissing.

When we came back the fqi lit a candle, and after the candle burned down the first glow of the sun appeared.

Then I looked, and the female was on top of the male. She had flipped him on his back, and she sank her stinger deeply into him while his legs ran in the air. It happened so suddenly. He struggled at first, but soon he stopped moving as she pinned him down and disentangled herself from the hairs that caught them together. Her jaws began to work on him. Her mouthparts moved like a machine upon his head. By the time the sun began to warm the tiles underneath me, she crawled across his half-eaten body into the darkest corner of the crack and rested.

Could it be the same scorpion that bit the young woman of our village? Is it perhaps the spirit of the woman who was killed, taking revenge? Sidi?

It is finished, said the fqi, the Widow's Breakfast. The female does not devour all of the male, only his head.

Only his head, repeated my father.

The white man and the white woman stayed all spring, and soon I went to work at the bathhouse. A few French and Germans had arrived and unboarded some of the bungalows along the path to the lagoon. Of course these tourists never used the public bath.

The man began to wear a zellab over his other clothes, and sometimes he smoked kif with the old men at the cafe, and the woman bought baboosh slippers. They shopped at the suq every week. I kept bringing the water. Several times my father visited them in the evening, and one time they ate seksu with us prepared by my father's sister.

It was as if they wanted to be like us, wearing the clothes and eating the food.

But they went more often to the beach by the Palace as the weather grew warmer, and when they stripped off the outer layers they wore the little bathing suits like underwear. Did they not realize that here, especially if you were a foreigner, there was always someone watching you? Not on purpose, to follow you. But let me say that the other tasks of the day could always wait if there was something to look at. Sometimes I had the thought, If I was the white man I could touch the woman whenever I wanted.

The bathhouse is located on the same side of the highway as the Project, across the fields where the suq is held. The building is divided into three sections, each warmer and wetter than the last. What you do is take your shoes off and hang your clothes in the first room and go and take your bath in the third room, then use the middle one for resting and cooling down. My job was to feed the furnace outside, which keeps the water in the fountain of the third room hot, and also to clean the floors at the end of the night. Men gave me a few centimes for watching their clothes or the things they brought with them, though no one ever disturbed these things, and sometimes I helped them with their buckets. The men's hours were in the morning and the evening. Only the smallest boys went with their mothers during the women's hours in the afternoon.

I had heard the women talk about the white woman. Once my father's sister came back from the bath with some friends and while they made seksu together they moved their mouths even more than they moved their hands. They said she was beautiful, that her skin was two different colors. Her breasts were like moons, they said, the patch of hair below her belly cut to the shape of a dark star, and the cheeks of her buttocks were whiter than the white sand on the Mother-of-Pearl coast. Some of them helped wash her long blonde hair, some helped wash other parts. They giggled as they told it, caressing the seksu with butter and oil.

After that when I was alone at the bath, I thought about the white woman and pictured her sitting there on the floor with the warm water pouring over her and the hands of the women touching her and washing her. Sometimes my hand went under my zellab as if I could not control it. Afterwards, I washed myself hurriedly, before anyone came. Would this never stop, I wondered, the touching myself?

For a time the white man came to the bath in the morning. He took off all his clothes, unlike the Moslems who leave the little pants on. His skin was striped too, the way they said the woman's was, so white underneath. Seeing his white penis made some of the boys giggle like women or children. I think he knew the other men talked about him, and soon he started coming late at night when no one else was there. He took a long time and used a great deal of hot water, many buckets, but he always gave me a dirham, and sometimes more.

Then one day, when it was almost summer, a soldier came to the cafe to announce that the King was coming. The Army was winning the war in the South, he said, and the King was going to lead a great march. A People's March, it was called, to take possession of our country's rightful ancient claims.

The King would not stay in the Summer Palace, he would only pass through town in his motorcade. Later, farther south, they would start walking. It could not be certain just what day he would come, or even if he would come for sure, but all the pictures and the flags were hung along the street in preparation for his arrival. I helped my father scrub the rooms and walls of the Palace in case the King wished to inspect it.

When I swept the courtyard, I looked in the crack where the scorpions had performed their Dance of Death. There was water there, deep in the foundation.

The Palace is sinking, I told my father.

Sinking! What is this? he said.

I have seen the water in the crack, I said.

Ahmed, you exaggerate things, my father said. It is that time in your life. The Palace is not one but many palaces. If this one sinks, as you say, another will be built on top of it.

After this speech, a long one for my father, he touched my head and then clapped my shoulder playfully. He used to do this when I was a boy, but it felt different now.

Now let's get back to work, he said.

Let me say all these preparations for the King took the whole day, and then I went to my job at the bath.

Late that night after all the men left I went behind the bathhouse to close down the dampers of the furnace. Across the field in the distance I saw the white man come out of the Project. He wore his zellab with the hood over his head, like the squatters from the countryside, but even across the darkness it was not difficult to tell who he was by the way of his walk, the long strides and arm-swinging and bouncing up on his feet.

He looked around. He could not see me where I crouched by the furnace. There was no one along the highway, no one even at the cafe or awake at the hotel, where all the lights were off. He went to a telephone pole in a dark place, crawled up a few steps, reached out and tore off one of the flags from where it hung above the King's picture.

He climbed down and stuffed the flag inside his zellab and walked quickly back into the Project. I went inside the bathhouse and began to mop the floors. A few minutes later the white man came to the bath.

Yak la-bas, Ahmed? he said. How's it going?

La-bas, I said.

Good. Would it be okay to take a bath now?

Waxxa, I said. His breath smelled sour from wine. I set down my mop and went and filled some buckets for him while he removed his clothes.

I have seen your father tonight, he said, as he wrapped a towel around himself like a woman.

You have drunk wine with him? I asked.

Yes, he said.

And the Madame?

Yes, the Madame too. Perhaps when you are older you will join us, he said.

La, I said.

No?

La, la! I said.

He laughed and went into the third room. I heard him splashing, pouring the buckets and filling more from the fountain. I stared at all his clothes hung and piled in the first room and then I began picking them up. Of course the flag was not there. I gathered everything into his zellab and went outside. I am not sure why I did this, I think I meant at first only to shake them out and straighten them up, but instead I started dropping the things as I walked around the building. I dropped one shoe behind one rock, the other shoe behind another. I threw his stockings, the kind Europeans always wear under their shoes, in different directions, east and west. Everything had the same soapy, sweet smell. Even the sweat of Westerners is like perfume. I buried the shirt with the writing on it under some sand and tied the legs of his pants around an argan tree.

I made altogether seven circles around the bathhouse, some bigger and some smaller. I counted them because there is magic in numbers, too, though I know they do not possess the powerful baraka of words. I sat down under the stars. As I listened to the ocean in the distance and the lagoon below, I realized there was salt water all over my face and I tasted it with my tongue but I could not distinguish between my sweat and the tears that were spilling out. I remembered the story of the Tuareg tribe, the Djbb Rish, scattering the camel's bas in the desert. Who am I, I wondered, to perform such magic? I heard the splashing of the white man inside. He will be finished with his bath soon, I thought.

I rose and walked around and picked up all the things from where I had put them. One by one I bundled them back into his zellab, and we entered the first room at the same time.

What are you doing? he asked.

Walu, I said.

Nothing? Nothing, Ahmed?

We just stood and looked at each other. He was naked, and I held his clothes in my arms. For a moment I thought I might cry again, but then I saw something in his eyes. There was something he was frightened of, too. This was the only time I had felt his fear.

I was only shaking out the sand, I said. Sometimes, when the water rises, the scorpions come inside.

He watched me carefully as I set his things down.

Would you like to have that shirt, Ahmed, the one with the writing? he asked.

Why do you offer this now? Is it that you and the Madame will be leaving soon, to go back to America?

Perhaps, he said. It is true that people live far apart there, but one day we must return to our home. She and I would like you to have the shirt if you want it.

Waxxa, I said. Then we will each, we will all have something to take with us, Monsieur.

Thanks for Covering Your Lane

I can't believe my luck that the TV reporter is interviewing me for the local feature *Heard in the Street*. The question this week, and it's a pretty good question I think, is "What animal would you most like to be in your next lifetime?"

My answer is Sea Otter! What can I say? If you've seen sea otters for even five minutes you know what I mean. The way they float on their backs with their whiskery dog heads scoping around like they are in charge of the whole ocean. Not in charge of exactly, maybe indifferent is more the right word. Like they are saying, Don't bother me with your little non-sea otter concerns. Because I am eating shellfish, cracking open crabs and lobsters with rocks and using my own belly as a table, I am grooming myself, I am meditating, I am floating on my giant water bed, maybe I am just maintaining my position from the shore. But if I choose at any second I could launch straight down to the bottom like a reverse cruise missile because I'm an unbelievably great swimmer too. I have the most valuable fur in the universe but I'm free now because I'm a protected species. By the way, my ancestors spit in your general direction for nearly hunting us into extinction.

I don't tell all this to the reporter or speak as a sea otter to him. I can never think of the right things to say at the time. I don't tell him that I love shellfish too but the closest we come in the VA cafeteria is fish sticks on Fridays. I forget to mention that we took a field trip once to the beach, south of San Francisco, but I didn't see any real otters, that I have only seen them in TV documentaries and in captivity, in the aquarium, or that I suffer from Memory Lapses along with Skin Rashes, Problems Thinking and Concentrating, Flashbacks of Gulf War, and Genital Itch.

I am excited though to imagine how I will look on TV. I wonder if I will sound normal. I know the other guys here at the hospital will get a kick out of seeing a close-up of my pink squarish face on the 6 o'clock news, repeated at 11 o'clock, *Heard in the Street,* with my name below in a little caption.

My name is Les Moore, but when I reach down my shirt to show the reporter my dog tags, they are missing.

My mother, who is dead, told me once she wanted to be a seagull in her next lifetime. Seagulls can fly like I do only in my dreams, she said. Plus they soar over the world's most beautiful scenery, and they eat anything they goddamn please. My mother was a Quaker and "goddamn please" was the strongest she ever swore. Later I realized that what seagulls eat is all the crap left over from what the other critters, like sea otters, don't want to eat, but that doesn't stop me from thinking of my mother whenever I see a seagull, which is pretty often in the Bay Area.

I won't say anything more about my mother. I want to leave her out of it. This is the very kind of thing Mimi, our therapist for Group, warned me about when she suggested I write up the whole thing—how one thing leads to another and another and pretty soon you don't know what belongs in your story and what doesn't. She says to just go ahead and put it all down, then we'll fix it up later.

"Try to tell the story that nobody else can tell except you, Les."

"What story is that?" I say.

"Tell about the dog tags," she says. Mimi has short hair in Day-Glo red and purple spikes, she has multiple ear piercings and she wears black lipstick and those retro narrow horn-rimmed glasses on the end of her nose, so she looks more like a Punk Librarian than a Clinical Psychologist. It's not my style exactly, but I like Mimi.

OK we're waiting for Mimi in the Group Room, me and Mickey and Jimbo and Spam, when *Heard in the Street* comes on at the end of the 6 o'clock news. I pop in a tape to record my 15 seconds of fame.

"Sea otter, huh, Les?" Mickey says, carefully avoiding b's and m's, the sounds he stutters on. These are special Speech Disorders called *betacism* and *mytacism*. In combination Mickey calls them *betamytacism*, a true diagnostic rarity, which he wrote down for me since he can't say it. Mickey is especially handy with the psychological jargon, like the way jail prisoners study the law to help get themselves released. He is equally expert with Post-Traumatic Stress Disorder (PTSD) and Gulf War Syndrome, and like me he supposedly has some combination of both. But he attributes the betamytacism to early, forceful potty training, his parents screaming "BM! BM!" hysterically, setting him on the john every five minutes, that's the way he tells it. Since Mickey is Mexican (his real name is Miguel), they may have been screaming in Spanish, I don't know if those are the same letters. Mickey got talked into enlisting by a green card recruiter who told him he could become a US citizen and go to college after Desert Storm, but he ended up here.

Jimbo's a short, wiry old black guy, with wrinkles like worms on his forehead, and he has wrapped his skinny arms around himself into a kind of chocolate cocoon. He rocks back and forth, nearly tipping over his chair. After seeing me on TV, Jimbo lets out his piercing hyena laugh that shows his crooked white teeth, gums, and tonsils. This is called Inappropriate Affect.

I replay the tape and Jimbo takes a long breath and does it again. His tonsils are purple.

"Let's *us* be the Sea Otters, Les," Spam says. He's a large, pale hairy man like you may picture a Russian. You don't usually notice how big he is because Spam's shy and he slouches like an ape, making the hair from his neck and back tuft out over the collar of his shirt, so you never forget how hairy he is.

"You've got the fur coat for it all right, Spam!" I say. Spam's hair is all gray and white, so I guess he would have to be an albino sea otter.

Spam and Jimbo are from the Vietnam War, which is when they discovered PTSD. Mickey says they used to call it Shell Shock or Battle Fatigue for the even older and mostly dead guys from previous wars. We are in an experimental program overseen by

Mimi that puts some of the Vietnam guys (Spam and Jimbo) with us Persian Gulf guys (me and Mickey), for going on field trips together to participate in the local community, sort of like a Coalition Joint Operation. What we do is swim three times a week at the community pool down the street.

"Fur coat," Spam repeats, he does that a lot (repeat things), and that's how the swimming group becomes the Sea Otters, and how I come to be writing this story, the only one I've ever written, despite my Deteriorated Penmanship, Difficulty Finding Words, and Excessive Salivation.

A few days later, let's say we have fish sticks for lunch so it's Friday, Mimi announces that we're on probation at the pool. Because it's the second time, the VA authorities are calling it Strike Two.

"Strike Three and you're out," Mimi says, glitter sparkling from her eyelids when she blinks. "Suspended, end of story." It is both a warning and an appeal to modify our behavior at the pool, at least for a while until we get off probation.

A group of sea otters is called a *raft*, which you can really picture, a whole bunch of otters floating on their backs and tied up together in the kelp to keep them from drifting apart in the waves or in a storm. The male and female sea otters make up separate rafts except at mating time. When they mate the male bites and holds the female's mouth and nose so she can't get away, for like an hour of rough sea otter lovemaking, leaving the female's snout bloody and scarred. This is normal for them, but people do not want to hear about cute, furry sea otters raping each other, so maybe Mimi will take this part out when she fixes the story up.

Our latest transgression is nothing violent, like Strike One it's just a minor violation of Pool Rules or some kind of locker room incident. But one of the regular customers has filed a complaint in writing. Mimi says when they do that, the pool people have to respond officially to protect themselves from a possible lawsuit.

"Especially when the customer who complains is a lawyer," Mimi says.

"Lawyer," Spam says.

I don't know what the head male of a sea otter raft is called. Top dog? I have to ask Mickey to look it up on the Internet, he is helping me with the sea otter facts. Mickey's got those school smarts despite growing up with gangs, but I was chosen head of the swim group for my leadership potential. Plus I have been on TV now. So I ask Mimi if I can conduct some private sessions of just me and the guys before each swim.

I figure what have we got to lose? If you've played baseball or softball you know that with two strikes you need to protect the plate, swing at anything you can reach, so you don't get called out on one that's close. If you don't want to leave your fate up to the Umpire, if you want to make the decision yourself, you'd rather go down swinging—at least that way you have a chance to hit one out of the park.

Mimi says OK so I will start with Public Shower Etiquette.

"All right Otters!" I say. You need to picture that the men's locker room at the pool has the same kind of communal center-pole shower we have at the hospital. "*One:* do not stare at other men's penises in the shower. If you are caught staring at another man's penis, avert your eyes in a sideways glance as if you were looking around at everything in general and his penis just happened to be in your field of vision."

Spam can detect minute differences in penis size and likes to catalogue them for us on the way back to the hospital. This is an exception to his general shyness. He says a name, describes someone's swimming style, or simply points to them, then offers his assessment of their whanger with his thumb and index finger, or thumb and pinkie spread apart for the larger specimens, as if he's measuring fish. If you don't pay close enough attention, he elbows you and repeats the fish measurements right in your face, then cracks up. You might even admire this kind of boyish enthusiasm in a 60-something polar bear of a man, but the problem is sometimes he starts doing it in the locker room before we leave. The staring and the measuring can be disturbing to the normal people who might be there, let's say your suburban dad and his preteen boy whose membership in the dick department is still a hairless little pencil-stub.

"*Two:* do not spend too much time washing your own penis."

"*Three:* in washing your penis, do not simulate any motion that may be remotely suggestive of masturbation."

"Masturbation," Spam says.

Jimbo rears back for a quick hyena cackle, a sign he's paying attention, and I catch his big wet brown eye for a second (the real one, I forgot to mention one eye is plastic). I don't know how he developed his obsession with genital cleanliness, if that is what it is, I just don't want us to get kicked out of the pool for it. Jimbo was a Tunnel Rat in Vietnam, one of the worst jobs you could have in my opinion. I saw a TV documentary about it. They loved finding a small black guy for this. Jimbo could fit into the tunnels as easily as the Viet Cong, plus he blended into the dark, *plus* the gooks were freaked out by black guys in general. Jimbo shaved his head for the heat and the lice, which increased the freakout effect. Jimbo was a famous Tunnel Rat at Cu Chi, the biggest tunnel complex in the south, he has all the medals.

One day, the story goes, Jimbo disabled about a dozen booby-traps while mapping a huge wing of Cu Chi that went right under the US military base there, used up all his ammo chasing down a VC colonel, then had to kill the colonel's whole extended family in a tunnel nest in hand-to-hand combat. Supposedly you could hear the screams up on the surface. One of the colonel's family poked out Jimbo's eye with a stick. Then they set off an alarm that started blowing up section by section of the tunnel complex, at one point burying Jimbo alive. Somehow he dug his way out but hasn't said a word since.

I review a couple other points—Mickey has Severe Butt Acne, I don't know if this is another symptom of Gulf War Syndrome, but it's particularly annoying when he bends over to rinse his ass—and then I sum up with, "In general, avoid any eccentric shower habits you may have developed from years of showering alone or in groups in the military. When in doubt, imitate the models who advertise shampoo or deodorant soaps on TV."

Actually Spam is the only one who can achieve a true lather on his stomach and chest. The rest of us have to get the lather worked up in our pubic hair and then spread it up to the trunk real quick to make it look like the TV showers.

When it's nice out, we walk to the pool, maybe we swing our army-issue canvas bags, even the older guys. Spam slouches but still bounces way up on his toes when he walks, and Jimbo limps on his artificial leg, I forgot to mention that he has only one leg in addition to one eye (booby trap). Mickey's cheek bunches up on one side with Chronic Eye Twitch. I walk like a normal person though I do wear dark wraparound sunglasses for my Increased Sensitivity to Light and long sleeves because of Unexplained Rashes. People look at us from their cars and driveways and kitchen windows. Sometimes they come out of their houses to gather up kids from the yard or retrieve their dog that Spam is trying to feed.

Live Oak Community Pool is on a quiet residential street, also named Live Oak Lane, near the VA. The one-story pool building with the office and locker rooms looks almost like another house except it's on a bigger lot and behind a low chain-link fence, like we have at the hospital. In the backyard by the pool there's one of the Live Oak trees that the neighborhood and street are named for. I always look for trees of that kind on streets with tree names, and I believe this is the only one left. I am afraid to touch it because Mickey says all the other Live Oaks died from a root disease, which I do not wish to get.

"You can't catch a tree disease, Les," Mickey says as we approach the pool. He claims to have some kind of farmworker knowledge on this even though he's from East LA. I still avoid touching the tree, or anywhere touched by squirrels or birds who have been in the tree.

"Disease is caused by germs, Mick, which are transferred by touch. I saw on a TV science show that, on a microscopic level, whenever two things touch they exchange tiny particles which have lives of their own." I tell him my theory of the Transitive Property of Touching, that is, if A touches B, and B touches C, then it's the same as A touching C.

"Which is why locker rooms are great for disease," I say. Once when I forgot my shower shoes I had to invent a special way of walking along the sides of my feet, to minimize skin contact where other people have walked. I established safe areas, which I still use, places where I know I've stepped before, places where I can always retrace my steps around the locker room and past the tree area and around the pool.

"You're losing it man," Mickey says. We go inside to change.

"Germs you think are dead can come back to life," I say. "These are called Doormat Germs."

If I think about an idea like this long enough it becomes like a voice inside my head that I talk to.

"Dorm-m-m-*mant*, not doorm-m-m-*mat*," Mickey says, but I am no longer sure if I'm talking to the real Mickey or the one inside my head.

Also:

Do not spit, hawk, blow your nose, or urinate in the shower.

Do not stand on the benches in the locker room to get dressed or hop up and down to put your pants on.

Do not hang your wet bathing suit and towel on other people's clothes.

Do not touch where other people have put their used wet things.

Picture the pool surrounded by a painted concrete patio people can rent out for children's birthday parties etc., with a brick barbecue and lawn furniture. There are special hours for Family Swim, Lessons, and Adult Lap Swim which is us. For Lap Swim the lanes are marked Fast (me), Medium (Mickey), and Slow (Spam). The slowest of the Slow lanes (Jimbo), along one edge, is shallow the whole length and has an entry ramp in addition to a ladder. We call it the Retard Lane, though Mimi says we shouldn't.

I love swimming. I used to be a thrasher but I watched the good swimmers and taught myself to breathe on both sides, in a rhythm, now I can do laps until I lose track of the number and the time. You have the lane dividers to guide you, plastic ropes with doughnut floats, and the black-tiled lane lines on the bottom. If there are nice looking women in nearby lanes you can look at them through your goggles and they can't really tell. Sometimes I flip over on my back and then front then back again, twisting like a sea otter.

Two differences between me and sea otters though. Number 1, I do not swim in my own toilet. Pools are clear and clean, like disinfectant. The ocean is dark with the crap of everything that lives in it, teeming with bacteria. I will have to get used to that if I die and actually become a sea otter, like my mother adjusting to a seagull diet. I know I said I wouldn't mention my mother again, but sometimes I wish I could talk to her about that, about adapting to life as a seagull. I hope it is everything she wished for.

Number 2, sea otters are outstanding divers. They can dive through water the way seagulls dive through the air. They hold their breath just like us but they can dive like a bullet 100 feet down, scrape a juicy sea urchin off the rocky seafloor, return to the surface and roll over on their backs and spin the urchin round and round in their paws to remove the stinging spines and then take a big juicy.... Uh-oh, better watch out for my mother swooping down to get that urchin!

Me, I stay on the surface. I tell this to Mimi as she looks over my story.

"Why, Les?" Mimi asks. She grips a pencil in one hand and twirls three or four earrings with the other, fingernails painted red and purple to go with her hair.

"I do not want to go down there."

"Down there," Mimi says, repeating things like Spam.

"I do not want a bunch of water over my head," I say. "I do not want all that pressure on my ears, on my lungs holding my breath. I do not want the chemicals burning my eyes, even through my goggles, like in Iraq."

Mimi underlines something and makes a note when I say *Iraq*.

"It doesn't matter anyway," I say, "because at the pool there is Absolutely No Diving Allowed, they have a sign."

I have a complete Memory Lapse as far as losing my dog tags. One day I had them, the next day they were gone, and I feel naked without them. You're supposed to wear your dog tags all the time, even here in the VA, so they can identify you if you're killed or fucked up. Now they say we're at war again, this time against Terror or Terrorism, I'm not sure which, but it seems we're at war all the time. You have two dog tags because one stays with your body and one is sent home for the military.

You could say people get a little superstitious with their dog tags. I have a routine where I roll them between my fingers a certain way, sort of like some people can twirl coins or poker chips on World Championship of Poker. I started doing it in Basic Training and refined my technique in Iraq. I can flip them end to end in both directions using the silencers for leverage, those are the little rubber gaskets that go around the edges and keep the tags from clanging together. When I do this it looks like I'm drumming my fingers on my collarbone.

The old dog tags made from World War II to the Vietnam War, which don't have silencers, had a little V-notch in the end of the metal. Supposedly the notch was for wedging between a dead soldier's front teeth. Then you opened the jaw and stuck the other end between the bottom teeth, and then kicked the guy's jaw shut permanently with the dog tags wedged in the teeth, that is the story you hear in the military.

Spam and Jimbo still have their notched tags so one day I ask Spam about it. I figure Spam should know because he got his nickname after his whole unit was ambushed on a Search and Destroy mission in Cambodia and he was picked up days later just sitting there among the bodies opening cans from everyone's c-rations.

"Spam, did you, um, go around and kick everyone's jaws shut with their dog tags?" I ask him straight out.

"No, Les."

"What *did* you do?"

"I guess I didn't do anything, I just waited for someone to come." Spam stares off into the distance like he's back in Vietnam and now I'm sorry I brought it up.

"The jaw-kicking story is an Urban Legend," Mickey says. He looks it up and finds that the V-notch was actually for holding the dog tags in the old embossing machine that printed out your name, service number, and blood type.

"Hey look at this, hajjis don't eat pork," Mickey says, following some side trail on the Internet about c-rations and SPAM, the canned meat product. C-rations is the old name for MREs (Meals, Ready to Eat), like gook is the old name for hajji, which is a *Middle Eastern* gook. These are the kinds of things you learn by putting Vietnam together with Iraq.

"That's why they didn't give us SPAM in the Gulf War," Mickey says, he means in our MREs, "to please the M-M-Muslim countries in the Coalition."

"Muslim," Spam says.

Plus:

Do not stop other swimmers to shake their hand and ask them how they're doing.

Do not attempt the butterfly stroke unless you actually know how to do it.

Do not race people when they try to pass you.

On TV they are showing the new Iraq War, it is much worse than the earlier one me and Mickey were in. Already the VA is overflowing with new post-traumatic stress cases, guys and even women now too with limbs blown off from roadside bombs and suicide bombers, and they are building a new wing on the hospital. There is a news story on the Rumaila Oil Fields, that is near Kuwait in southern Iraq, and suddenly I see myself back in Basra in Operation Desert Storm.

Let's say we are doing mop-up, they have already bombed the crap out of the city, buildings are crumbled, there are bodies in the streets. You can hear concussion thuds in the distance where we are carpet-bombing the retreating Iraqi Army before the ceasefire. My orders are to cover Lane Romeo-Juliette-Niner (that is military talk for Lane RJ9, the name of this street on our surveillance map) until the battalion completes its sweep of the area. I find shade next to some kind of ruined government building or bank, the only trees are some palms in the distance by a dried-up canal. I squat down to drink some water, and then I realize I'm alone for what seems like the first time in years. I twirl my dog tags quickly from thumb to pinkie, pinkie to thumb, I can do it with both hands now without even thinking. Black clouds rise over the ruins and I feel a blast of hot sandy wind, smell the burning oil.

Across the street are two dead hajjis, Iraqi teenagers in bloody robes, maybe Shiite resistance fighters killed by the Republican Guard on their way out. The wind ruffles their clothes and their hair. I remember a picture of Armageddon from a Sunday School book when I was a kid, it had fires and darkened skies and people cowering by dead bodies, and now I think maybe I am seeing the future. Not Heaven but Armageddon. Death and Destruction, the caption said. I told my mother about the picture—she was trying me out with some other church, because there was no Friends Meeting (the name of Quaker church) available where we were living—and she said, "That's just some people's imagination." The Quakers don't care much about hellfire and brimstone. They think God lives inside of everyone. Also they are pacifists so they would refuse to fight in a war like this.

Burning oil and radioactive battlefields as far as you can see, toxic chemicals, dark swarms of sand flies carrying parasites, clouds of poisonous pesticides, Depleted Uranium dust from our weapons everywhere in the shrapnel, on the ground, in the smoke, in the air. My eyes sting inside my fogged up goggles, my nostrils are on fire, and I think, Why the fuck didn't *I* become a Quaker?

I hear a voice saying Don't forget to take your nerve gas pills, oh and by the way they may cause brain damage.

The Army doctors say there's no such thing as Gulf War Syndrome, everything is in my head. I'm not sure, but sometimes, like now, I think I am talking to the TV.

And:

Do not trap large fart bubbles underwater in your trunks then release them to make "volcanoes."

Do not go into the office dripping wet to report small pieces of dirt, drowned insects, or dead leaves on the bottom of the pool.

Do not discuss politics with the lifeguards, or ask them on dates.

Do not pee in the pool.

When it's crowded you have to share a lane with several people and Circle Swim, which means go Counterclockwise around the center line. If I get stuck Circling with a couple assholes who won't let you pass even at the ends, sometimes I resort to the Retard Lane, where it's less crowded and you can just fly by people.

The Retard Lane is used mainly by (a) extremely fat people who jog and jiggle along the bottom and (b) actual disabled people like Jimbo, who has to disattach his artificial leg to swim. Let me say that little Jimbo loves that leg even though it's a ridiculous pink color, he is still waiting for an African American prosthetic. Anyway Jimbo doesn't seem to mind that we call it the Retard Lane, maybe because sometimes there are civilians worse off than him in the physically disabled department.

Take Captain Pike for example. I forget his real name, he is an attorney and dresses real nice. He must have his clothes custom tailored, because although his head is somewhat normal, his body is dwarf size and he has a back hump the size of a basketball, his spine is twisted like a pretzel, his arms and legs are like straws with the little hinges in them. He wears ankle-to-thigh steel braces and walks with two canes. I don't know if he was born like this or had some terrible accident. He walks so slowly that by the time he changes into his swimsuit, drags himself out to the pool on the canes, undoes the braces and clanks them onto the concrete next to Jimbo's pink fake leg, and works his way down the handrail into the Retard Lane, we can usually finish our laps, shower, and dress.

Spam named him Captain Pike from the original *Star Trek*, because nobody can remember the name of the woman that Captain Pike falls in love with in the pilot episode. The woman is horribly injured in a starship crash then put back together all crooked and disfigured by the Talosians. The Talosians botch the job because they've never seen a human before, so they don't have a model. That is what they say, but they never explain why they would put her together so crooked when the Talosians themselves are at least symmetrical. Anyway Pike himself is severely burned and mangled in a radiation accident and lives in a futuristic, full-life-support wheelchair. But the Talosians have the Power of Illusion or something so they can let Captain Pike and the deformed woman think they are young and beautiful again, fall in love, and live out the rest of their lives on Talos IV like they're normal. I wish we had some Talosians here.

OK so one of the dead Iraqi teenagers isn't really dead. He gets up and yells something at me, it sounds like *Mohammed!* or *Jihad!*, everything they say sounds like that, like they're clearing their throat all the time. He fires a round right into my leg before I can barely piss and shit my pants. You don't hear much about messing yourself, definitely not from the Embedded Reporters for the new war who are still babbling on the TV about Operation Whatever, but believe me this happens to a lot of people. It's like a bucket of ice water is dumped over me, I'm emptied out with fear, and then just as quickly my whole body is on fire with sweat and adrenaline.

What surprises me the most in this scene is how much the bullet hurts. It's like getting hit by a shovel full force. After that it's almost a relief to focus on the pain instead of my fear.

I drop my dog tags and pull up my M16 and squeeze off round after round, wildly at first but then homing in on the hajji, until the boy is really dead, this time for sure, his body jerking and bouncing with each hit.

Then let's say I empty the clip into the other kid too just to make sure.

When the medics come I am holding my leg, sitting in my own crap, and singing to myself, to the tune of "I Wish I Were an Oscar Meyer Weiner,"

> *Oh I wish I were a Quaker like my moth-er.*
> *That is what I'd truly like to be.*

*'Cause if I were a Quaker like my moth-er,
Everyone would be in love with me.*

I am still singing when they load me in the back of a Humvee.

Presently, the TV that was showing the new Iraq War changes to an SUV ad, then a preview for a new Reality Show where people injured in car wrecks will be brought to a fake hospital and compete for medical care while trying to figure out who are the real doctors and nurses, something like that.

I go to the real hospital window and look down, we're on the third story if I forgot to mention that, and I see Mimi get into her car in the parking lot below. She moves the rearview mirror to check her hair and jewelry. I never thought before about how much maintenance those colorful spikes and piercings might require. I doubt she'll leave this in the story, but I wonder for a second if she has a date after work.

And finally:

Do not try to push or pull people's dogs into the pool, they are not allowed.

Do not spend too much time underwater ogling the women swimmers through your goggles.

Do not stand up on the lane dividers in the pool or try to walk on them like a tightrope or straddle them and bounce up and down yelling Whoopee Ride 'Em Cowboy.

Remember, Absolutely No Diving Allowed.

Today it's raining so an orderly takes us in the van. I like going in the van because I can press my face against the tinted window and look back at the neighborhood people without them seeing me. When we get there Captain Pike is in the parking lot. He drives a specially-equipped bigass Buick. One day in summer he had shown us the hand controls for the gas and brakes.

"It's like Tiger Woods's Buick," he had said, also showing us his golf clubs in the trunk. I think this stuck with us because, although he may be well off, Captain Pike looks about as much like Tiger Woods as we do.

Now Spam goes over to have another look at the buttons and levers in the driver's seat. Spam is somehow fascinated with Captain Pike, who pushes the door open and begins the long process of shifting his legs around to get out. Spam watches for a minute or two, then reaches down and scoops Captain Pike up like he's going to carry him to the locker room.

"*Please* put me down," Captain Pike says.

"Spam's only trying to help," I say.

"I don't want your help," Captain Pike says.

"He's an attorney," I remind Spam, who drops him back into his seat like a live hand grenade, and all of a sudden I realize that Captain Pike must be the one who got us on probation in the first place.

"Attorney," Spam says, and a light goes on for him and Mickey too, *lawyer, written complaint,* Strike 2. We all look at each other.

"Fuck Tiger Woods!" I say to Captain Pike, in his face through the driver's window. It seems inadequate but it's all I can come up with, and it feels good. Captain Pike seems a little scared by the outburst, while Jimbo cracks up about Tiger Woods all the way into the locker room.

During the rainy season they keep the lane covers on the pool to preserve the heat. If there aren't very many people, like today, you have to uncover your own lane by rolling up the blue styrofoam, and then you're supposed to re-cover it when you're done. That's the hard part, getting out of the pool and crouching on the wet concrete, after you've gotten all warm, and rolling the mat back out again. In case you forget, in the winter months they put out a big sign on an easel, "Thanks for Covering Your Lane."

Mickey and I uncover our lanes quickly, we help Spam and Jimbo with theirs, then we all slide into the warm water and swim swim swim swim, Jimbo in the Retard Lane, Spam in the Slow Lane, Mickey in Medium, and me of course in the Fast Lane. After a while I notice something shiny on the bottom directly below, something metal stuck down in the drain. The drain is in the deepest part of the deep end, the number on the side says *9 Feet* which I suppose for the remainder of my lifetime as a human I will pronounce *Niner Feet* in my head.

Is it maybe a couple coins dropped from someone's trunks, like hidden treasure?

As I pass back and forth, turning my neck opposite ways to alternate my breathing, the light reflects off the metal at different angles through the leaves and dirt that collect around the drain. Now I can see there's also something attached to the coins, floating above the drain, waving in the water like sea urchin stingers. I feel this strange attraction, and I wonder if this is how sea otters spot their food. But for me the bottom is like another universe, I'm hypnotized by the sparkling light in its wavy reflections. Even on this cloudy day the patterns of light shimmer on the pool floor like the constellations at night, you can see them almost right in your face, but you'd never try to actually go there. You'd never try to go there because it's too far and there's no air and you can't hold your breath that long, the pressure on your head and ears would be unbearable, your eyes would bulge out and burn when you opened them, your eyes would burn burn burn and your goggles would not protect you.

You'd never go there because the only way to get that deep, way down to the very drain of the deep end, would be to dive in from the side, all at once. You'd have to get physically out of the pool and dive in from the edge, but there's Absolutely No Diving Allowed says the sign, and thanks to Captain Pike the Sea Otters have Two Strikes already.

No, no, you'd never do it unless the shiny, shimmering objects beckon to you and say: Maybe I am your dog tags.

Returning in the van everyone seems to realize we will be suspended from the pool. We are silent for a while. Then Spam starts doing Captain Pike with his fish measurements. We are well aware of the length and girth of Captain Pike's surprising sausage pecker, along with Spam's exaggerated version of it, but Spam is very determined and animated in his presentation and we all start cracking up.

"Good one," Mickey says.

"Hup!" Jimbo says, his forehead wrinkling like strands of black licorice. It's almost like a hiccup yet more than that, and Mickey and Spam and I all turn to look at him, since if it counts as a *word*, which I'm not really sure it does, it would be Jimbo's first in over three decades. I will have to ask Mimi. If we show some signs of progress, then maybe she can get permission for a new experimental program like we had with the Sea Otters.

The rain stops, I unfog the window and see, above the trees, the construction workers start back to work on the rooftop of the new hospital wing. Looking through the van window is like watching TV. There far away a man pounds nails in a steady rhythm. The air is thick like water, and across the distance the sound arrives at the top of his stroke instead of the bottom. I try to match my heartbeat to his hammering. You can do this for short periods of time if you try hard enough. It's a trick I guess, I don't know if it means anything. I think, my heart pounding, that after work these men will go home, have beers, and take showers.

Pelican Stamina Triple Double Dactyl*

1.
Birdishly-fervishly,
Pelican, stamina,
Two words that hang on the
Tip of your tongue;

Face it, your gray matter's—
Cerebrovascular

---

* The double dactyl, also known as Higgledy Piggledy, is a comic form of light verse with stringent requirements for structure and prosody. It consists of two quatrains, each with three double-dactyl lines (dactylic dimeter: /˘˘/˘˘) followed by a dactyl-spondee pair, or choriamb (/˘˘/). The two choriambs must rhyme. The first line is a nonsense phrase and the sixth line a single double-dactylic word, ideally one that has never been used previously in other double dactyl poems.

Mental capacity—
No longer young.

2.
Schmelican-schmamina,
Pelican, stamina!
Two words interred in your
Noggin's Noun Jail,

Not where you think they are;
Neurolinguistically,
Memory-wise you just
Agingly flail.

3.
Hallaballoozabah
Pelican stamina
Both now together so
Hard to forget.

How do they stay up so
Aerodynamically,
Gliding and swooping like
Marionettes?

About the author

Richard Holeton is author of the hypertext novel *Figurski at Findhorn on Acid* (figurskiatfindhornonacid.com) and award-winning short fiction. Recipient of fellowships from the National Endowment for the Arts, MacDowell, Dora Maar House, and the California Arts Council, he's taught writing at Cañada College, San Francisco State, and Stanford University. He lives in the San Francisco Bay Area on unceded ancestral land of the Ramaytush Ohlone.

richardholeton.com

Made in the USA
Monee, IL
11 August 2025

23116519R00174